MW01482061

This special signed edition is limited
to 350 numbered copies.

This is copy **244**.

The
Lovecraft Chronicles

The
Lovecraft Chronicles

by
PETER CANNON

with illustrations by
JASON C. ECKHARDT

Subterranean Press 2008

First Edition

ISBN 978-1-59606-134-7

Subterranean Press
PO Box 190106
Burton, MI 48519

www.subterraneanpress.com

To my sisters

Contents

"The Knopf deal is probably the closest Lovecraft ever came to having a book published in his lifetime by a mainstream publisher. If he had done so, the rest of his career—and, it is not too much to say, the entire subsequent history of American weird fiction—might have been very different."

—S. T. Joshi

"How he would have enjoyed seeing a novel of his in a Boston bookstore; how he would have loved to do some sightseeing in his beloved old England!"

—Earl Wells

"I had fully realized, in an abstract way, that I would probably live till about 1960."

—H. P. Lovecraft

The
Lovecraft Chronicles

Clarissa

Chapter 1

There was no possibility of getting a seat to myself that day. The Providence bus was more than half full by the time I boarded, but since I was planning to start my new book my choice of companion for the next two hours scarcely mattered, so long as he or she wasn't a chatterbox, like my mother. The safest prospect I decided, as I walked down the aisle, was a gaunt, middle-aged gentleman, possibly a minister or undertaker, to judge from his plain dark suit—who was too absorbed in writing a postcard on the valise in his lap to notice my approach. When I asked if the place next to him was free, he looked up and gave a start, like some frightened animal. His face flushed above his old-fashioned collar before he managed to say, in a high-pitched, genteel New England voice, that the seat was indeed empty and I was welcome to it.

I was embarrassed as well, yet also rather pleased, that a stranger should at first sight find me so intimidating. He made no move to help me lift my suitcase into the overhead rack, but then I was already a large girl by fifteen. I settled into my seat and opened *Cold Comfort Farm*, while he continued his postcard writing. The driver announced final call and, after an unpleasant burst of exhaust fumes, the bus was soon rattling through the nondescript streets of downtown Hartford.

Cold Comfort Farm has since become one of my favorite novels, but I'll admit it was an effort to concentrate on the story. Stella Gibbons' English social satire was a shade too subtle for an American schoolgirl, even one as advanced as I was. Seeking other distraction, I found myself stealing glances at my seat-mate, who had shifted closer to the window and arranged his valise so as to avoid, I was sure, any chance brush of knee or elbow. After finishing his postcard, he immediately started another, as fluidly as a chain-smoker lighting his next cigarette. The jolts and rumblings of the bus hardly disrupted the flow of his pen.

With his mousy, short-cropped hair flecked with gray, long jaw pocked with ingrown whiskers, and deathly pallor (the pink had soon faded), he would never have been cast as a leading man. Maybe as a sidekick, say, for Peter Lorre or Sidney Greenstreet. Here, I began to imagine, was a sinister character with a mysterious past. Shyness has never been one of my shortcomings. During a pause in his scribbling, I took the plunge and asked the obvious question:

"Are you a writer, mister?"

The way the pen twitched in his hand suggested that I had again caught him off guard. Nonetheless, he turned toward me and said, hesitantly and not unkindly, "Yes, I do write, young lady, but merely as a means of self-expression."

This struck me as evasive. I persisted.

"When you're not writing postcards what kinds of things do you write?"

"I write letters…"

"Come on, mister, you know what I mean."

"…and on occasion, in an effort to capture on paper that fleeting sense of wonder produced by dream images or landscape vistas, a tale of supernatural horror."

"Supernatural horror? You mean like *Dracula* and *Frankenstein?*"

"Yes, those are two of the classics in the genre."

"I've seen the movies. My mother wasn't going to let me, but each time I convinced her I was mature enough to go—with her of course. They were both a little juvenile in my opinion, not especially scary." As an early and indiscriminate fan of all motion pictures, I didn't want to wax enthusiastic in front of an adult whose tastes were apt to be a lot more sophisticated than mine in his chosen field. In fact I'd been riveted by both films, and more than once had closed my eyes during the scarier parts. At least I hadn't hidden my face in my hands like my mother.

"You are more charitable than I," he replied. "I saw the beginning of *Dracula*, but couldn't bear to watch it drag to its full term of dreariness, hence I walked out. I would have drowsed through *Frankenstein* had not a posthumous sympathy for poor Mrs. Shelley made me see red instead."

As usual, my instincts had been right. This was a man not easily impressed.

"Have any of your own stories been made into pictures?" I ventured.

"I shall never permit anything bearing my signature to be banalized and vulgarized into the kind of flat infantile twaddle which passes for 'horror tales' amongst radio and cinema audiences!"

I'd clearly struck a nerve there. I tried to shift to safer ground.

"Would I have read any of your books, mister?"

There was only the slightest pause before he answered this one, in a tone that was almost matter of fact.

"My modest effusions have yet to achieve the dignity of collection between cloth covers. They have appeared exclusively in the cheap magazines."

"Which magazines? Maybe I've read one of your stories!"

"*Weird Tales* has been virtually my only outlet, but under present editorial policy this market is all but closed to me."

I was not familiar with *Weird Tales*. In general I looked down on the pulps, unlike the movies, as a vulgar form of popular entertainment. Was this how he made a living—or was it only a hobby? In the light of his glum remark, I hoped for his sake it was a hobby. Perhaps he really was a clergyman or undertaker.

"What's your name, if you don't mind my asking?"

"Not at all. I am H. P. Lovecraft."

"Is that your real name?"

"Indeed, although I am probably the only bearer of the name Lovecraft in the United States."

"You have no children?"

"No."

"Are you married?"

"I am a bachelor. I live alone."

I sensed I was treading on delicate ground. In the silence that followed he finished his postcard. I was about to return to *Cold Comfort Farm* when I heard him mutter:

"And may I be so bold as to ask your name, young lady?"

It was my turn to be surprised. What a relief not to be always the one asking the questions.

"Clarissa Stone," I answered.

Stone was not my family's original name. When my Russian grandparents landed on Ellis Island, it had been far from Anglo-Saxon sounding. This was a personal detail, however, that I felt was inappropriate to share on first meeting an individual who appeared to be every inch the fastidious Yankee.

"And what brought you to Hartford, Miss Stone?"

"My Aunt Kitty, that's my mother's sister, and her husband, Uncle George. They're both teachers at Miss Porter's in Farmington." I wasn't hesitant to suggest that a relative of mine was associated with one of the classiest girls schools of the Old American elite. "Farmington's pretty in a picture postcard kind of way, but to be honest I would've preferred spending the weekend in New York."

"New York City?"

"That's right. We used to live in the Village, where my father taught at N.Y.U. He's an English professor. When Brown University offered him a job, before the Crash, he couldn't resist. Do you know New York?"

"I once lived in Brooklyn," he said, "but Providence is my one true home. Providence is my world."

"Providence is boring."

"My dear Miss Stone, how can you say such a thing?"

"There aren't nearly enough movie theaters in Providence, not like New York."

"There's the good old Strand in Washington Street."

"What does Providence have to equal the Metropolitan Museum?"

"We have the Art Club in hilly Thomas Street, not to mention the School of Design museum."

"And what about Carnegie Hall? Where's the Providence equivalent of that?"

"I myself am not particularly musically inclined," he said after a pause, "but years ago my younger aunt used to attend the Friday afternoon symphony in Boston."

He made this pathetic comment with such solemn dignity that I dared not laugh, much as I was tempted to. Rubbing in the cultural superiority of New York to Providence any further would have been cruel.

"What I really miss are the people," I continued.

"I confess I have my friends in New York whom I miss, too, Miss Stone. It has been my custom of late to visit them after Christmas."

"Were you visiting friends in Hartford, Mr. Lovecraft?"

"I was meeting a client of mine in need at short notice of my literary services. I am a free-lance revisionist."

"A free-lance what?"

"A free-lance revisionist, a term I consider more accurate than freelance editor, since I usually engage in wholesale revision if not actual ghostwriting." So this was how he earned his daily bread. "Coincidentally, after concluding business, I accompanied my client on a tour of Farmington, which must rank as one of the most exquisite villages in America, with its lovely colonial houses shaded by a magnificent plentitude of ancient elms. While you were staying with your relatives, did you happen to see the one dating to about 1650, with overhanging second story?"

"No. Did you?"

What soon became clear, as I sat listening in awe to the ensuing monologue, was that Mr. Lovecraft was a passionate antiquarian, devoted in particular to the eighteenth-century architecture of his native New England. While none of the towns where the bus stopped at intervals in our eastward journey compared with Farmington, my companion was quick to point out any house or feature of a house— a gambrel roof, a scroll pediment, a square column—that pleased his fancy. Only when I managed to drop the fact that my father was an expert on eighteenth-century English literature, and hint that I might have something interesting to say on the subject if given the chance, did he remember his manners.

"God bless Grandpa's old bones!" he exclaimed. "Forgive me, Miss Stone, for rambling on like a puling lackwit. At times I get carried away by my enthusiasms. In truth I am more accustomed to epistolary conversation than the face to face variety. Tell me, with whom of the esteemed authors of that fabled Augustan age is your learned father acquainted?"

"The novelists mostly—Richardson, Fielding, Smollett. Then there's Boswell."

"I am a tremendous admirer of Dr. Johnson, Miss Stone, though it is the poets such as Mr. Pope and Mr. Thomson who please me most. In my metrical novitiate I was, alas, a chronic and inveterate mimic, allowing my antiquarian tendencies to get the better of my abstract poetic feeling."

"So you're a poet, too?"

"I once composed reams of imitative verse but no longer do so now that I have attained some modicum of literary self-understanding in old age."

At fifteen all adults seem old, but for a man in his forties, as I guessed him to be, to call himself "Grandpa" and otherwise emphasize his advanced years showed a certain lack of self-confidence.

"I write poetry myself," I said. "Dorothy Parker and Edna St. Vincent Millay are my models. Do you know their work?"

"I am aware of Miss St. Vincent Millay by reputation. A friend connected to the real literary world once offered to introduce us in the Village, but I declined. It has never been my policy to fawn on the great. I confess I have not heard of the other poetess you mention."

"You don't read the *New Yorker*?"

"No, I do not. That magazine's vein of urbane, sophisticated humor is not meant for the little old lady from Dubuque, their editors say. Well might they proclaim it unfit for the old dreamer from Providence!"

Was the man trying to be funny? It was hard to tell.

We discussed books for a while, but it soon became clear that my seat-mate didn't keep up with current mainstream fiction. He admitted that he had all but ceased to look over new books, since his interests in recent years had become so definitely antiquarian. He had never heard of Stella Gibbons.

When the topic returned to poetry, he offered to have a look at whatever of my own verse I would feel comfortable sharing with him. He hastened to add, his long grave face coloring again, that of course this was purely as a courtesy from an old gentleman to a young lady, not a business proposition. I thanked him for his generosity and said I would seriously consider it.

After we crossed the state line into Rhode Island, Mr. Lovecraft resumed his rhapsodies, this time about the surrounding countryside. The low brown hills with their bare trees, as yet showing no sign of the spring that was around the corner, held no magic for me. But for him they were the seat of ineffable marvels, seemingly because his mother's family, honest farmers mostly, had inhabited the area for generations. When the sun came out, after what had been a typical March afternoon, cloudy and gray, his voice rose almost an octave in his excitement over the contrast between light and shadow on the landscape. When the bus reached a height on the road that afforded a glimpse of the spires of the state capital, glowing in the sunset toward the horizon, he became positively ecstatic. "Where bay and river tranquil blend, and leafy hillsides rise," he began. I soon realized he was reciting a poem. It went on for several stanzas.

"That was beautiful!" I said, with more or less genuine enthusiasm. "What's the title?"

" 'Providence,' " he said, as if it were the name of the woman he loved.

"Who wrote it?" I said, as if I didn't already have a good idea of the answer.

"I did, Miss Stone."

"I didn't notice any heroic couplets, Mr. Lovecraft."

He laughed, and for a moment the veil dropped to reveal a relaxed human being behind the formal facade. In the next instant he was again the grim Puritan, explaining that in his few poetic attempts of recent vintage he had adopted a more natural style.

As the bus neared the terminal in downtown Providence, I said I would need to know his address in order to send him my poetry. I didn't really care that much what critical advice he might have. While I was only half aware of it at the time, I did, however, want an excuse to stay in touch with this potential new friend, without appearing too forward.

"I live at 10 Barnes Street," he said. "I apologize for not having a card."

"That's all right. I'll remember. We live fairly close by, on Blackstone Boulevard. Say, how are you planning to get home?"

"By foot."

"Would you like a lift, Mr. Lovecraft? My mother's picking me up in her car."

"You are very kind, Miss Stone, but I prefer to walk. That way I can pause to admire the sunset fire reflecting on the fanlights of College Hill doorways if I so choose."

I didn't insist. The way he avoided my eye indicated that he was once again feeling that embarrassment he'd displayed at the start of our journey. Perhaps he was only mindful of the proprieties, and accepting a ride from a young lady he had just met was just not the thing for a man in his position to do. He was, though, gentleman enough to offer to take my luggage down from the overhead rack. I said no thank you, I could manage. With my free hand I gave him a friendly wave before heading up the aisle. I didn't look back, but I was confident that I hadn't seen the last of Mr. H. P. Lovecraft.

So fate, or perhaps Providence, introduced me to the master of weird tales. In the future I would sometimes wonder what different courses our lives might have taken without this chance meeting. In the future, too, I would eventually learn that *the "client" who had prompted his trip to Hartford and with whom he had toured Farmington had been his erstwhile wife, the former Mrs. H. P. Lovecraft.*

Chapter 2

Yes, I know, by italicizing the final clause of that last sentence I'm guilty of the same cheap rhetorical trick as you know who. To be fair, after reading most of the Lovecraft horror oeuvre, I appreciated that this was a device he tended to favor only in such short, punch-ending tales as "In the Vault," "Pickman's Model," and "The Outsider"—or "The Dunwich Horror," his one long story to prostitute itself to pulp standards. In his later, more mature work he was usually a more subtle stylist. But I'm getting ahead of my story.

That evening, after my return from Hartford, my parents asked me over the dinner table about my weekend with Aunt Kitty and Uncle George. I was happy to oblige them, making a point of describing at length the Episcopal church service we had gone to that morning. It was clear to me that my two young cousins, who attended Sunday school, were unaware they were half-Jewish. I admit I said this in an effort to needle my parents, for whom the topic of religion was taboo. If they didn't try to hide or deny their Jewishness, they never discussed it either, not in front of me at any rate. At some level I'm sure my mother envied her sister for having married a gentile, moreover a member of the old New England aristocracy. On the other hand, she could take comfort in having secured for a husband the next best thing—a brilliant scholar who was a wholly secular Jew. Probably my father couldn't have gotten a job at an exclusive school like Miss Porter's, but as a tenured professor at a prestigious Ivy League university, who was he to complain?

And who are you, faithful reader, to complain if I'm no self-effacing Watson or over-awed Boswell? I'm perfectly aware that you couldn't care less about Clarissa Stone. In order to understand my relationship to Howard Phillips Lovecraft, however, you have to know something about me and my family. Given the role I was to play in the life of the great author, I feel I'm entitled to be a little self-indulgent.

"I sat next to a strange man on the bus today," I said after I had finished my account of Aunt Kitty and Uncle George's ultra-Anglo-Saxon home life. My parents had responded in monosyllables, unwilling apparently to give me the satisfaction of rising to the bait. "I was planning to read my book, but—"

"Honey, I hope you…I mean, you can't be too careful. The people who ride buses—I don't mean you of course, you're just a student—but some grown men, they—"

"Oh, don't worry, Mother. He was a gentleman, a prissy type wearing one of those old-fashioned detachable collars. If anything he seemed frightened of me."

My father smiled and said, "Knowing my Clarissa, I'm sure you talked the poor man's ear off the whole trip."

"On the contrary, Dad, he did most of the talking."

"What about?"

"Architecture mostly. By coincidence he'd also visited Farmington over the weekend. He just gushed about the colonial buildings there."

"Did he tell you his name?"

"Lovecraft—H. P. Lovecraft."

"That's an odd one. Wonder what he changed it from." My father laughed. "Did this Mr. Lovecraft say what he did for a living?"

"He's a writer. He publishes stories in magazines like *Weird Tales*."

"A pulp, huh?"

"He's also a free-lance editor or revisionist, as he calls it. He even offered to critique my poetry."

My parents exchanged glances. "Oh, honey, you didn't promise to see this man again, did you?" my mother said.

"I invited him to hitch a ride with us from Union Station, as a matter of fact, but he said he preferred to walk. He wasn't about to accept any favors from me."

I further assured my parents of my new acquaintance's respectability, and in the end my father said he saw no harm in my sending him some of my poetry if I so wished. As someone who grew up in exotic and suspect New York City, I didn't have a lot of friends at Miss Abbot's, the Providence girls' school where I was a sophomore. Despite its liberal if not bohemian reputation, I had yet to fit in there. (I wouldn't have touched proper Miss Porter's with a ten-foot pole, by the way—nor they me probably.) The teachers and the course work were by my exalted standards run-of-the-mill. To his credit, my father was wise enough not to discourage me from a pursuit that had evidently piqued my jaded teenage interest.

After helping my mother rinse the dishes, I typed out three of my better poems, poems that in my view my English teacher had insufficiently appreciated, and put them in an envelope addressed to Mr. H. P. Lovecraft, 10 Barnes Street, Providence, R.I. I also wrote him a brief letter, reminding him who I was and saying how thrilled I would be to have a professional writer read and assess my work. I urged him to be honest. I could take criticism—at least from people I respected. As an additional favor, I asked that he send me a copy of the poem he had been kind enough to recite on the bus.

A few days later I returned from school and there it was on the table in the front hall—a thick plain envelope with my name on it in flowing script. The address of a New York bookseller was crossed out in the upper-lefthand corner, but on the back, squeezed into the bottom corner of the flap, were the name and address of my travel companion. Grabbing my prize, I rushed upstairs without going to the kitchen for a snack, my usual after-school routine. Thankfully my mother appeared not to be home, but I closed my bedroom door to ensure I wasn't disturbed.

The letter consisted of several thin sheets, each side filled with a spider-like hand that was hard to read at first. The opening page consisted largely of courtesies, commenting on the agreeableness of my company on the Providence coach the previous Sunday, the "honour" (he used English spellings) of receiving an epistle from an intelligent and talented young lady such as myself, and so on. The politeness of it all was a wonder.

Then he settled down to the business at hand, a lengthy analysis of the three poems I had been so kind to mail him. My adult self would be embarrassed to quote even short passages from these immature and awkward effusions, but you can well imagine that they amounted to feeble imitations of certain favorite contemporary poets. My mentor's advice, never less than unfailingly tactful, had mainly to do with mechanics—the importance of regular rhyme. As for content, he complimented me on the sincerity of my sentiments, leaving it unclear whether or not he actually approved of them. He declined to comment on the subtle erotic pun in one poem—maybe it was too subtle. All and all, though, I was tremendously flattered.

On both sides of the last sheet was "Providence," thirteen stanzas following a simple ABAB rhyme scheme. It was a joyful, lyrical poem and certainly technically superior to any verse I was capable of—and yet there was something missing. I read it again and then it hit me. There weren't any people in the poem, unless you counted the dead: "stern fathers 'neath the mould…airy hosts…grey ghosts." Even the narrative voice came across as vague. Who was this guy so nostalgic for the past and bits of landscape and old buildings? His pretty images weren't about to make me like living in a small, dull provincial city any better. Hearing "Providence" for the first time on the bus it had sounded marvelous, but studying it on the page I could tell it wasn't first-rate. If this was a typical specimen, then Mr. Lovecraft had not been falsely modest about his poetic abilities. (Later, when I read his sonnet cycle, "Fungi from Yuggoth," I had to revise my opinion upward.)

Of course, in the reply I later wrote I chose only to praise "Providence." I could be tactful too. Naturally I thanked him for reading my work so carefully and for his suggested revisions. I decided it would be pushing it to send him any more of my poetry, and instead went on at some length about T. S. Eliot, parroting something I'd read about "The Love Song of J. Alfred Prufrock," in an effort I suppose to impress him with my seriousness. The fact is I wasn't sure what I as a fifteen-year-old girl had to offer in return, yet I didn't want our correspondence to end after only a single exchange of letters.

I shouldn't have worried. The eldritch gentleman responded to my second letter as warmly as he did to the first, possibly relieved to have found no juvenile verses enclosed. On the other hand, in his second missive, wholly unprompted, he included more of his own work: a clipping or cutting, as he called it in his British fashion, of a long poem called "Waste Paper: A Poem of Profound Insignificance," which he asked me to return; and a pamphlet entitled *Further Criticism of Poetry*, which he said I was welcome to keep.

"Waste Paper" proved to be a parody of Eliot's masterpiece, *The Waste Land*, showing that if Mr. Lovecraft didn't appreciate modern poetry he at least had a sense of humor. In the accompanying letter he remarked that earlier in the year he had attended a reading by "the enigmatical & celebrated T. S. Eliot—interesting if not quite explicable." *Further Criticism of Poetry* amounted to a set of formal guidelines consistent with the advice he'd given me earlier. In his letter he explained that he had written it for the National Amateur Press Association. He had once been an officer of the rival United Amateur Press Association, and now after a long lull was once again becoming active in the field. While it often fell short of its ideals, he asserted, amateurdom had the merit of championing literary expression free of commercialism.

Well, as my father's daughter I was aware, as Dr. Johnson put it, that nobody but a blockhead ever wrote except for money. What sensible grownup would waste his or her time on unpaid writing? In my reply, after checking with my father as to the exact wording, I quoted Dr. Johnson and asked Mr. Lovecraft if he agreed with the sage's opinion. I don't think I did this as a deliberate goad, though from the somewhat defensive response I received it was obvious I had touched on a sensitive topic. He went on at some length to explain that the good doctor was given to exaggerated rhetoric and in any case could not be blamed for failing to esteem a branch of aesthetic development that did not blossom until the century after his death.

He also enclosed a copy of an amateur press publication from 1917, the *United Amateur*, which contained a piece called "A Reminiscence of Dr. Samuel Johnson," by "Humphrey Littlewit, Esq." This odd name was just one of the several eighteenth-century pseudonyms he was fond of assuming in his early amateur days, he explained. In this delightful sketch, the narrator, purportedly born in 1690, reminisces in mock eighteenth-century prose about Johnson and his literary circle. Toward the end he shows the doctor some doggerel rhyme he's revised, but the Great Cham of Letters is unimpressed. If I hadn't suspected it already, this was conclusive evidence that Mr. Lovecraft not only had a sense of humor but could laugh at himself.

Up to this point I had jealously kept his communications to myself, but here was something I had to share with someone I knew would truly appreciate it—my father. That afternoon, before he returned from the campus, I left the *United Amateur* on his desk in the study, opened to the first page of "A Reminiscence of Dr. Samuel Johnson."

In the evening, at the dinner table, my father did not start as usual by holding forth about his day in the classroom. Instead he turned to my mother and said:

"I found the most extraordinary item on my desk when I got home, Ruth. Do you know anything about it?"

"What are you talking about, Henry?"

"The *United Amateur*? 'A Reminiscence of Dr. Samuel Johnson'? Humphrey Littlewit?"

"What?" By this point any fool who knew my mother could tell she didn't have a clue.

"Ah, I should've known," Dad said, looking suddenly at me. "You were asking the other day about one of Johnson's aphorisms. Where in the world did you come up with this, this pastiche? It's one of the cleverest things of its kind I've ever read."

"Mr. Littlewit himself sent it to me."

"You mean the author—"

"Yes, Dad. I know he's over two hundred years old and gets tired easily, but when I wrote him—"

"Wait a minute. Is this 'Mr. Littlewit' the same as your Mr. Lovelace?"

"Dad, it's Lovecraft, not Lovelace!"

"Well, next time you write Mr. Lovelace, I mean Lovecraft, you can tell him for me I think his wit is nothing to belittle. With your permission, Clarissa, I'd like to show this *jeu d'esprit* to some of my colleagues in the department. I'm sure they'll get a big kick out of it too."

When my father came home at the end of the week he was pleased to report that his prediction had been correct. Other members of the English faculty had been just as tickled by "A Reminiscence of Dr. Samuel Johnson" as he was. Perhaps, he suggested, we ought to invite the ancient author over sometime. My mother, who was in charge of all social matters, reluctantly approved, since she still had reservations about the suitability of my having an older single man as a friend. My father countered that if the fellow was a pervert he was a learned pervert and should at least be good company for one evening.

In my next letter I described what a hit "A Reminiscence of Dr. Samuel Johnson" had made in the Stone household, as well as among the Brown University English department. I added that my parents were curious to meet him. Was he free for dinner some night? I didn't try to hide my own eagerness at this prospect. I had to wait nearly a week for the reply.

Mr. Lovecraft felt highly complimented that my father and other professional scholars, genuine authorities on eighteenth-century literature unlike himself, had seen fit to praise such an ephemeral effort. As for my family's generous invitation, he was, to his deep regret, too busy for the moment to accept. In particular, he had to finish revising a long short story for a writer friend. This task was especially demanding because he had to rewrite the tale in his own words while remaining faithful to his friend's original concepts. In addition, he and his aunt had to look for a new place to live, as they had decided to consolidate households. While he didn't say so, I gathered the reason for this move was economic. I was disappointed, but partially mollified by his promise to get together when his schedule allowed. In the meantime he wasn't too busy to remain in "epistolary conversation."

So our relationship was stuck on paper, where we continued to address each other as "Dear Mr. Lovecraft" and "Dear Miss Stone." More than once after school as the weather got warmer I took a detour and walked past what he playfully referred to as "Tenbarnes," an unremarkable double-house of Victorian vintage. If I wasn't lucky enough to spot him through a window, then perhaps I might run into him strolling in the neighborhood. But I never did. When I asked him about his daily schedule, he admitted he tended to sleep during the day and work through the night. As much as I would have welcomed it, a bachelor gentleman was not about to invite a proper young lady to visit him at home.

Then in early May came the announcement that he had found a new home, the top floor of 66 College Street, on the crest of College

Hill near the main gates of the university. He expected to move by the middle of the month. His aunt, Mrs. Gamwell, would join him a couple of weeks after that. During this period there was a gap in our correspondence, followed by his longest letter to date, describing in rapturous detail his new quarters, which for colonial charm beat any Georgian relic in Farmington. Now that they were settled in, he said in closing, his aunt would be pleased if I might stop in one afternoon for tea. With an older female relative in residence, it would appear a visit from a proper young lady was permitted.

On the appointed day, shortly after the end of the school year, I walked south on Waterman Street toward the campus, turned right past the John Hay Library, and went a short distance downhill to 66 College. Since my correspondent's last letter had included a drawing (not bad, but obviously the work of a non-artist), I had no trouble recognizing the two-story yellow house, with monitor roof and wooden fanlight above the doorway. The place was set in from the sidewalk, amidst a little grassy court. At the top of the stoop there were two bells, one marked "Shepherd."

When I rang the other, unmarked bell, a faint voice called "just a minute," and soon afterwards I heard the clatter of footsteps on uncarpeted stairs—and then a thumping, crashing noise ending in a loud thud. Fearing some calamity, I tried the door, which fortunately was unlocked. I was glad I was careful to open it only a few inches, for when I poked my head in I saw *an elderly woman sprawled on the floor behind it, moaning in pain and clutching her leg!*

Chapter 3

So my first visit to 66 College Street got off, literally, on the wrong foot! I had scarcely asked the poor woman what I could to do help when Mr. Lovecraft appeared at the top of the stairs. "My dear aunt…"

"Oh, Howard!" she cried. "Please call an ambulance. I think I've broken my ankle."

Though Mrs. Gamwell was evidently in great pain, she apologized for her clumsiness, stumbling on the stairs in her rush to answer the bell. This was no way to greet a guest! That she could make this little joke suggested that her injuries couldn't be too serious.

A minute or two later, after making an emergency phone call, Mr. Lovecraft was kneeling with me by his aunt as she lay on the floor, assuring her that an ambulance was on its way. He didn't actually take her hand or otherwise lend physical support, but his tender and solicitous words to her while we waited showed the depth of his feeling.

At last the ambulance arrived, and it seemed the most natural thing in the world for me to accompany both accident victim and nearest relative on the ride across town to Rhode Island Hospital. There in the emergency room we learned that Mrs. Gamwell had indeed broken her ankle. It would have to be put in a cast and she would have to stay in the hospital.

Throughout this upsetting business my companion maintained a sort of stoic calm. I couldn't tell whether he minded my presence. At any rate, he didn't object to my sitting with him in silence while we awaited the doctor. When the doctor did bring word that Mrs. Gamwell was resting comfortably in her room and could receive visitors briefly, Mr. Lovecraft made it understood that he wished to see his aunt alone. As a non-family member, I felt this was only appropriate.

Only when we left the hospital together did the situation become awkward.

"Miss Stone," he began, "I cannot tell you how grateful I am for your help in this crisis. You have done too much already by coming to the hospital. Allow me to give you some money for a taxi. Your parents—"

"My parents aren't expecting me home yet. It's only five." Hardly more than an hour had passed since I had called at 66 College with such unfortunate results.

"Why don't we share a taxi, Mr. Lovecraft?" I continued. "I'll pay."

"My dear Miss Stone, you mustn't. I was going to walk home."

"Then I'll walk with you."

We argued some more, but when I insisted I was going to walk the mile back to College Hill, unescorted if he wasn't gentleman enough to keep me company, he gave in. He set a brisk pace and I would have demanded he slow down had we not been forced to stop every other block or so for red lights. He also betrayed his annoyance, if that's what it was, in the way he spoke of the Providence commercial district, its handful of skyscrapers a pathetic imitation of the monstrous monoliths of "the pest zone." I could guess that he meant New York City.

We were both a bit breathless by the time we reached the top of College Street. The shadows were beginning to lengthen in the late afternoon sun. A warm breeze rustled the branches of a tall elm tree, full of spring greenery, that stood in the grassy court in front of the house. It was in fact a lovely day.

"Miss Stone, you have been most kind," said Mr. Lovecraft at last.

"Aren't you going to invite me in?" I replied.

"Miss Stone, I—"

"The least you can do is offer me some tea. Or better yet, I'll make you some!"

Mr. Lovecraft refused to meet my eye. Then, looking furtively left to right, as if he feared the neighbors might catch him in some shameful act, he muttered, "You are quite the persistent young lady. Very well then. Come in."

I followed him into the house and up the stairs, careful to mind my step. At the head of the stairs was a hall and beyond, through a paneled door that opened with a latch, was the study. It was a square room, filled with mostly antique furniture: chairs, desks, and large central table, which was heaped with books and papers. Bookcases occupied most of the wall space. The only obviously modern fixture was a typewriter on a table in a corner. Mr. Lovecraft was soon pointing out the features of the 1800 period that charmed him so: wide floor-boards, small-paned windows, colonial mantel and fireplace, with chimney cupboards.

"I keep half-expecting a museum guard to come around and kick me out at five o'clock closing time!" he exclaimed.

"Well, it's past five now and I'm ready for some tea, with a little milk please. As I said I'd be glad to make it, if you'll just show me—"

"No, no, Miss Stone. You are my guest. Please wait here."

After he left the room, a magazine on top of one of the piles on the central table caught my eye. It was the July issue of *Weird Tales*, with a fiend on the front cover aiming a dagger at the heart of a scantily clad woman. I picked it up and took a seat in a Morris chair near a corner window. The contents page listed a story entitled "The Dreams in the Witch-House," by H. P. Lovecraft.

I had read the first couple of pages by the time my host came back, a steaming mug in one hand and a plate with two doughnuts in the other. He set these on a side table next to the Morris chair.

"Aren't you having anything?" I asked.

"My coffee's in the kitchen, if you'll again excuse me."

When he returned, with cup and saucer, he explained that he didn't care at all for tea, which his aunt preferred, though he was exceedingly fond of coffee, with four or five lumps of sugar.

"Yuck!"

"My sweet tooth has no limit, Miss Stone," he said, settling himself in a rocker by the central table. He shifted some papers to make room for his coffee. "I love to snack on chocolate, while ice cream or pie—blueberry, mince, or apple, with ice cream on it—forms my favorite dessert. I can't get enough ice cream, and frequently make a full meal of it in the summer."

"You mean you'll eat ice cream for dinner and nothing else?"

"That is so, young lady."

"Do you like any foods other than dessert?"

"I like nothing better than a good old New England turkey dinner, with gravy and cranberry jelly and all the trimmings. Fortunately, I was able to partake of several such feasts during the past autumn and winter."

"Well, it might not be the season, but I'll make sure my mother fixes a good old New England turkey dinner when you come over to our house."

"Miss Stone, please…"

Evidently the idea of accepting kindnesses from me or my family was hard for him to take. Against such a defense the best policy was to attack.

"Don't you think it's time you stopped calling me Miss Stone? I wish you'd call me Clarissa."

"Miss Stone, for an old gentleman to address a mature young lady—"

"For chrissakes I'm only fifteen!"

For once he was at a loss for words.

"Why you are a mere child," he murmured at last. "I thought… you look as if you were close to attaining your majority."

"I wrote you I was a sophomore—a sophomore in *high school*," I said, flattered by the unintentional compliment but unwilling to give up the offensive just yet. "What did you think I was, a moron who had to keep repeating tenth grade?"

"My dear Miss Stone—"

"Clarissa."

"Forgive me, *Clarissa*," he said, with the trace of a smile, "for assuming you to be older than your actual years." I believe he was relieved to find he was entertaining a girl in her teens instead of a nearly grown woman.

"Thank you…Mr. Lovecraft."

"Ah, in all fairness, you must no longer address me by my patronymic. Would it be too much to ask to call me 'Grandpa'?" He was now actually smiling.

"How old are you?"

"I am in my forty-third year."

It was my turn to be surprised. I would have guessed him to be closer to fifty than forty.

"That's too young for anyone to be called Grandpa. No, if you don't mind I'd rather call you H. P."

The smile disappeared. "You're not the first to call me that," he said in a low voice.

"That's how you sign your stories…H. P."

"Indeed."

"I've just been reading your story here in *Weird Tales*," I said, sensing that it would be imprudent to dwell further on the name issue. "I like the witchcraft stuff at the start, but don't the characters ever talk to each other? I flipped ahead and couldn't find any conversations."

While I finished my tea and second doughnut, I listened to a disquisition on the theory and practice of the weird tale. Apart from his inability to write it, he asserted that dialogue tended to draw too much attention to the human point-of-view. In any sincere work above the pulp level the focus had to be on the given violation of natural law, not the fictional characters. In other words, effect was everything—people counted for next to nothing.

"You care about your aunt, don't you?"

"Miss Stone—pardon me, *Clarissa*—I'm speaking of literary aesthetics."

"Yes, but isn't what a writer says in his fiction often a clue to what he really believes?"

This led to some extended debate, which he appeared to enjoy even more than I did, perhaps because I was out of my depth. I simply wasn't as well read nor was I a professional author who knew about these things from experience. The best I could do was try to divert him to the personal from the abstract ideas he expounded with such passion.

I decided asking him for more tea might break the conversational flow, so instead I inquired about Mrs. Gamwell. There had been a close familial bond between them, he acknowledged, since he was a boy. His aunt had been a popular member of the younger Providence social set and had brought the principal touch of gaiety to his grandparents' rather conservative household. He hinted at some loss or tragedy in later years, leaving me to wonder whether a Mr. Gamwell had played any significant role in her life. Caught up to the present, he worried about the expense of her hospital stay, not to mention the disruptions her invalid state was sure to bring to both her schedule and his own.

"I'd be happy to do what I can," I said. "My family doesn't have any plans to go away this summer, except maybe for short visits to New York."

"I much appreciate your thoughtful offer," he said, "though I'm afraid only I can attend to the mass of work that threatens to engulf me." He gestured with his coffee cup toward the stacks of papers on his table.

"Are you writing a new story?"

"No, repeated rejection has all but dried up original composition. I must apply my pen to the usual revision jobs, as well as to answering correspondence."

"You like to write letters, don't you?"

"At times it seems as if I spend all my waking hours in letter-writing."

"Just how many people do you write to?"

"At last count I had some seventy-five regular correspondents. The trouble is many of them require research, work, or extended argumentative replies. I must start to prune, but how am I to get out of epistolary obligations without coming across as snobbish or uncivil!"

The taste of doughnut in my mouth suddenly turned sickly. All along I had assumed myself to be part of an exclusive club, one of the lucky few who could claim H. P. Lovecraft as a pen pal. To learn that I was merely one of dozens and dozens came as a humbling blow.

"Who are these people?"

"Amateur press colleagues, fellow writers of supernatural horror, readers of *Weird Tales*…"

"And you consider them all your friends?"

"Indeed, I do. My correspondents constitute my social world, as I know hardly any congenial souls in Providence."

"Okay, Mr. Lovecraft," I announced, rising to my feet. "I can take a hint. Not only did I almost kill your aunt this afternoon, I've been wasting your valuable time for months!"

The next instant I burst into tears. My host remained seated in his rocker, apparently too stunned to take his cue. I was hoping he would at least stand up and offer some consoling words, but when he stayed put, regarding me as if I were a witch or other horrible creature of his imagination, I decided to make my exit. I ran out of the study, but took care not to go too fast down the stairs.

Chapter 4

Two days later it arrived—an apology running to several closely written sheets. It opened "My dear Clarissa" and was signed "E'ch-Pi." The hundreds of words in between boiled down to his saying how sorry he was for having offended me. When he had casually remarked that he knew few congenial souls in Providence, he of course hadn't meant to suggest that I numbered among the uncongenial. He was guilty of an unpardonable act of thoughtlessness, owing no doubt to his lack of ordinary daily contact with people. In truth, in the months since our meeting on the Hartford coach, he had welcomed my always fresh, bright, and energetic point-of-view. I suspected some of this was bull, but all in all I don't think I could have wished for a more handsome apology.

In my reply to "H. P." (whose "phonetic" initials I refused to imitate—too silly), I apologized for my behavior. At times I could be oversensitive, I admitted, as my mother knew only too well. I tended to take as slights off-hand comments from others who hadn't meant to wound. It was I who had imposed on his kindness, insisting he give me tea when he must have been preoccupied with concern for his poor aunt. I asked how Mrs. Gamwell was doing and whether she felt up to receiving visitors. "Please," I wrote at the end, "let me know if there's anything I can do to help either of you." Where before I had signed my letters "Sincerely" or "Sincerely yours," I closed "Your friend, Clarissa."

As tempted as I was to follow up by phone, I sensed that to get in touch by this modern means would be too direct, a violation of our epistolary protocol. When I received no response to my letter after a few days, however, I gave him a ring, having first determined that only his aunt was listed with information.

H. P. did sound startled to hear my voice, but he quickly repeated the essence of his last letter—and apologized for not yet responding to my latest. His aunt was doing fine, he added, and would welcome a visit from me at my convenience. The following afternoon? Yes, that would be all right. No, there was nothing I could do for him at the moment… It was clear he wasn't used to chatting on the phone, so when he hinted that he had some work to do, I let him go.

The next day my mother, who had shopping to do downtown, drove me to Rhode Island Hospital. There I found Mrs. Gamwell in a semiprivate room. She was lying in bed, with her wounded ankle, encased in plaster, hanging from a sling. I gave her a bunch of begonias, for which she thanked me warmly while a nurse went in search of a vase. At her request I pulled a chair up to her bed. I immediately felt at ease with this woman, who in contrast to her nephew came across as naturally sociable.

"How good of you to come see me, Miss Stone," she said. "At last we have a chance to get acquainted."

"It's the least I could do, Mrs. Gamwell. I feel guilty. If I hadn't—"

"Tush, girl. It was an accident. No one's to blame. Let's say no more about it. We have better things to talk about. You must start by telling me all about yourself."

Had H. P. told her nothing about me—or was the old lady just being courteous?

"Where do you go to school, dear? Hope High?"

"No, Miss Abbot's."

"Mercy me. Why that's where I went to school."

"Didn't H. P. tell you I was a Miss Abbot's girl?"

"You know, dear, he might have mentioned the fact, the day you and I were supposed to have tea. Falling downstairs must have knocked it out of my silly old head."

We discussed Miss Abbot's for a bit. I didn't try to hide my less than enthusiastic feelings about the school—or about Providence. I wasn't exaggerating too much when I told her that meeting her nephew on the Hartford bus had been the most exciting thing to happen to me since my family moved from New York.

From this it was an easy step to a subject of greater interest to us both, Howard Phillips Lovecraft, who she confirmed was her nearest living kin. Howard's mother, Susan, the prettiest of the three Phillips sisters, had died in 1921. Her other sister, Lillian, had passed on just the previous year. She made no mention of her nephew's father—or of any other male relations of her own generation. I was eager to ask more questions about the family, but knew well enough not to press.

"Dear Howard," said Mrs. Gamwell. "He works so hard for so little. A writer's life can be so discouraging. I don't know how he bears it. I'm sure I would've given up long ago. And now he has me, his crippled aunt, to worry about."

"Mrs. Gamwell, I wish there was something I could do. But I get the feeling that H. P., that is, your nephew, doesn't want my help. For instance, when I invited him to my parents' house for dinner, he said no. Of course, he had excellent reasons and was very polite, but still…"

"Howard was always a shy boy, Miss Stone. You must understand."

"But turning down invitations from your friends isn't normal!"

"You mustn't take it personally, dear girl. It's just that Howard can sometimes take traditional Yankee reserve too far."

"But I know he and my father would have so much to talk about. Dad's read a story of his, the one about Samuel Johnson, and thought it was a peach—and Dad should know, being an expert on eighteenth-century English literature!"

"Pardon me a moment, dear," Mrs. Gamwell said, wincing slightly as she shifted her foot in the sling. "There, that's better."

I asked if she needed another pillow or the nurse. She shook her head.

"You know, Miss Stone, you're right." She sighed. "Howard should make more of an effort to get out locally and see people—especially nice, educated people, even if they do come from New York." She smiled. "Tell you what. Ask my nephew again to come for supper. I'll see to it that he accepts this time."

"Oh, Mrs. Gamwell, thank you!"

"Howard should eat good solid meals more often. I'm afraid I'm no help in the kitchen, even when both legs are in working order."

"I know H. P. likes turkey," I said, my mind already on the menu, "but turkey might not be so easy to get at the market this time of year. Are there any other foods he likes—or doesn't like?"

"Seafood. He simply detests all seafood, despite his New England upbringing. In the old days, when my father, Whipple Phillips, presided over the dinner table…"

As I listened to the woman reminisce, I realized that H. P. wasn't the only member of his family capable of rambling on if given half a chance. And while she may not have been as gifted a story-teller as her nephew, I nevertheless welcomed the chance to learn more of the family history.

When at last I said I had to go meet my mother in front of the hospital, Mrs. Gamwell said how pleased she was to meet me. She hoped I would come see her again soon. I promised I would. Then she made a final, somewhat curious comment:

"One word of advice, Miss Stone. If my nephew is at all stand-offish it may be because you remind him of someone."

"Who?"

"It's not just your looks but also your manner."

"Who, Mrs. Gamwell?"

"Never mind who, dear. Someone suffice it to say that Howard used to be close to and feels, well, sorry about now."

"A lost love?"

"I've said too much, Miss Stone. You mustn't keep your mother waiting. And please, when you next see my dear nephew, don't let on that you're aware of…of what I just told you."

"Oh, I won't, Mrs. Gamwell," I said. "I swear I won't."

"We Miss Abbot's girls have to stick together." The old lady smiled.

In the car I recounted to my mother the substance of my conversation with Mrs. Gamwell. If this lady with her genteel background was impressed that I came from a nice family, well, that was in Mother's view a point in Mr. Lovecraft's favor. But before I reissued my dinner invitation, she would have to check first with my father. My having an older man as a friend troubled her. Why didn't I get to know boys nearer my own age? Perhaps it was a mistake my going to an all girls school. When she was my age… I didn't argue, because I was pretty sure I could rely on my father to give me what I wanted—and in fact Dad did come through when he got home from the John Hay, where he was doing some research. As far as he was concerned, the author of "A Reminiscence of Dr. Samuel Johnson" was still welcome for dinner.

I wrote him a short note that evening. Two days later H. P. R.S.V.P.ed—by phone. By the time I realized to whom my mother was talking she'd hung up.

"That was your Mr. Lovecraft, Clarissa."

"Mother! Why didn't you let me speak to him? What did he say?"

"He didn't say much, dear, but his voice… It was just the sort of voice you'd expect a ghost-story writer to have—spooky, haunted."

"Mother!"

"Or maybe it was the connection."

"Mother, don't be a goof. Is he coming for dinner or not?"

"Yes, dear, everything's set—for Friday, at seven."

At seven that Friday evening I was in front of my dresser mirror, applying the final touches to my hair and makeup. Mother had given me permission to put on a smidgeon of blush and lipstick. I had of course chosen to wear my prettiest summer dress. It was too warm for stockings.

When the doorbell rang, I proceeded calmly downstairs. It had been decided that I would be the one to greet our guest on his arrival.

"Good evening, young lady," said H. P. when I opened the door.

"Hi there!" I said. "Glad you could make it!"

He stood tight-lipped on the threshhold, looking pale and lean in a baggy white tropical suit. In one claw-like hand he clutched a straw-boater, in the other a box of Hershey's milk chocolates.

"Come on in, H. P. Say, that's some snappy suit you're wearing."

"Thank you. It was a gift from a dear friend, the late Henry S. Whitehead, of Dunedin, Florida."

When he failed to compliment me on my dress, I attributed the oversight to nervousness rather than bad manners. It may have been my imagination, but to me this forty-two-year-old man, alias "Grandpa," had the timid, self-conscious air of a teenage boy meeting his girlfriend's parents for the first time.

My parents by now were waiting in the front hall.

"H. P., I'd like you to meet Ruth and Henry Stone… Mother, Dad, this is Mr. Lovecraft."

H. P. bowed to my mother and handed her the box of chocolates, while he gave my father a quick, jerky handshake. "Can I get you a drink, Mr. Lovecraft?" Dad asked as we moved into the living room.

"A ginger ale, if you wouldn't mind, Mister…or is it Professor Stone?"

"Please, it's Henry. And we can offer you something harder if you wish."

"I prefer ginger ale all the same, thank you. Fruit juice would be equally agreeable."

"I hope you don't mind if I fix myself a gin and tonic, Mr. Lovelace...sorry, Mr. Lovecraft. I know repeal won't be official for another few months. I'd be a bad host to flaunt the law in front of a guest who cares about such niceties."

"Not at all, sir. It is your home. Far be if from me to impose my standards on you."

This was not a good start. Teetotaling Puritan meets booze-loving liberal. Though they were practically the same age, at this rate I was sure Dad would address H. P. as "Mr. Lovecraft" all evening, when he wasn't addressing him by the name of the villain in *Clarissa*, while H. P. would avoid calling my father anything at all. I could have cringed with embarrassment.

While Dad fixed drinks at the bar-cart by the kitchen door, my mother and I watched H. P. survey the living room. We possessed no antiques or family heirlooms as such, and I could guess that the art-deco furniture and contemporary paintings which we did have weren't to his taste. When Mother commented on the warm, sticky weather we'd been having, H. P. replied that he'd been very much enjoying it.

We all sat down around the coffee table after Dad brought the drinks. I was on the verge of asking H. P. about his aunt's health, when our cat, Fiorello, stepped into the room. My parents had allowed me to get a kitten when we moved to Providence, a place where, in contrast to our Manhattan apartment, it could have a yard to play in.

"Why bless my ears and whiskers, isn't he the handsome young gentleman!" exclaimed H. P. as Fiorello sniffed at his trouser leg. When Fiorello leapt into his lap, our guest positively beamed.

"I hope you like cats, Mr. Lovecraft," said my mother.

"Like cats? Mrs. Stone, I am a lifelong ailurophile!"

Here at last was some common ground. While H. P. stroked Fiorello, who responded to this attention with loud purrs, he extolled the virtues of the feline tribe. Clearly cats ranked in his estimation up there with colonial architecture and ice cream.

"Do you have a cat yourself, Mr. Lovecraft?"

"Alas, Mrs. Stone, I do not. As a boy I was so devastated by the loss of my sable-furred Nigger-Man that I haven't had the heart to replace him with another."

"You had a pet cat named Nigger-Man?" I asked.

"Yes, child. He was black as coal."

At this point my father said something about Samuel Johnson having been fond of cats, and soon the two men were deep into conversation about eighteenth-century England. My father's remarks on "A Reminiscence of Dr. Samuel Johnson" made H. P. blush, but modesty didn't prevent the author from explaining at some length the background of its composition and publication. If there was little I could contribute, I was at least satisfied that the ice appeared to be broken. When my mother excused herself, I decided to join her in the kitchen.

Dinner itself was a success, I thought. Mother roasted a chicken in lieu of a turkey, serving it along with baked potatoes, green beans, and a salad. For me, as meals at home went, it was nothing that special. For H. P., however, it was a veritable feast, given how he devoured more than one helping of everything. Between mouthfuls he praised my mother's cooking most eloquently. Conversation otherwise focused on major topics of the day: President Roosevelt, the Depression, the New Deal, Hitler and the Nazis. Again the men dominated the serious discussion.

My parents drank wine, while H. P. stuck with ginger ale. He said he didn't care for milk, which was my meal-time beverage. By dessert—banana splits with three different kinds of ice cream (my choice)—he had relaxed to the point where, with only slight prompting from them, he was calling my parents Henry and Ruth. They in turn dropped the Mr. Lovecraft, but were a little confused whether to address him as Howard or H. P. To judge from his smiles, either way was fine with him.

After dinner our guest declined my father's invitation to join him in a cigar. We had overwhelmed him with our hospitality. He could impose no longer. At the door, hat in hand, H. P. bowed to me and my mother, looking neither of us in the eye. He and my father shook hands and in the next instant he was gone.

I was dying to know what my parents thought of H. P., but wasn't about to ask. Fortunately, they had drunk enough wine at dinner to be more open than usual in front of me. Back in the kitchen, where we all helped with the cleaning up, Dad spoke first:

"A man who loves cats can't be all bad. And he does have an impressive knowledge of my own field for an amateur. I like his politics too. A bit surprising to find someone of his class a New Deal supporter."

"His attitude to race—or to what's going on in Germany—doesn't seem terribly progressive," said Mother.

"In that respect he's no worse than the majority of educated white people in this country, I'm afraid."

"He was so proper, Henry. I thought he was never going to stop calling us Mr. and Mrs. Stone."

"A traditional type of Yankee, Ruth. Doesn't drink. Doesn't smoke. Doesn't screw."

"Henry!"

"Pretend you didn't hear that, Clarissa," Dad said.

"You think he's totally repressed then?" Mother continued.

"Probably, but there's one thing that makes me wonder. The way he shook hands. He tickled my palm."

"So?"

"Among some circles that's considered a kind of signal…"

"Henry, do you think Clarissa should be hearing this?"

"Shush, Mother. Dad, what do you mean a signal?"

"Well, ladies, I hear the palm-tickle, as it's called—and I emphasize that I know this only from what I hear—is a come-on used by—"

"Dad!"

"—by fairies."

"Dad, H. P. is not a fairy!"

Chapter 5

I mean to say, it was pretty outrageous for Dad to suggest that H. P. might be queer, and in fact over the weekend I got my parents to concede that even if our guest was a deviate he'd have to be crazy to telegraph his inclinations to a stranger, all but certain to be normal, and risk a punch in the nose. While H. P. might be an odd bird, he knew better than to insult his host at first meeting.

"Okay, Clarissa, you win," Dad said. "The man's an innocent—so innocent, I'll bet, that if any attractive female were to crawl into bed with him he'd insist on using a bundling board."

"What's a bundling board?"

"Look it up in the dictionary."

Dad could be annoying that way, making you work to learn something when he could easily have told you the answer himself.

Monday morning there was a letter in the mail addressed in a familiar script to "Professor and Mrs. Henry Stone." Since Mother was out doing errands, I had to wait for her return before I opened it.

"Clarissa, please," said Mother, simultaneously setting down her shopping bag and snatching the envelope.

"I was only saving you the trouble," I replied.

"Well, my goodness…your Mr. Lovecraft does have a lovely way with words, doesn't he? As handsome a thank you as I've ever received, I'm sure."

"May I see?"

"I do wonder, though, why he's afraid to call us Henry and Ruth."

Mother handed me the letter, then headed for the kitchen. It didn't take long to read. It was only a couple of paragraphs, gracious and formal ("Dear Professor and Mrs. Stone," it began), with an affectionate reference to Fiorello but no mention of me whatsoever. I was glad Mother wasn't there to see the disappointment on my face. Hiding my emotions has never been my forte.

I consoled myself with the thought that H. P. would be sending me a thank you separately, but when after a couple of days nothing further came I decided it was time to renew the offensive. I would visit Mrs. Gamwell again. The weather continued fair, and it was a perfect day for a long walk.

At the hospital the old lady was resting in her chair, looking more comfortable than before. An array of cards and flowers by her bed and in the window suggested she had no lack of well-wishing friends. For a moment I feared she might be tired of visitors, but her warm smile reassured me. I first asked about her ankle, which she reported was healing nicely if still very sore.

I didn't have to inquire about "dear Howard." Mrs. Gamwell, as I had hoped, was eager to relay her nephew's impressions of dinner chez Stone: he had enjoyed himself immensely, my mother was a marvelous cook, my father an engaging and brilliant conversationalist. In short, he had been positively overwhelmed by my parents' hospitality. I should have been relieved to hear all this, and yet I couldn't be sure H. P. had been entirely candid, even with his beloved aunt. Despite the compliments, might he prefer to keep his social distance? In his old New England eyes might we appear too "foreign"?

I wasn't about to share my anxieties with Mrs. Gamwell. Instead I encouraged her to reminisce, to tell me more about her parents and her sisters. To my surprise I learned that she had had a brother, Edwin Phillips, who had overseen the family's business affairs after the death of their father. They had once lived in a big house on Angell Street, with servants and a stable, long since torn down.

"Howard was fourteen when the house had to be sold," she said. "He took it very hard."

"Poor H. P.!"

"His high school years were difficult. Nervous trouble, you know, and then his mother wasn't particularly well herself. For a long time Howard hardly left his room."

"Didn't he have any friends?"

"Not by then. For some reason the local boys he used to go bicycling and play detective with had disappeared. Thank heavens he got involved with those amateur journalists when he did or he might still be stuck in his room."

It occurred to me that in some sense H. P. was still stuck in his room, that is, he hadn't fully recovered from an awkward adolescence. Perhaps that accounted in part for his appeal. He was scarcely more mature than I was.

"Mrs. Gamwell, do you think your nephew would mind if I just dropped by College Street later today?" I said. "It's on my way home from the hospital."

"I don't know, dear…"

"Oh, Mrs. Gamwell, please."

"…a young lady just dropping by unannounced, for no good reason, why Howard might—"

"Mrs. Gamwell, please!"

"All right, dear. I have an idea. During his last visit we agreed he'd take some of the extra flowers back to the house—people have been so generous!—but we both forgot. I know he'd like these peonies. You can tell Howard I sent you."

Once again I had reason to thank Mrs. Gamwell. On her instructions I removed the peonies from their vase and wrapped them in some brown paper for ease of carrying. I said I would be back to see her soon.

When I rang the bell at 66 College, I heard H. P.'s thin, high-pitched voice call from the upper regions to enter. The door was unlocked. It was as if I was expected. Had his aunt phoned from the hospital to say I was coming?

H. P. was waiting at the top of the stairs—in his shirt sleeves. This was my first sight of him without a coat and tie. He immediately turned crimson. You would have thought I had caught him in a towel after his bath.

"Why Miss Stone…Clarissa…this is a surprise!" he stuttered.

"Hi there, H. P.!" I replied, determined to ignore his embarrassment. "These flowers are for you. Do you have something I can put them in?"

By now I had crossed the threshold into the study and was casting an eye about for a suitable place to set the flowers. Then I saw that H. P. had company. A trim little man in his thirties, dressed in what looked like Oriental pajamas, had risen from the Morris chair and was regarding me with an air of puzzled bemusement.

· "Hello, missy," he said, extending his hand. "I'm Ed Price. Some people call me 'Malik, the Peacock Sultan,' but you can call me Ed." Ed gave me a conspiratorial wink.

"Malik...Ed, may I introduce Miss Clarissa Stone," H. P. muttered.

"Pleased to meet you," I said, shaking hands.

"The pleasure's all mine, Clarissa," said Ed, clasping my hand with both of his. "I'm so glad this isn't going to be a stag outing after all."

H. P. was positively red-faced by now. "Say, Howard," said Ed, finally dropping my hand. "Does your girl friend bring you flowers every day?"

To avoid further misunderstanding, I explained that the peonies came courtesy of Mrs. Gamwell and they needed to be put in water promptly. H. P. went off in search of a vase, while Ed invited me to have a seat and stay awhile. He was a big talker, and in short order I learned the biographical essentials. Ed, or E. Hoffmann Price, as he was known to his readers, wrote fiction for the pulp magazines. He was in the process of moving and was making a driving tour of the northeast. He used to live in the French quarter of New Orleans, where H. P. had visited him the year before. They had recently collaborated on a story, "Through the Gates of the Silver Key," which the editor of *Weird Tales* had just rejected, but no matter, they'd written the thing for the fun of it. This was the tale, I realized, that H. P. was working on when he claimed he was too busy to come for dinner.

In the meantime H. P. had rejoined us, having found a vase and cleared a space on the central table for the flowers. I was curious to hear more from Ed about New Orleans, but our host interrupted and started to describe his trip there the previous June. When Ed commented that they had stayed up for twenty-eight straight hours, H. P. corrected him: to be precise they had spent twenty-five-and-a-half hours together. Ed said to me that it hadn't been exclusively an intense one-on-one session, thanks to the arrival of some members of the Vieux Carré crowd. H. P. added that they did go out at one point for coffee at the French market across the street.

At any rate, staying awake all night was evidently no hardship for either man. They had visited St. John's churchyard at four that morning, the climax of a tour of Poe sites along Benefit Street. Had I arrived much earlier I would have found them both dozing. I wondered where Ed might be sleeping, then it occurred to me he must be using Mrs. Gamwell's room. Or, if H. P. really were queer…but no, Ed was obviously not the type, even if he did lounge about in Chinese pajamas.

Then the door bell sounded.

"That must be young Brobst," H. P. exclaimed. While H. P. called down the stairs for this latest visitor to enter, Ed explained that Harry Brobst, a Providence friend of Howard's, had accompanied them on their midnight prowl. I was shortly introduced to a large, rangy boy in his early twenties with a friendly, open manner. I liked him instantly. So this was who H. P. had been expecting when I delivered the flowers.

"Mind if I put some of these in your refrigerator, Howard?" said the new guest, who was carrying a brown bag.

"What you got there, Harry?" asked Ed.

"Six bottles of beer."

"And what are you going to do with so *much* of it?" asked H. P.

"Drink it," said Harry. "Only three bottles apiece."

"That's about right for our blighting, blasting, searing curry in the true East Indian fashion," Ed replied. "Not the pallid, gutless, quite innocuous sauce for women and children… Say, I don't mean you, missy. You are staying for dinner, aren't you?"

I glanced at H. P., who looked as if he had just swallowed a mouthful of blighting, blasting, searing curry. Nobody said anything.

"Notwithstanding her mature appearance, Miss Stone is but a girl," H. P. finally quavered. "No doubt her parents—"

"Ah, come on, Howard," said Ed. "I did the shopping. I know we've got enough for four. I could spare her one of my beers."

"I'd be happy to buy more beer," said Harry.

H. P. clutched the study door for support. The color had drained from his face. He seemed on the verge of fainting.

"You okay, Howard?" said Ed.

"I wouldn't want to impose on Mr. Lovecraft's hospitality," I announced in my coldest voice. "And even so, he's right. I'd have to telephone my parents and ask permission."

"It's set then!" cried Ed. "Where's your phone, Howard?"

The phone was in the living room, in Mrs. Gamwell's half of the apartment. On the way I peeked into Mrs. Gamwell's bedroom, where the unmade bed and scattered clothes indicated a temporary male occupant. Fortunately, both parents were home, and after some debate— the presence of two other men complicated the issue—Dad convinced Mother that I could remain at H. P.'s, as long as I was back by nine o'clock, dinner or no dinner.

"These friends of Mr. Lovecraft's, are they like him?" Mother asked.

"Exactly. A couple of schoolmarms. Don't worry."

"All right, Clarissa. But if you're not home by nine, I'll send your father after you with half the Providence police force."

"Don't worry, Mother. These fellows are real gents."

And they were, too. While H. P. and Ed worked in the kitchen on the curry, a dish they claimed they'd been discussing for months in their letters, Harry entertained me in the study with tales of his adventures as an intern at Butler Hospital, the local nut hatch. I asked him how he and H. P. had met. He said he had written his favorite *Weird Tales* author a fan letter, which led to an irregular correspondence. When he knew he would be moving to Providence for this three-year program in psychiatric nursing, his literary hero had urged him to get in touch upon arrival. That was in February of '32. Since then they had gotten together every so often for a walk or a meal. Well, I thought, at least someone found it easy to become H. P.'s friend in Providence.

Since he had no dining-room table, H. P. had to clear the papers and books off the big table, where the flowers made a handy centerpiece. From one of the chimney cupboards he produced some old family china and silver that he said he scarcely ever used, along with some threadbare linen napkins. They made quite the contrast with the brown beer bottles. I declined Ed's offer of a beer, and took his second suggestion of a glass of ice water. H. P. drank hot coffee. From time to time he eyed Ed and Harry apprehensively as they guzzled their beer.

Having tasted curry in New York, I knew what to expect. Despite Ed's boasts that it would draw blisters from a Cordovan boot, the dish he finally served wasn't all that fiery. It was delicious, though, consisting of highly spiced lamb and white rice. A lettuce and tomato salad would have been the perfect accompaniment, but I guessed no one else present was concerned to eat fresh vegetables.

Since H. P. and I were at opposite ends of the table, with the peonies between us, and I had already chatted at length with Harry, I talked mostly to Ed. Or rather I listened to Ed. He was not only a writer, I learned, but also a West Point graduate, a war veteran, a student of Arabic, an amateur fencer, a champion chess player, and an astrologer. This last was of particular interest. I had never had my chart done, and Ed promised he would do mine before he left Providence.

I was enjoying myself, but I was keeping an eye on my watch. I knew I was doing something adult and I didn't want to give my parents an excuse to forbid any future social outings. By 8:30 we had finished the last of the curry and I said I had to leave. Both Ed and Harry pleaded for me to stay longer but I was firm.

"Please stay seated everyone," I said as I got up. Ed rose to his feet.

"Can I give you a ride, Clarissa? The Ford's parked right outside."

"No, thank you, Ed," I replied. "Like H. P., I prefer to walk."

"You sure?"

"Very sure."

"Well, then, you'll just have to come back tomorrow for our motor tour of the countryside."

"Good-bye, Ed."

"Can I see you out the door first?"

"I—"

"I have something else to ask about your horoscope—"

"Ed, that's enough!" yelled H. P. stumbling out of his chair. He bumped the table hard enough to knock over the vase of flowers.

Chapter 6

I was home a few minutes before nine. My parents had finished their dinner and were on the back porch, Dad smoking a cigarette, Mother nursing a glass of sherry. They greeted me as they normally did, apparently in no hurry to probe me about my evening. Dad made a few banal remarks about the beauty of the fading light. I knew, before I turned in, that I would have to give some account of dinner chez Lovecraft.

Just how much to reveal was the question. I began by admitting I'd been wrong to call Harry and Ed schoolmarms—schoolmarms didn't drink six bottles of beer between them. Ignoring Mother's little gasp of shock, I went on to describe how astonished H. P. had been at their alcoholic capacity. Dad chuckled, while Mother tittered nervously. Ed was a pulp writer like H. P., while Harry kept the psychotics in line at the hospital where he worked. I said nothing to suggest that Ed's attentions to myself had verged on the over-friendly, nor did I mention H. P.'s "accident." Before I left, "they" had invited me to join them tomorrow on a tour of the countryside. This sparked a disapproving murmur from Mother, but to my relief no more than that. I went to bed feeling I'd passed muster.

In the morning I was awakened by the ringing phone. It was unusual to get a call that early, and I opened my door a crack the better to eavesdrop. I could hear Mother down the hall:

"…why that's very kind of you…Clarissa did mention…I've never been to that part of Rhode Island…I'm not sure…may I call you back?"

It had to be Ed. A minute later my mother was knocking on my door.

"I just got off the phone, Clarissa, with a Mr. Price," she said.

"That's one of H. P.'s friends I met last night," I answered from my bed.

"He's invited all of us to go motoring with him and your Mr. Lovecraft."

"Swell!"

"He was quite the charmer and it does sound like a treat. I have nothing pressing to do today. I don't know about your father."

I had mixed feelings about my parents joining me on the excursion, but once I came down for breakfast I realized I had no choice. After some discussion, Dad said he preferred to stay home and work on an essay, so if Mother wouldn't mind doing chaperone duty solo…

I phoned H. P. to accept. Ed answered and said they would pick us up at the house in half an hour. Howard was still asleep, but he was sure his host would welcome more company. The Ford could comfortably accommodate four.

When they arrived, H. P. was wearing his summer suit, while Ed was sporting a loose, embroidered shirt that looked vaguely Middle Eastern. I guess Ed was what you would call a true Bohemian. Mother and I wore lightweight traveling dresses. Ed decided I should ride up front next to him, while the other two took the backseat.

We roared south out of Providence on Route 1 in "Great Juggernaut," as H. P. had dubbed Ed's jalopy. We must have been making a good forty-five miles an hour. Conversation wasn't easy in that rattletrap at that speed, but what I did hear from Ed about his astrological studies was fascinating. H. P. filled in Mother, as best as I could tell, on the "plantation" country we were all about to see for the first time.

At some point we turned off the highway onto a side road that led into some dense woods. I can't say I was overly excited by the sightseeing aspect of the trip. This corner of Rhode Island was empty, apart from a few scattered farms and villages. We toured an old mill, helped ourselves to some mulberries growing outside some other historic building, then after asking directions of a local bumpkin went in search of a house with an unusual roof of colonial vintage. Unlike the previous places, this was a private residence. H. P.'s nerve almost failed him when a man answered his knock and he had to explain how we'd like to have a look inside. Ed and I were less interested in the interior than the others, and after a while went outside to wait by the car. We were in the middle of nowhere and Ed was telling me how pretty my dress was, so I suppose I shouldn't have been wholly

surprised when he suddenly slipped his arm around my waist. Well! I hadn't decided whether to slap his face or scream when H. P. and Mother emerged from the house. Ed immediately dropped his arm.

Mother said nothing directly, but insisted that we return at once to Providence, without stopping for lunch. H. P. was speechless, but from his stern, Pilgrim-father expression I could tell he felt we deserved to be put in the stocks. Ed was as affable as ever, agreeing that perhaps it was time to head home. I automatically followed Mother into the back. The two men rode up front. Nobody tried to talk above the noise of Great Juggernaut until we reached the city and exchanged the briefest of good-byes.

A couple of days later came the letter from H. P., for both me and my parents, apologizing at length for Ed's unmentionable behavior. The way he dressed was to be pitied but his worst sin, in H. P.'s view, had been his efforts to inculcate me with the false and pernicious notions of astrology! Needless to say Ed never did do my chart. If Mother fretted a good deal in the aftermath of our country outing, I made it equally clear that I had in no way encouraged Ed to take liberties. Dad said he knew he could count on Mother to do a good job as chaperone—and you had to hand it to Ed for his chutzpah.

Still, I had to wonder when I might see H. P. again. In the circumstances I wasn't about to make the first move. Fortunately, H. P. phoned that same evening—to invite me to meet yet another out-of-town visitor! A female visitor, he quickly added, the daughter of a friend of a friend from California. She was staying in the boarding house across the street from 66 College, and he was sure she would welcome the company of someone other than the old gentleman in the course of her Providence sojourn.

The next day H. P. and his guest came over for tea. My parents had said they wanted to meet this new friend of H. P.'s too. Was it natural generosity—or were they now wary and in need of reassurance? In the event Miss Helen Sully turned out to be a perfectly presentable woman ten years or so older than myself. She was also very pretty in a china doll sort of way—which I admit didn't endear her to me at first. But as she chatted in a shy, golly-gee voice about this or that Providence landmark that her host had shown her earlier in the afternoon and of her travels to date along the eastern seaboard, I warmed up to her. She was obviously no sophisticate. H. P. contributed little to the conversation, being mainly occupied with stroking Fiorello, who as before had settled on his lap.

The next morning Mother dropped me off at the waterfront for the Newport boat. H. P. and Helen were waiting on the dock, he in his summer suit and straw boater, she in an outfit far more chic than my own girlish attire. For a moment, only a moment, I was, yes, jealous.

H. P. handed me a ticket. "What do I owe you, H. P.?" I said, opening my purse.

"Why nothing at all. You are my guest today."

"Oh, come on, H. P. You don't have to."

"I insist. It would be ill-mannered of me not to show a young lady all due courtesy."

I didn't push it. No doubt it was important for H. P. to demonstrate that he at least knew how to behave in the company of the fair sex, especially after what had happened on our last trip together.

Since the sun was shining we sat out on the deck, where H. P. kept up a running commentary on the geography and history of Narragansett Bay. When he pointed out the site where hot-headed rebels burned His Majesty's revenue cutter *Gaspee* in 1771, it was clear that his sympathies were with the mother country. In between lessons, I learned that Helen came from Auburndale, California, where her mother was good friends with an artist and writer named Clark Ashton Smith. This Mr. Smith and H. P. had corresponded for years though they'd never met. Helen and H. P. had exchanged a few letters before meeting for the first time the other day. H. P. always addressed Helen as "Miss Sully," I noted, while she called him "Mr. Lovecraft."

In the ladies room Helen told me she wished he would call her Helen, even though she found him so fatherly, or even grandfatherly, she couldn't imagine calling him anything other than Mr. Lovecraft. I said it had taken me ages to get him to use my first name. Even now, I confided, he probably preferred to call me Miss Stone. We decided he ought to be challenged on the matter.

"H. P., Helen and I have been talking," I said once we'd rejoined him on deck, "and we agree it's time you stopped being so formal with her."

"I, formal? How do you mean?" he answered in his most pompous voice.

"I mean, why don't you drop the Miss Sully and simply call her Helen."

"If you wouldn't mind, Mr. Lovecraft," added Helen.

"Certainly, I am no surname addict," he replied.

"Ha!" I exclaimed.

H. P. chuckled. "I seem to remember having a similar conversation with you, Clarissa."

"Yes, and you'd still rather not call me Clarissa."

"Perhaps I should devise some Latin cognomen instead, as I have done for other friends of mine. Like Belknapius for Belknap Long."

"Belknap told me in New York that you sometimes call him Sonny," said Helen.

"On the other hand, Clarissa already has the ring of the pure Latin of the Caesars."

"It means bright or shining," I said. "Though, of course, I was named for Samuel Richardson's heroine."

"Ah, yes, one of the literary giants of the neo-Augustan Age. Speaking of which, you may observe an architectural survival of same on the Aquidneck shore. Behold, the steepled-skyline of old Newport!"

Old Newport, that is, the town's eighteenth-century section, turned out to be shabby at best, derelict at worst. More to Helen's and my taste were the "cottages" of the wealthy along Bellevue Avenue. We strolled on Cliff Walk, which afforded a distant view of the St. George School, with its Gothic chapel tower and neo-Georgian belfry, a vision which H. P. likened to an English landscape and moved him to recite some archaic verse. This time I didn't have to ask who the author was. We ate an ice-cream lunch at the Newport Creamery—which I insisted was my treat. H. P. protested at first but I was determined.

Most memorable, however, was the Truro Synagogue, the oldest synagogue in America, where H. P. had to wear a crepe-paper yarmulke. All he needed was some facial hair, Helen said, and he could pass for a Talmudic scholar. H. P. remarked on the wisdom of the Hebrew fathers in consigning female members of the congregation to the upper galleries. Throughout our time in Newport he avoided first names, instead addressing us collectively as "young ladies" or, when I suppose he was feeling especially playful, "children."

The return trip was uneventful, and I parted from Helen assuming I had seen the last of her before she headed for Boston and points farther north. I liked her, but I was glad she lived in California.

Early the next morning the phone rang. This time Mother got me out of bed to take the receiver. It was Helen. She said she wanted to say goodbye again, how much she had enjoyed our Newport tour, how generous Mr. Lovecraft had been to pay for everything, including her boardinghouse bill. Finally, she confessed what was really on her mind:

"Oh, Clarissa, I just have to tell someone before I leave Providence." She was catching the Boston train later that morning. "Last night Mr. Lovecraft took me to this church cemetery, down a little hill."

"St. John's churchyard, I bet." It was the same place he had entertained Harry and Ed.

"Yes, that's the one."

"Well?"

"Mr. Lovecraft said Edgar Allan Poe liked to go there."

"Go on." I was trying not to sound too interested.

"Then he began to tell me strange, weird stories in a sepulchral tone."

"Sounds like H. P.'s idea of fun."

"Not my idea! Something about his manner, the darkness, and the eerie light that hovered over the gravestones got me so wrought up that I began to run out of the cemetery."

"No!"

"He followed close at my heels, and my one thought was that I had to get to the street before he, or whatever he was, grabbed me. I reached a street lamp, trembling, panting, and almost in tears, when he caught up with me."

"What did he say?"

"Nothing. But he had the strangest look on his face, almost of triumph!"

Chapter 7

As much as I was tempted to ask H. P. about his chasing Helen out of St. John's churchyard, I of course didn't. I would no more have mentioned it than I would have said anything further to him about Ed's antics. No doubt H. P. would have been mortified to realize that I was even aware of this incident, so fraught was it with Freudian undertones. (My knowledge of Freud was quite superficial at age fifteen, as you might expect, but later I was to learn a great deal about the theories of the father of psychoanalysis.)

The route toward ingratiating myself with H. P. clearly remained through Mrs. Gamwell. I had determined that he was in the habit of visiting her afternoons, so I made a point of stopping by the hospital late one morning, when I calculated my chances were best to catch her alone. This time I brought a gift box of Schrafft's chocolates, not the finest available admittedly but a cut above Hershey's.

The old lady was sitting in a chair, her injured foot propped on a stool. She had a new cast, of more manageable size. The same get-well cards decorated the window and side table, but there were fewer flowers. When I asked how she was doing, she said the doctors would soon be sending her home. Why, then, did she sigh and look so glum?

"What's wrong, Mrs. Gamwell?"

"Dear me, I don't know how we're going to survive."

"Survive what? I mean, a broken ankle can't be that serious."

"I shouldn't burden you with my problems."

"Please tell me. I really want to help."

"No, dear, it's unfair to you. I mustn't."

"You're beginning to sound like your nephew, Mrs. Gamwell," I said. "You self-reliant Yankees need to learn to depend more on others."

"You cosmopolitan city folk—you do care, don't you?" she said, with a faint smile. "A few years back, when I visited Howard in New York, I met such gracious people. The senior Mr. and Mrs. Long, for instance…"

Eventually she returned to her present woes and I heard the bad news. I could have guessed. Her accident had put a severe strain on the family finances, of which she had been in charge since her brother Edwin died. Now Howard had gone over the accounts and confirmed her worst fears. It wasn't just hospital costs—they would need to hire a nurse to attend to her at home. How were they going to afford it? Howard could look after her needs only up to a point.

"Oh, Mrs. Gamwell, let me be your nurse!"

"Dear girl, no!"

"I don't mean a real nurse," I said. "More of an assistant. I could be your legs—you know, do your shopping, run errands, that sort of thing."

"My dear, you mustn't," she protested, but less vehemently than before.

"It would help H. P."

She hesitated. I almost had her.

"Wouldn't you rather spare him doing routine chores," I continued, "when he could be writing?"

"I do have friends," she said, in a last effort to think of an excuse not to accept my offer.

"Not many as young and eager as I am, I bet."

"My, but you are persistent, Miss Stone."

"It's Clarissa. You better get used to calling me that because you're going to be seeing a lot of me."

About a month after her fall, Mrs. Gamwell came home to 66 College Street, in a taxi, as I heard when I stopped in the next morning. (My offer to arrange for one of my parents to transport her from the hospital had been politely refused.) A plain woman in a white uniform, who identified herself as Mrs. Gamwell's nurse, answered the door. I've forgotten her name, but she knew who I was. Upstairs the patient was in bed, a pair of crutches within reach. H. P. was not up yet.

Mrs. Gamwell brought me up to date on her situation since we last saw each other in the hospital. The day before Howard had done the marketing, but he hadn't realized how low they were on tea. Would I be a dear and go down to the Weybosset Food Basket at the base of the hill and buy a package of Lipton's? From her change purse on her bedside table she extracted the exact amount and handed me the coins.

I performed this small errand cheerfully, as I would any number of other duties during the old lady's convalescence, including light house work, usually dusting or sweeping. The nurse prepared tea and toast for her breakfast, but sometimes later in the morning I made a pot of tea. This gave me the chance to snoop in the kitchen. In the cupboard was a bottle of ketchup, some canned goods—instant coffee, cocoa, baked beans, spaghetti—and a heap of sugar packets from a variety of eateries up and down the Eastern seaboard. The contents of the icebox were even less inspiring—a hunk of cheddar cheese and a jar of mayonnaise. The boarding-house across the street provided Mrs. Gamwell with her two main meals. Often a friend stopped by the boarding-house and brought her lunch or what she called "dinner," after the old New England fashion, while I gathered H. P. retrieved her supper in the evenings.

Though I came in nearly every morning for at least an hour or two, I never saw H. P. From time to time I could hear his step creaking on the floorboards behind the closed door of his study. Once Mrs. Gamwell told me he had gotten up early and taken the boat to Newport with a friend visiting from New York. On another occasion she announced that he had gone to Cape Cod to stay for the weekend with yet another New York friend and his family. It was only because he was sure the nurse and I were taking such good care of herself, she assured me, that he felt he could make this longer excursion. Otherwise I had no idea whether he was grateful for my presence or not. Perhaps he had a lot of work to catch up on.

Mostly I just kept Mrs. Gamwell company, at her bedside or next to her on the living room sofa, where she could answer the phone and listen to the radio. When I said I worried about H. P.'s diet, she shook her head. A man who stood nearly six feet tall should weigh more than 140 pounds. While his mother was alive he had eaten well enough, and for a short period after her death he had grown positively plump, thanks to—

"Thanks to who, Mrs. Gamwell?"

"Oh dear, I shouldn't have said."

"Said what?"

"Nothing, dear girl."

"Please, Mrs. Gamwell, you can tell me."

Mrs. Gamwell sighed. I sat up straight and put on my most concerned adult expression.

"All right, then, I'll tell you," she said finally. "I hinted at it in the hospital. The truth is, Howard was once married. That's why he moved to New York. He didn't tell anyone until after the wedding, not even his nearest and dearest. Lillian and I were so surprised and so hoped things would work out. But they didn't, and after a couple of years Howard came home."

"What happened to, uh, Mrs. Lovecraft?"

"She offered to establish her business here in Providence, but that just wasn't acceptable. So Howard filed the papers for divorce."

"I'm sorry."

"Don't be, dear. It was better for everyone—though I will say in her favor, it was she who fed Howard, stuffed him like a Thanksgiving turkey she did!"

I coaxed a few more details from Mrs. Gamwell about H. P.'s former wife, such as her name: Sonia Greene. She was a Russian by birth and a hat-maker by trade. They had met at a convention of amateur journalists, in Boston. Later Howard had visited New York, where she was living at the time, and some sort of romance must have blossomed. They had exchanged many letters over the next year or so, but had no real experience of life together before taking the plunge into matrimony. Marriage was hard, as Mrs. Gamwell well knew. She and her husband had parted after their teenage son, Phillips, had succumbed to T.B. (A second child, a daughter, had died in infancy.) Howard had been very fond of his young cousin, who had engaged him in a steady and stimulating correspondence. This was the origin of her nephew's love of letter-writing.

"I don't know why I'm telling you all this, Clarissa," said Mrs. Gamwell, who was beginning to get teary. "Remember, this is private—just between us. Howard mustn't know."

"Mum's the word, Mrs. Gamwell," I said. "Thanks for trusting me."

"I think it's time I had my bath," she said, dabbing her eye with a handkerchief. "Please tell the nurse I'm ready for her."

"Oh, one last thing. Is your nephew in touch with his former wife?"

"Yes, but just as casual friends."

"Has he seen her since their divorce?"

"Only once to my knowledge, and that was this past spring—in Farmington, Connecticut."

I retired to the living room, where I had plenty to think about until the old lady needed me again. Did H. P. carry a secret torch for Sonia? Would he ever admit it to me if he did? And why didn't he tell me the truth about her the day we met on the bus? Unable to come up with any satisfactory answers to these tantalizing questions, I started to read the July issue of *Weird Tales*, which I'd bought the day before on the newsstand. I had been meaning to read H. P.'s story ever since getting an advance peek that fateful day Mrs. Gamwell broke her ankle.

I wish I could say that I liked "The Dreams in the Witch-House" better than I did. It was about a student who moves into an old house haunted by a witch and her familiar, a rat with a human face. It mixed witchcraft with the fourth dimension and Einstein's relativity theory. In the end a priest takes a cross and—

Well, I'll leave it at that, just in case anybody's reading this who hasn't read the complete works of H. P. Lovecraft several times over. The oddest thing was, there was no dialogue at all. The hero has no friends or family—he just has the bad luck to rent a room in the wrong house. And the weird phenomena he observes simply weren't that interesting. Even I could tell "The Dreams in the Witch-House" was a dud.

Of course, it was a gem compared to the other stories I bothered to read in the magazine. Fun in a trashy way, though, was "The Horror in the Museum." This story was full of scary creatures in a London wax museum and the two main characters actually had conversations.

Fortunately for H. P., as I was to learn the day Mrs. Gamwell returned to the hospital to have her cast removed, others, better qualified than me to judge, thought more highly of "The Dreams in the Witch-House." This time Mrs. Gamwell accepted my offer of a ride to the hospital and back. Since I'd hardly caught a glimpse of him of late, I didn't know how H. P. felt about this act of charity. My parents, who were aware through me of their financial plight, were happy to oblige.

That day in early August my father was free to take the wheel of the Chevy. H. P. and Mrs. Gamwell were waiting on the sidewalk at the appointed pick-up time, he with a brown envelope under his arm, she on her crutches.

"You look well, H. P.," I said, as if I hadn't minded his avoiding me. "Where did you get that tan?"

"On the Newport boat," he said, not meeting my eye, "whilst entertaining my friend James F. Morton. The weather was especially sunny, even finer than it was the day you and I and…and Helen visited the ancient seaport."

Dad got out of the car and introduced himself to Mrs. Gamwell, who thanked him for being so kind as to drive her to the hospital. H. P. murmured his thanks. I held her crutches while both men made sure she was settled comfortably in the backseat, where I soon joined her. H. P. climbed in front.

"How's the writing going, Mr. Lovecraft?" asked Dad, as we set off down the hill. Dad's tone was friendly, but I could guess he wasn't going to take any chances of coming across as too familiar, hence the "Mr. Lovecraft."

"I have been occupied with my usual revision work, sir."

"Have you written any new stories?"

"My program has been too feverishly crowded to permit me to write anything new."

"But you did have one published in the latest *Weird Tales*," I chimed in. "I thought it was swell—'The Dreams in the Witch-House.' "

"A tale that most emphatically fails to satisfy me," declared H. P. Then he turned to my father and said, "Might I trouble you to stop at the corner, sir, so I may mail this envelope?"

"Sure thing," said Dad. He slowed down and stopped opposite a mailbox near the foot of the hill.

"Howard is being overly modest," said Mrs. Gamwell as her nephew leaned out the window to drop the envelope in the mailbox.

"H. P. modest about his work?" I said.

"This morning he received a letter from an editor asking to see some of his stories," she continued. "He'd already read one…well, Howard can tell you better than I."

"Dear aunt," stammered H. P.

"Oh, H. P., that's so exciting!" I said.

"Please, it is nothing to work up a temperature over," he said, blushing through his tan.

"I'll be the judge of that," I said. "What happened?"

"Yes, Mr. Lovecraft, do tell us," said Dad. "Is this an editor at a New York house?"

The rest of the way to Rhode Island Hospital we heard the details. A friend of H. P.'s, Sam Loveman, had connections with the real literary world in Manhattan. He had shown an editor acquaintance of his "The Dreams in the Witch-House" in *Weird Tales*. The editor had written H. P. and asked to see more of his fiction. As we had just witnessed, he had responded by mailing the publisher a batch of his best tales. However, he wasn't feeling sanguine:

"Like other such requests I've received, this one means little. Editors merely scout around to make sure they don't miss anything good—but they don't really want the kind of stuff I write. Sooner or later this batch will come back with the usual polite regrets."

"Who did you say the publisher was?" asked Dad.

"Alfred A. Knopf."

Chapter 8

Over dinner that evening my father filled in my mother on our expedition to the hospital. Mrs. Gamwell would have to spend another week in bed. It was likely to be winter before she was fully on her feet again. The burden for her nephew, though, was partially lightened by the possibility of being published—by no less a house than Alfred A. Knopf.

"That's wonderful, Henry," said Mother. "Mr. Lovecraft must be thrilled."

"If he is, Ruth, you'd never know it."

"H. P. likes to assume the worst," I said. "That way he can't be disappointed."

"Knopf isn't in the same league as, say, Scribner's or Doubleday," said Dad. "Still, if I were Mr. Lovecraft…"

"Don't we have friends in New York who know Alfred and Blanche Knopf?" said Mother.

"That's right, the Bombergers," said Dad. "Phil's a jobber."

"What's a jobber?" I asked.

"Look it up, Clarissa."

"Come on, Dad."

"Okay, a jobber's a kind of middle-man in the book trade. The point is, Phil might be able to put in a good word with the Knopfs for Mr. Lovecraft."

"I don't know if H. P. would like that," I said.

"Why not?" said Dad.

"He'd think it was cheating."

"Well, that's the way the real world works, Clarissa. If he hasn't figured that out by now, heaven help Mr. Lovecraft."

Divine intervention my parents couldn't provide, but they could do what was humanly possible for H. P. The question was, should they proceed with or without his knowledge? We finally agreed that I should first try to sound him out on the idea, though I was sure he would be against it. In any event, as Dad pointed out, praise from us guaranteed nothing. His fiction would have to measure up in its own right.

Through the dog days of August I continued to minister to Mrs. Gamwell, sparing her nurse and nephew the small chores and errands that otherwise would have been theirs. By now I had my own key to the house, and could come and go as I pleased. Once, when H. P. ventured into Mrs. Gamwell's half of the apartment, I asked him whether the Knopf editor had responded yet. He made his usual self-deprecating remarks about his prospects, then went into a spiel about how grateful he was for all I was doing for his aunt. This made me feel a little better about his recent lack of attention to myself.

I still hesitated to raise the subject of my parents' possible influence with the Knopfs. Then one morning, as I mounted the stairs of 66 College, I heard the sound of a typewriter. This may in fact have been the first time I had heard H. P. typing, which was surprising. After all, this man was a writer—he must do a lot of typing. The study door was ajar, and inside H. P. was hunched in front of an old typewriter, pecking away with two fingers.

"Excuse me, H. P.," I said. "Are you busy?"

Clearly he was busy, but instead of dismissing me, as I was half-expecting him to do, he asked me to come in.

"I have just finished a letter," he said, trying to sound matter-of-fact, "to Mr. Allen G. Ullman."

"Who's he?"

"The editor at Knopf who originally asked to see some of my stories."

"He's going to publish you!"

"Alas, no. According to my friend Sam Loveman, Mr. Ullman simply wishes to consider a larger selection of my work. I am sending him another eighteen stories, practically everything of mine I have not repudiated."

"He must be really interested if he wants to see more."

"I daresay nothing will come of it in the end," said H. P., "based on past experience."

"You've almost had a book published before?"

"*Weird Tales*, Putnam's, and Vanguard have all approached me about possible book publication."

"What happened?"

"Negotiations in each case fell through."

"I'm so sorry, H. P. Did they give any reason?"

"In his rejection letter the Putnam editor said my tales were not subtle enough, too obvious and well explained, besides being too uniformly macabre in mood. This last point is sheer nonsense—unity of mood is a positive asset in a fictional collection. He added some slices of bologna about later discussions concerning a volume in which the heavier tales might be sandwiched in betwixt lighter ones—the herd must have its comic relief!—but I never heard from him again." H. P. spoke with all the bitterness of a bride who had been repeatedly stood up at the altar. I couldn't bear the thought of yet another feckless suitor breaking his heart.

"May I see your letter, H. P.?"

"If you wish." He pulled the page he had been typing out of the machine and handed it to me. "Please let me know if you spot any typos."

The letter opened with the customary courtesies I knew so well from H. P.'s letters to me. Okay, if a little flowery. Then he began to describe the enclosed stories: "The Tomb" was "stiff in diction"; "The Temple" was "nothing remarkable"; "The Outsider" was "rather bombastic in style and mechanical in climax"; and so on. Every one of his tales was faulty in some fashion. I was stunned, but not too stunned to speak my mind when I finished this sorry excuse for a sales letter:

"H. P., you're nuts!"

"What?"

"This is a terrible letter. You'll never get published by apologizing."

"I am simply stating the truth."

"No, this is just your usual self-effacing crap."

"Miss Stone, I—"

"It's Clarissa, dammit!" I was starting to lose my temper. "Look, H. P., do you want a collection of your stories published or not?"

When he didn't immediately reply, I answered for him: "Of course you do! You deserve a book of your own. But you're going about it in the wrong way. Here, let me show you the right way. Where's your typing paper?"

While H. P. got up and fished in a drawer for a fresh sheet of paper, I sat down in front of the typing table. Spring semester I had taken a typing class, which taught you not only how to touch-type but how to write a proper business letter. When he asked if I wouldn't prefer to do a draft on the back of an old letter first, I said that wouldn't be necessary. At last he produced a clean sheet of paper and I set to work, using his letter as a guide. It didn't take long. I kept H. P.'s polite introductory and concluding remarks, but cut out all the self-criticism in the middle.

"There, I think you'll find this a big improvement," I said, passing him the finished letter.

H. P. studied the page, his lips tightly pursed. "I suppose this will do," he said, too proud apparently to thank me. "Your typing is impeccable."

"Didn't you ever learn to touch-type?"

"I cannot bear a typewriter, nor compose anything of importance on one. It is, of course, perfectly adequate for careless and hasty letter-writing"—like his letter to the Knopf editor?—"where no delicate plot-nuances have to be managed, and where the most slipshod sentence-structure can get by without criticism. I never employ a typewriter except when absolutely forced to do so."

"You ought to hire a secretary, H. P."

"I hire a secretary?" He laughed. "In the past, in exchange for my revisionary services, friends have prepared typed copies of my tales, thus sparing me a session at the cursed machine. Nowadays, however, my manuscripts are so full of finely-written interlineations and marginal insertions that I trust no one but myself to read them. In any event, I could never afford a professional typist."

"Don't be so sure, H. P. Just wait till you get your first check from Knopf!"

I offered to package the bundle of stories he was sending to the Knopf editor, but he wouldn't hear of it. I watched carefully as he stuffed the typescripts in a large envelope, afraid that he might replace my letter with his original. After sealing and addressing the envelope, he placed his version, I was relieved to see, in a drawer. He kept a supply of discarded, blank-on-the-back letters, he explained, for use in story composition. When I offered to take the envelope to the post office, he said he was about to go for a walk and would mail it himself. Perhaps his aunt was in more need of my assistance than he was at the moment.

After H. P. left, I realized I'd forgotten to mention how he might benefit from my family's Knopf connection. Should I raise the topic with his aunt? As it turned out, I didn't bring it up with her either. On this particular day Mrs. Gamwell was tired and not in a talkative mood. When I ventured to ask her opinion of her nephew's stories, she admitted it had been a long time since she had read one but she was sure he still wrote very nicely.

That evening I told my parents about H. P.'s less-than-professional approach to selling his fiction:

"So you see, I was so busy helping him with his letter, I forgot to say you knew someone who knew the Knopfs."

"You mean to tell me, Clarissa," said Mother, "that you actually rewrote Mr. Lovecraft's letter for him?"

"There wasn't much to rewrite. I just cut out the parts where he said his stories were lousy."

"And you say he types with only two fingers?" said Dad.

"That's right. Hardly better than hunt and peck. H. P. says he hates the typewriter—or, in his words, 'the cursed machine.' "

"My God, and this man calls himself a writer? He needs all the help he can get. I'm going to write Phil Bomberger first thing tomorrow morning."

Later in the month I was to perform another unexpected typing job for H. P. Again, I arrived one morning to find his study door open and made bold to enter. As before, he didn't protest. I figured as long as I intruded only once in a while I was safe. H. P. was seated in the Morris chair, reading some sort of manuscript.

"What's that H. P.? A letter?"

"No, it is not," he said in his best pedantic manner. Then he smiled faintly, and continued in a lighter tone: "As it happens, I have just finished writing a story."

"Swell."

"It is the first new thing I have done in more than year, not counting that collaboration with...with the Peacock Sultan."

"The Peacock Sultan?"

"Ed Price." H. P. colored, then hastily added, "I confess that credit for this recent fictional attempt is in part due to you, Clarissa. I cannot tell you how much I appreciate your encouragement in this Knopf affair. While I may have felt annoyed the other day, I see on reflection that you were right to redo my letter to Mr. Ullman."

"Has Mr. Ullman replied yet?"

"No, he has not."

"You'll tell me when he does, won't you?"

"Certainly."

"What about this new story. Are you going to submit it to *Weird Tales*?"

"It is unlikely I will do so, for reasons I have already explained to you. I will first circulate a carbon to certain members of my epistolary circle who are wise in the ways of fiction. Something about the tale dissatisfies me profoundly, and I hope one or all of them might help identify the problem. Of course, before that, it has to be typed."

"I'll type it for you!"

"Please, Clarissa, no. I have a delinquent revision client in mind for the task."

"H. P., I thought you said these days only you could type your manuscripts."

"Well, to be precise, I was thinking of two recent unplaced tales of mine, both fiendishly long and including hideously complex revisions. This latest effort is much shorter and is largely free of corrections and interpolations."

"How long is it?"

"I cannot say exactly, somewhere in the vicinity of ten thousand words."

"That doesn't sound too long. May I see it?"

H. P. rose from his chair and handed me the manuscript. It was written in pencil, but seemed legible enough.

"'The Thing on the Doorstep,' huh? Good title. May I read it?"

"If you wish."

"I can read it while I'm here this afternoon. Then we can discuss it and if we both agree I'm up to the job, I'll proceed. Okay, H. P.?"

At this he pursed his lips and looked studiously at the papers and books heaped high on the central table.

"Okay, H. P.?" I repeated.

"Very well, Clarissa," he said at last. "I will consider the possibility.

Now if you will excuse me"—he waved a hand toward the pile of books and papers—"I have a great deal of work to do." "Sorry, H. P. I'm just trying to help."

"I know you are, Clarissa," he said. A second or two later, as I stepped into the hall, I heard him mutter, "Thank you."

Mrs. Gamwell was sitting at the kitchen table, sipping a cup of tea. She invited me to join her, which I did. There was nothing I could do for her immediately, she indicated, except keep her company. When she asked what I was carrying, I said it was her nephew's new story, which maybe I was going to type.

"Howard has written a new story? How nice. He only writes a story when he's in the right mood—a good mood."

"He didn't tell you he'd written a new story?"

"No, dear. He's been so busy trying to catch up on his work we haven't had much time to chat. Besides, he's about to go away—"

"Go away?"

"Yes, as a reward for all he's done for me while I've been incapacitated I've given him a belated birthday present—"

"A birthday present!"

"—enough money for him to take a vacation trip to one of his favorite cities, Quebec."

"I didn't know it was his birthday. When was it?"

"Last Sunday."

"I wish he'd told me."

"As I said, dear, Howard's been very busy. You mustn't mind." She went on to explain how much he liked the old Canadian city settled by the French and how important it was for him to get there before the cold weather set in, but I wasn't in any mood to listen.

"Mrs. Gamwell, if you really don't need me today," I said, "I think I'll go home. I'm not feeling very well."

She offered me more tea, but I said it wasn't my stomach that needed soothing. At the head of the stairs I saw that H. P.'s study door was closed. I guess I could have knocked and asked if it was all right to take "The Thing on the Doorstep" manuscript with me, but I decided I had already bothered him enough that day.

Chapter 9

I suppose I really had no right to feel hurt. Probably H. P. never allowed anyone to make a fuss over his birthday. All the same, had I found out in advance, I would have been tempted to plot a surprise party—though the only person I would have known to invite was Harry Brobst. Still, I bet I could have persuaded Mrs. Gamwell to give me the names of other potential guests. H. P. had to have more than one friend in the Providence area.

In the meantime, the least I could do was give him a belated birthday present. And what better present than a neatly typed copy of his new story? For a day or two I worried that at any moment I might receive a frantic phone call or note requesting the return of the manuscript, but none came. Perhaps H. P. had already left for Quebec. I decided to stay away from 66 College Street for the time being, unless summoned.

"The Thing on the Doorstep," which I could read easily because I was used to H. P.'s script from his letters, turned out to be a lot more interesting than "The Dreams in the Witch-House." It was almost like a supernatural Sherlock Holmes story, with a Dr. Watson type recounting the adventures of his more talented and eccentric friend. It had some real tension and suspense, plus the most disgusting ending! That rotting, smelly corpse that couldn't talk on the phone was worse than anything I'd ever seen in the movies.

The gruesomeness, however, wasn't the most disturbing thing about the story. The poetic hero, Edward Derby, has some big psychological problems, while his wife Asenath is a true horror—a woman who thinks she can be "fully human" only if she's a man! In fact, she's possessed by a man's consciousness, that of her *father*. Pretty weird. A Freudian could have some fun with "The Thing on the Doorstep."

As I typed, I noted certain oddities of style. For instance, instead of normal conversations the story had long-winded monologues spoken by one character only, Edward Derby. Why couldn't Dan Upton, the narrator, talk back? Maybe because of his lack of social contacts H. P. found it hard to imagine two people having a real exchange of words. My job, though, was not to tell H. P. how to improve his story. After all, I was no "free-lance revisionist." But I couldn't resist making one correction, where the narrator mentions the "principal" of what appears to be a private girls school. I knew from experience that private girls schools don't have principals—they have headmistresses.

The day after I finished typing "The Thing on the Doorstep," I received a picture postcard of Quebec's Hotel Frontenac, which H. P. described as "Cyclopean" (now that was a word I had to look up in the dictionary). The card was full of H. P.'s usual eloquent architectural observations. In a P.S. crammed below the address he said he was eager to hear what I thought of his new tale.

It was Mrs. Gamwell who phoned soon after to say that her nephew was home from his travels and might I be free to stop by one afternoon—with the manuscript I had "borrowed."

When I walked over to College Street, I was carrying not only the original pencil draft but also the typed copy, along with a carbon on which I had corrected every typo, wrapped in colorful tissue paper and concealed in an oversized handbag. I had considered attaching a card, but decided that would have been overdoing it.

I let myself in with my key. At the top of the stairs H. P.'s study door was ajar. The familiar Yankee-accented voice bade me enter. Inside the windows were open, for while the sun was lower in the sky, the late summer breezes continued to be balmy. H. P., wearing a loosened tie and shirt sleeves, rose from behind the center table and bowed. He looked tired, like a businessman after a grueling trip who hasn't had time to eat or freshen up. He was just able to manage a smile, probably because he spotted the manuscript of "The Thing on the Doorstep" in my hand.

"I truly enjoyed it, H. P.," I said, sincerely enough, passing him the pages across the table before taking a seat in the Morris chair.

"Did you, Clarissa?"

"I did. The characters were, well, almost like real people, especially the hero. Is Edward Derby based on anyone you know?"

"You ask the most personal questions, young lady. I should say my doomed protagonist is based on no single individual, but is rather a composite portrait. I shall name no names. I realize that it is against my usual principles to try to render human character in any depth. Here, however, I decided to experiment, providing what I hope more discerning readers will deem a plausible psychological background."

He went on to admit that he had of late attended a number of lectures at the university on psychology. He was coming more and more to appreciate how coddling can warp childhood development. One friend of his in particular was still tied to momma's apron strings at age thirty. I was curious to ask H. P. why he chose to give Edward Derby a father but no mother, but he suddenly changed the subject.

"I suppose, Clarissa, you wish to discuss the matter of your preparing a typed copy of the manuscript?"

"Yes, H. P., but before we do, I have something for you." I pulled the present out of my handbag. "Happy birthday!"

"My birthday was weeks ago!"

"I know. Your aunt told me."

H. P. had turned pale pink, but after only a moment's hesitation he took the gaily colored package and opened it. In another moment he was gaping in wonder at the contents.

"O Gawd, O Montreal! You have certainly done a professional job, young lady. And you have supplied a carbon as well."

"I checked it against your pencil copy twice. I corrected a few typos, and in one place, you should be aware, I made a change."

"You changed my text?"

"Yes. Where you refer to the 'principal' of the Hall School. I think you really mean 'headmistress.' "

H. P. did a pretty good imitation of what I believe in comedy is called a slow burn. But after I had explained the social and educational distinctions, he nodded and conceded I was right.

"You know, Clarissa, as a rule I never allow editorial tampering with my stories."

"It must be hard being perfect, H. P."

H. P. blushed again.

"I am once more in your debt," he muttered. "How can I repay you?"

"That's easy. Let me be your secretary."

"I don't need a secretary."

"You will when Knopf accepts your story collection and you're besieged with all sorts of offers—movie sales, for example."

"Clarissa, please."

"I assume you haven't heard yet."

"No, I have not."

"That reminds me. Dad has a friend in publishing who knows the Knopfs. Dad's asked him if he can put in a good word for you, or at least nudge the process along." The last I knew, my father had written Mr. Bomberger, but hadn't heard back. "Hope you don't mind."

"Don't mind?! Why if a bonafide book bearing the name H. P. Lovecraft should materialize, I guess I'll know who to thank for the miracle. What then won't I owe to you and your family!"

H. P. shuddered and hid his face in his hands.

"I am very tired, Clarissa," he said at last, looking up but refusing to meet my gaze. "I believe my aunt may want a word with you."

"Okay, H. P. I'll see you later."

At the door I remembered I had forgotten to ask him about Quebec. How rude of me. But I kept going into Mrs. Gamwell's side of the house.

I found the old lady in the living room, in her accustomed chair next to the radio. A pair of crutches lay within reach. I asked about her health, and she replied that she was coming along nicely. So nicely, in fact, that they had felt free to dismiss the nurse. And with a newly installed electrical device on the front door she could now let visitors in without going downstairs.

"So you see, dear," she said, "we no longer need you to come by as regularly as you have over the summer. You've been a great help, both to me and my nephew. We do appreciate your kindness. But I think it would be best for everyone at this stage if you came over only when there's real need."

"Oh, Mrs. Gamwell."

"You understand, don't you, dear?"

If I understood anything it was that H. P. was trying to get rid of me, despite or because of all I had done for him. I wasn't about to show I minded, though, and told Mrs. Gamwell I did understand. I had nothing more to say. Mrs. Gamwell was mumbling something about returning their house key, but I was too agitated to comply with her request. I was out the door and around the corner by the John Hay Library before I burst into tears.

I hadn't been looking forward to the start of school, but now I welcomed it. New classes and new teachers, together with afternoons playing field hockey, meant I couldn't spend every waking hour moping. My parents did their best to cheer me up. Mother even went so far as to offer a fall weekend in New York, to shop for my birthday in November. Even this prospective treat didn't excite me much. I considered writing H. P. and trying to get our relationship back on its original epistolary basis. But that was no longer enough. I wanted to see H. P., to be his friend face to face.

I had one card left. I still had my key to 66 College Street. Of course, I could have just mailed it back, or slipped it under the door, but to be safe I would have to deliver it in person. If neither H. P. nor Mrs. Gamwell was going to ask for its return, I would just have to wait for the right opportunity to do them the favor.

That opportunity came at the end of September. Dad finally did get a letter from Mr. Bomberger about H. P.'s proposed story collection. The gist of it was this. The editor at Knopf who had first approached H. P. had apparently consulted the editor of *Weird Tales*, to see if the magazine could guarantee a minimal sale to its readers. The magazine could not. Mr. Bomberger, however, spoke to the Knopf editor on the phone and said that from his experience as a jobber this type of book did sell well to the trade, that is, through regular bookstores. People sick of the Depression took solace in escapist fiction like Mr. Lovecraft's. He advised the Knopf editor to publish.

Well, this was good news! The next best thing to actual acceptance— which I felt was bound to follow. I decided I was going to be the first person to tell H. P. his luck was about to change. I wasn't going to phone or write first. I wanted to surprise him. I would stop by after school, claiming my purpose was to give Mrs. Gamwell back her key, then I would casually mention what my father had heard from Mr. Bomberger.

The next day, on my way home that afternoon, I stopped at 66 College Street. I could have let myself in, but decided it would be more polite to ring. I heard Mrs. Gamwell calling from an upstairs window who was it. I said it was me, Clarissa, and I had come to return the key. I opened the door as soon as it buzzed. At the top of the stairs H. P.'s door was closed. I continued down the hall into the living room.

There Mrs. Gamwell was sitting in her accustomed chair. She had a magazine in her lap, but she was staring straight ahead, as if dazed.

"Is anything wrong, Mrs. Gamwell?"

"Oh, Clarissa, you won't believe it, my dear nephew—"

"Is he hurt?"

"No, no, it's just that…" Then she broke into tears. A moment or two later, as she dabbed her eyes with her handkerchief, she smiled and declared: "Howard's book has been accepted!"

Chapter 10

"hat's wonderful, Mrs. Gamwell!" I exclaimed, trying to sound as if I was really surprised. "H. P. must be overjoyed!"

"I noticed the letter in this morning's mail, with the Knopf return address," said Mrs. Gamwell, dabbing at her eyes with her handkerchief. "I was tempted to wake Howard up, but what if it contained bad news? I couldn't tell from looking at it.

"I decided to put the letter on top of Howard's mail where I usually leave it, at his place at the kitchen table, and wait. I happened to be heating some water for tea when he appeared for breakfast. I didn't say anything, but I knew he'd spotted it right away. He wished me good morning, or maybe afternoon (I was too nervous to notice the time), and went ahead and made his coffee. Then he sat down and scanned his mail as if it were a normal day's delivery. So brave!

"At last he gave me a pained look, like a child afraid to open his Christmas stocking because it might be full of coal instead of candy. Then he said that he had better get it over with. I could hardly bare to watch him slit the envelope. It was only a second or two after he started reading that he let out a whoop like an Indian. In the next instant my proper, strait-laced nephew was waltzing me around the kitchen, wholly mindless of my injured ankle.

"When he'd recovered his poise, he showed me the letter. It was from Mr. Ullman, the editor at Knopf, saying they wanted to publish his book and pay him a thousand dollars!"

Once more Mrs. Gamwell started to sob. "You don't know how much this means to us, Clarissa. We're so happy."

At this I could no longer restrain my emotions. I was drying my tears with a spare handkerchief that Mrs. Gamwell loaned me when I noticed H. P. standing in the doorway, grinning like a ghoul after a good night's grave-robbing (if I may use a Lovecraftian simile).

"Congratulations, H. P.!" I cried and rushed over and gave him a huge hug. If H. P. didn't reciprocate with quite the same fervor, at least he didn't resist. When I pulled away his face was flushed—for once, if I'm not mistaken, with triumph rather than embarrassment.

"Thank you, Clarissa," said H. P. "I am immensely pleased, as you can well imagine, with this fantastic turn in my literary fortunes."

"We'll have to have a party to celebrate!"

"Now let's not go overboard, young lady."

"You're going to be rich and famous, H. P.!"

"I doubt that, but at least Grandpa and his daughter won't be standing barefoot in the breadline this winter."

"Howard, I think we ought to offer our visitor some refreshment," said Mrs. Gamwell.

"By Azathoth, I have forgotten my manners. Clarissa, do you not take milk in your tea?"

I sat with H. P. and his aunt in the living room for the next hour, trying to get them to talk about what they might do with the thousand dollars. But other than some travel for him, and some new clothes for her, neither was inclined to speculate. It wouldn't do to count one's Old Ones before they hatched—or unfroze, quipped H. P. (I was coming to learn that playful if cryptic references to his mythical monsters was a sign of high spirits.)

When I was ready to go, I turned to Mrs. Gamwell and asked her where she would like me to put the house key. Instead of answering she looked at her nephew.

"I know I should've given it back last time I was here. It was very rude of me not to."

"I think you may need that key, young lady," said H. P., "assuming you are agreeable to a modest business proposal. You once made me an offer…" Here he paused to fumble with a packet of sugar. I sipped my tea, in no hurry to help him out.

"To speak plainly," he resumed, "I can now afford a regular typist, on a per job basis, thanks to this gift from the great god Knopf. I hope you will accept."

"Oh, H. P.!" I was tempted to rush over and give him another hug, but instead I showed Yankee restraint.

"You need not respond now. I realize you have returned to school. I would not want any work you might do for the Old Gentleman to interfere with your studies."

No girl who has waited untold eons for her suitor to pop the question could have been as pleased as I was to hear these words. Again, though, I wasn't about to betray the extent of my feelings.

"I'll have to ask my parents," was all I said. "I'll let you know."

H. P. saw me to the head of the stairs, where he made a final speech: "You must forgive me, Clarissa. I know that at times I have failed to…to appreciate you. But please do not think I am ungrateful. I have no way of knowing for certain, of course, but I strongly suspect that if I had not rewritten that letter to Mr. Ullman at your insistence, his reply might have been entirely different. Thank you."

"You're welcome, H. P."

Was this the moment to mention Mr. Bomberger's role? Considering all I had done for H. P. that he hadn't recognized, I had no qualms about taking for the time being a little more credit than was rightfully mine.

"Good-bye, Clarissa," said H. P. giving my hand a quick shake with cold, claw-like fingers. He had disappeared behind his study door before I could try for a last hug.

Mother and Dad were nearly as excited as I was about H. P.'s good news, somewhat less so about his job offer. Did Mr. Lovecraft expect me to do his typing at College Street or at home? His letting me keep my house key suggested the former. Was he going to pay me by the hour or by the page? And what about my school work?

In the end everything was sorted out. H. P. explained over the phone to Dad that his wasn't the easiest handwriting to read. As I typed I might well have to consult him frequently, until I got used to his crabbed scrawl. His aunt, Mrs. Gamwell, would serve as chaperone, it went without saying. Two afternoons a week, on those days when my school load was lightest, ought to be right to begin with. I would be paid forty cents an hour.

I started the day after H. P. received a check from Knopf for the first half of his advance. He said that he would receive the second half on publication of the book, which was provisionally titled *The Outsider and Others*. The final contents had yet to be determined, but H. P. figured that Mr. Ullman would end up using about twenty of the twenty-five stories he had originally supplied for the editor's consideration. If all went according to schedule, the collection would appear the following spring.

With the promise of a real book to his name H. P. was moved to reconsider what he called his "repudiated work," in particular two short novels, each longer than a hundred pages. At the time of composition the prospect of typing such a mass of material had been too daunting. The one novel-length fiction of his that he had made the colossal effort to type—*At the Mountains of Madness*—had been rejected by "Farnie the Fox," or Farnsworth Wright, the editor of *Weird Tales*. This had been a devastating blow.

But now things were different. In his last letter Mr. Ullman had indicated an interest in seeing a novel from the Old Gentleman. He still lacked the courage to submit *At the Mountains of Madness* to anyone else, but in little more than a month in 1927 he had written a lengthy paean in prose to his native Providence. *The Case of Charles Dexter Ward* or *The Madness Out of Time* (H. P. had not yet settled on the title) might well make an honorable successor to *The Outsider*, notwithstanding its status as a cumbrous, creaking bit of self-conscious antiquarianism. Preparing a fair copy from the heap of handwritten sheets would be my first task.

Typing *The Case of Charles Dexter Ward* (the title I preferred) occupied me for the rest of the fall. I sat at the typing table in H. P.'s study, while he worked at the central table that served as his desk. I was amused to find that much of the novel was written on the backs of old letters. A case of Yankee thriftiness if ever there was one. At first I had the devil of a time reading the text with its numerous interpolations and crossings-out. I had to interrupt H. P. every few minutes, it seemed, and even he couldn't always decipher his own hieroglyphics. I will say, as my pace picked up, that I began to enjoy the novel for itself, with its leisurely, understated style, even though the hero was a lonely egghead fixated on the past.

During this period H. P. produced two new stories, one a recasting in prose of some of his "Fungi from Yuggoth" sonnets, the other an elaboration of a dream about an evil clergyman in a garret full of forbidden books. A few of his stories, he told me, were literal transcriptions of his nightmares. H. P. did not send these new tales on the rounds of his literary circle, but instead submitted them, along with "The Thing on the Doorstep," directly to the editor of *Weird Tales*. Wright had written to offer his congratulations on the Knopf deal and to say he had decided after all to take "Through the Gates of the Silver Key." He was eager to see more Lovecraft fiction. Farnie the Fox snapped up these three new tales immediately.

Mostly though, from what I could observe, H. P. was busy doing what he liked best—writing letters. As the news of his literary coup spread, the congratulatory notes and telegrams began to pour in. An announcement in the November *Weird Tales* of a forthcoming Lovecraft volume added to the deluge. H. P. showed me the letter Helen wrote him but not the one he received from Ed on the subject. I had to sneak a peek at Ed's while he was conferring with Mrs. Gamwell in the living room. I had gotten only a glimpse of a reference to "that saucy gal Friday of yours" when I heard H. P.'s step in the hall. Hastily sticking Ed's letter back in the middle of a batch of opened mail, I exclaimed:

"Do you really have to reply to everyone who writes you, H. P.?"

"A gentleman always answers his mail, Clarissa," he replied.

"What if the other person isn't a gentleman?"

H. P. hesitated a moment, then said, "Once, I admit, I did cut off one correspondent—an aspiring young author who was so tactless as to write certain mutual friends that he did not plan to end up like Grandpa, limited to a single market. I do not take kindly to back stabbing. Nor do I appreciate young ladies examining my mail without my permission."

"Sorry, H. P. It's just that I could help you with at least some of this stuff. You know, reply to fan mail that you shouldn't be wasting your time on."

"Please, Clarissa," he said, beginning to sound really testy, "let me be the judge of how I spend my time."

"Okay, H. P."

I backed down for the moment, but over the weeks, without being overly inquisitive, I was able to figure out who his most important correspondents were—and to get at least some idea of their personalities. First there was Frank Belknap Long, a New York writer who liked to think of himself as a decadent aesthete, though at age thirty he was still living at home with his parents. H. P. was particularly grateful to his "favorite grandson," also known as "Sonny," for introducing him to the work of the Welsh master of the weird, Arthur Machen. (I would later have the chance to judge Frank's boyishness for myself, but that's another story.) The writer-friend H. P. most admired was Clark Ashton Smith, a gifted poet and artist as well as fictionist. As I already knew, Smith was pals with the Sully family in Auburndale, California. Then there was Robert "Two-Gun Bob" Howard, a rural Texan who resembled the musclebound barbarians he wrote about for the pulps. He also lived at home with his folks. The one member of his circle who H. P. thought might make a name for himself in the literary mainstream was a young Wisconsin native, August Derleth (or "Comte d'Erlette"). H. P. was impressed by Derleth's ability to produce cheap pot-boilers at the same time he was contributing poignant human sketches to the little magazines.

The rest of the field consisted of wheedling revision clients, juvenile readers of *Weird Tales*, pesky amateur journalists, and old ladies who shared his fondness for cats. One of the most pleasing aspects of his new residence, H. P. asserted, was the view out his study window of the garden below, where as many as six or seven cats were often to be seen lazing in the sunshine. H. P. called this "feline sodality" the Kappa Alpha Tau or K.A.T., since the neighborhood was filled with fraternity houses. He even designed some special "Kappa Alpha Tau" stationery for replying to fellow worshippers of Bast, "the cat-headed goddess of Aegyptus."

I'm getting ahead of myself a bit here, but it became increasingly plain that somebody had to do something to prevent H. P. from becoming totally enslaved to his letter-writing fans. I seized my chance after Christmas, when he went to New York for a week to visit friends. I had received permission to come over to 66 College Street in his absence to work on my typing tasks.

I had already helped H. P. to organize a list of people to whom he wished to send Christmas cards. Using this as a guide, I was able to determine fairly easily who should and who should not receive the form letter I had prepared with the help of a duplicating machine in the Brown English Department. (I think my father must have assumed that this scheme had H. P.'s approval when he agreed to let me come into his office for this purpose.) Shortly before New Year's, in my employer's obsolete George Kirk Booksellers envelopes (but with stamps that I paid for out of my own pocket), I mailed nearly a hundred letters to people in most of the states in the Union. The letter thanked the individual for writing, but said that due to Mr. Lovecraft's professional obligations he was unable to reply personally. He apologized and hoped, time permitting, to respond at a later date. Each one closed: "Sincerely yours, Clarissa Stone, Secretary to Mr. Lovecraft."

While I wanted to avoid the fight that surely would have ensued had I asked H. P. beforehand, I was confident that he would eventually see reason and not give me hell. I will say, though, I was feeling more than a little anxious when early in the new year I arrived at 66 College Street and found him back from his New York sojourn, scribbling away at the large central table in his study.

"Good afternoon, Clarissa," he said without looking up. "I hope you enjoyed your holiday."

"Farmington was as picturesque as ever, H. P." My parents and I had spent Christmas with my aunt and uncle, an occasion filled with all the usual family rivalry and tension, not that I was about to bore H. P. with the details. "How was New York?"

It had been a notably social visit, he said, including a New Year's Eve party at Sam Loveman's place in Brooklyn Heights and lunch with the writer A. Merritt at the Player's Club in Gramercy Park. Another highlight was stopping by the Knopf offices, where he met with his editor, Mr. Ullman, who introduced him to no less a personage than good old Alfred A. himself. They discussed Arthur Machen, a fellow Knopf author, whom Mr. Knopf had had the pleasure of calling on at his London home. Then, in his best graveyard manner, H. P. said:

"While in the pest zone I met one of my new correspondents, a collector of rare books named Herman C. Koenig. Mr. Koenig showed me a rather curious missive that bears all the hallmarks of a meddlesome young lady. Would you be so kind as to give the Old Gentleman an explanation?"

"I was going to tell you, H. P. I didn't realize Mr. Koenig was someone you wanted to keep corresponding with. My mistake. I'll be glad to write him, or any of the others, and say I'm sorry."

"Do you mean to say Mr. Koenig isn't the only one to whom you sent this…this…" For once H. P. was at a loss for some horrible metaphor.

"No, I sent out ninety-five, maybe ninety-six, such letters." Better to be wholly open about the extent of my campaign, I thought. "Don't worry, I bought the stamps myself. I also noted the names of all recipients. If there are others besides Mr. Koenig who should be reinstated on the Lovecraft A-list, just tell me and I'll make amends."

When H. P. finally spoke I could barely hear him:

"Miss Stone, a gentleman always answers his mail."

"Mr. Lovecraft, a gentleman doesn't always have to reply to every fool who can put pen to paper," I retorted. I was determined to hold my ground.

"Miss Stone, I hope you will excuse me. I have no need of your services for today. Please go."

Chapter II

To my relief H. P. soon got over his anger. A couple of days later I received a note saying that while he couldn't condone what I had done he realized that I had acted in what I perceived to be his best interests. In my reply I apologized again, but was firm in restating my view that a famous author shouldn't let himself get lost in letter-writing. The next time I visited College Street, H. P. admitted that I was right. He would have to cut back. From now on he would pass on to me any correspondence that didn't require his personal response. It was a small concession, but it was a step in the right direction.

By this point such disputes between us were rare. Since the good news from Knopf H. P. had been altogether happier, more relaxed. And if in my role as his secretary I didn't feel exactly loved, I did feel...appreciated. About a month after he received the first part of his advance, H. P. took me to the movies, to celebrate my sixteenth birthday. (I was only a little disappointed when "Aunt Annie," as Mrs. Gamwell now insisted I call her, also came along.) The main feature was *Berkeley Square*, about a man who travels back in time to the eighteenth century and possesses the body of his ancestor. It reminded me of a sunnier version of *The Case of Charles Dexter Ward*. H. P. was enthralled with the fidelity to the atmosphere of the period, but over dinner at the Biltmore afterwards he questioned the mind transfer business. Where had the consciousness of the hero's ancestor gone while his descendant occupied his body? I told him he had done a much better job with a similar idea in "The Thing on the Doorstep."

Apropos of the eighteenth century, one afternoon while I was working at 66 College Street, a delivery man arrived with a couple of heavy cartons. These turned out to be filled with old books, including an early edition of Boswell's *Life of Johnson*. H. P. had bought the lot earlier that day, he explained. These books had once been part of his grandfather's library, the bulk of which had been sold after Whipple Phillips's death to a local second-hand bookseller. Thanks to the money from Knopf, he could finally afford, after nearly thirty years, to retrieve what remained of this lost family legacy from the dusty shelves of this same bookseller. H. P. positively hummed as he made space in his already crowded bookcases for these new volumes.

H. P. also spoke of realizing an even greater dream—recovering his grandfather's old house, where he had spent his boyhood. I made a point of walking past the place one afternoon, on Angell Street several blocks east of the Brown campus. It was a large, rambling Victorian, not at all the sort of colonial mansion I imagined would be H. P.'s dream house.

On another occasion his short-cropped hair looked neater and trimmer than usual. When I complimented him on his haircut, H. P. admitted he had been to the barber for the first time since purchasing a self-barbering device for a dollar several years earlier.

These truly were the halcyon days. H. P. dealt with the usual petty problems and demands of his trade with unfailing good cheer. When some callous fan attacked a story by Clark Ashton Smith in some obscure journal, H. P. wrote several tart letters in Smith's defense. In letters to one of his New York literary pals he must have exhausted a whole bottle of ink quibbling over punctuation, spelling, and facts in an article that he had written for a journal of Dutch history. At the request of a fan who was planning a new magazine, he wrote a short autobiography which he titled "Some Notes on a Nonentity." I told him he would soon have to retitle it "Some Notes on an Entity"—or better, "Some Notes on a Mensch."

For Thanksgiving H. P. did something he had been wanting to do all his life—consume the traditional feast on the historic soil of Plymouth, Massachusetts. He afterwards told me that the day was spectacularly warm—up to 68 degrees in the afternoon—and he spent it all in the venerable Pilgrim town, going over the familiar sights and unearthing many new ones.

When the copy-edited manuscript of his story collection arrived the second week of December, H. P. gladly put all lesser matters aside. He agreed with me that it was far more satisfying to focus his energies on his forthcoming book, now called *The Call of Cthulhu and Other Weird Stories*. His editor had decided that this was a catchier title than *The Outsider*—and that it would help attract the readers of *Weird Tales* magazine. I had to wonder, though, whether it was smart to have such a strange word in the title. H. P. had to give me a lesson on how to pronounce *Cthulhu*.

He and Mr. Ullman had also settled more or less amicably on the final contents, a total of eighteen stories covering the full range of his work. The only real bone of contention had been the inclusion of the serial "Herbert West—Reanimator," which H. P. regarded as hack work written down to the herd level. The Knopf editor, however, had seen it in its original magazine appearance and thought it would nicely balance the more cerebral tales. H. P. admitted that he didn't care for some of the Knopf copy-editor's suggested changes, though on the whole I gathered he was far more willing to accept editorial tampering from her than from his amateur friend with whom he had niggled over the Dutch history article. He was grateful that the copy-editor had no quarrel with his British spellings.

It wasn't all business at 66 College Street. One afternoon I arrived to find a Christmas tree standing in one corner of the living room. H. P. said that it was the first tree that they had had in a quarter of a century. I was delighted when he asked me to help him and Aunt Annie decorate it. Their old-time decorations were long dispersed, so he had laid in a new and inexpensive stock from Woolworth's— colored lights, shiny round ornaments, a star for the top, and loads of tinsel to hang from the branches like Spanish moss. "Grandpa" and his elderly invalid aunt went about this traditional Yuletide rite like a couple of carefree kids.

A few days before Christmas, on my final visit to 66 College Street for the year, I brought over a couple of presents. One was a holiday basket of fresh fruit, which I set beside the tree in the living room. It was too bulky to fit underneath. While I was aware that H. P. regularly picked up his evening meal from the boarding house across the street, at other times he seemed to eat only cheese and sugary snacks like doughnuts. Increased solvency had made no discernible impact on the frugal Lovecraft larder.

The second present was a black ornament with ears and a cat's face. I was in the act of hanging this on the tree when H. P. emerged from his study. He thanked me for the gift, which he declared a perfect likeness of good old "Nigger Man."

By this point I had the run of the kitchen, where I often made myself a cup of tea, to warm myself up after coming in from the cold. Not that I really needed it, since H. P. tended to keep the radiators turned on high and refused to open the windows, even a crack. After a couple of hours I couldn't wait to get out in the chill air again! At some stage he explained to me that he was hypersensitive to cold, and even became physically sick if exposed for too long to subfreezing temperatures.

On this afternoon H. P. said he hoped that I could stay later than usual to join them for a little Yule festivity. I wasn't long at my typing chores before H. P. said it was time to retire to the living room. There the tree lights were already aglow in the late afternoon gloom. On the coffee table were a teapot, cups, and a single coffee mug. From the kitchen Aunt Annie emerged with a plate of gingerbread cookies shaped like pine trees and Santas. No, she hadn't baked them herself, they were the gift of a neighbor. Conversation turned to our respective Christmas plans. On the 25th they would be eating a turkey dinner at the boarding house. I said that my parents and I would be driving that morning to Farmington, to celebrate Christmas with my aunt and uncle.

I'll admit it made me somewhat self-conscious to be talking about Christmas with these nominal Christians, though neither of them as far as I could tell was a churchgoer. Were they even aware that I was Jewish? And if so, what did they think of me and my family adopting their holiday? At sixteen I had no use for religion as a system of belief, only as it related to social standing. Fortunately, the conversation moved on to the immediate issue of whether or not to open presents.

"I admit I'm very curious to see what Clarissa has given us," said Aunt Annie. My fruit basket, wrapped to disguise its contours, dwarfed all other presents in sight.

"I vote we open our presents now," I said.

"Very well, ladies," said H. P., setting down his coffee mug. From under the tree he produced two small packages. "Merry Christmas, Clarissa," he said as he handed them to me.

"Thank you, H. P."

I in turn picked up my present and set it in between my two hosts, who were sharing the sofa. H. P. allowed his aunt to do the opening honors.

"My goodness, dear girl," exclaimed Aunt Annie when the cornucopia of apples, pears, and bananas lay revealed. "Thank you so much. Now, Howard, when I tell you you should eat more fresh fruit and vegetables you'll have no excuse."

H. P. merely smiled as he helped himself to another gingerbread cookie.

In the meantime I had opened my presents—a copy of Edna St. Vincent Millay's *Fatal Interview* and a catnip mouse. H. P. didn't have to explain that the mouse was for Fiorello.

It was time to go. I gave Aunt Annie a hug, and even H. P. almost reciprocated when I did likewise to him. It was only after I got home and looked at my new book more closely that I noticed the inscription on one of the front pages: "Best seasonal wishes to my favourite adopted granddaughter." It was signed "Grandpa." I was in heaven, even if of course Aunt Annie took first place in his affections as his blood "granddaughter."

Yes, to be honest, I had by this point developed what could only be called a schoolgirl crush on H. P. I know that now with hindsight. But that didn't blind me to his faults, nor did it stop me from challenging him when I thought somebody had to tell him when he was wrong. I soon had provocation to do so.

Early in the new year I finished typing the manuscript of *The Case of Charles Dexter Ward*. What a task! I felt I had truly earned my forty cents an hour. The important thing, though, was that my boss was pleased. I didn't have to worry. H. P. praised my work to the stars after reading the text through and spotting only minor typos. These I easily corrected, and on my way home for the day I stopped by the post office and mailed the manuscript to Mr. Ullman. (This time I didn't need to help H. P. with his cover letter other than to type it.) Since the temperature was well below freezing that afternoon, H. P. didn't dare to venture outdoors himself.

I knew, because he had promised, that he would give me a new typing job the next time I came over. This turned out to be a lengthy essay entitled "Cats and Dogs." H. P. was sure that as a fellow ailuro-phile I would approve of his extended argument for the superiority of the feline breed to the canine. He had written it some years before as his contribution to a meeting of his New York literary club that he couldn't attend in person. Recently one of his correspondents to whom he had loaned the manuscript had urged him to try to place it professionally.

Full of learned lore and playful humor, "Cats and Dogs" was a wonderful piece of writing, as I discovered when I read it through. If I had any criticism of the style, it was that it was too wordy. Some of the paragraphs went on for ever. As for content, one thing bothered me in the second paragraph, a sentence that began: "I have no active dislike of dogs, any more than I have for monkeys, human beings, negroes, cows, sheep, or pterodactyls." Granted the tone was tongue-in-cheek, I felt that this distinction between human beings and Negroes (I knew it should be capital "N") was embarrassingly racist.

"H. P., before I start typing, I have a question," I said.

H. P. looked up from his table where he was engaged in his cus-tomary letter-writing.

"Yes, Clarissa?"

"You say something here I'm sure you don't really mean." I read the bit cited above aloud.

"Well?" said H. P.

"H. P., you're suggesting that Negroes aren't human beings."

"It is merely a jest."

"Not everyone is going to think it's funny."

"Young lady, I wrote this *jeu d'esprit* for a few friends. None of them took the slightest offense."

"I bet none of them was black."

"Miss Stone—" H. P. spoke sharply, but my reply was sharper still:

"A private joke is one thing, Mr. Lovecraft, but don't forget you're now trying to sell 'Cats and Dogs' to a professional editor."

"Miss Stone, in one story of mine I named a cat Nigger-Man, in honor of my boyhood pet. The editor did not object when he ac-cepted the tale for publication."

"Who was that?"

"Mr. Edwin Baird, of *Weird Tales*. A far more discerning editor than his capricious successor, I might add."

"When was this?"

"The year was 1923, Miss Stone."

"Mr. Lovecraft, it's 1934. You can't insult people because they're members of a so-called inferior race. It may have been okay in the eighteenth century, but not today."

"Miss Stone—"

"Who do you think you are, Adolf Hitler?"

I hate to admit it, but I was fast losing my temper. H. P., his normally chalk-white pallor nearly scarlet, stared at me in speechless horror. I was sure he was about to dismiss me for the day, if not for good. Finally, though, he simply said that it would be better to drop the matter, since we both had work to do. I agreed to let it rest. We didn't exchange another word until I got up to leave.

As I was putting on my coat, H. P. said out of the blue that Samuel Johnson had been devoted to his African valet and had made the man his heir. He added that his grandparents' household had included one black servant. He remembered Delilah fondly. In the aftermath of our little set-to, I had remembered that *The Case of Charles Dexter Ward* included two minor Negro characters. Just before I said good-bye, I told H. P. that I thought his portrayal of "old Asa and his stout wife Hannah" had been sympathetic. (I could have added "and condescending," but I refrained.)

Chapter 12

At our next meeting H. P. was even more conciliatory over his racist slur in "Cats and Dogs." He admitted to me that the friend who had urged him to try to get it published had also pointed out the inappropriateness of the distinction between human beings and colored people. This friend had even recommended "tradesmen" as a substitute. I had already left out "negroes" in the typescript, and it was easy enough to indicate an insert. Suggesting that "tradesmen" didn't qualify as human beings was acceptable, though the implied snobbery still wasn't to my liking.

When I told H. P. so, he said that he had been a different person in 1926, the year he wrote "Cats and Dogs." While he liked to fancy himself an eighteenth-century gentleman, he had become in the real world of today a socialist. He was all for political and economic reform, which was why he supported President Roosevelt and the New Deal. The previous year, shortly before FDR's inauguration, he had composed an essay, "Some Repetitions on the Times," formulating his views on what he believed had to be done to alleviate the misery of ordinary citizens—including tradesmen. These views were nothing very original in themselves, but it occurred to him that he might have me type up the essay at some point, with an eye toward possible publication. That said, he wasn't going to get rid of the amusing contrast between human beings and tradesmen in "Cats and Dogs."

H. P. shortly was to discover another category of creatures that he might wish to distinguish from human beings—bird lovers. The winter was particularly cold, and H. P. rarely ventured outside, but one Sunday he braved the frigid temperatures to go meet a friend of a friend from Vermont staying with relatives a few blocks away. Besides Miss Dorothy Walter (he didn't say whether she was attractive or not, but I gathered she was no Helen Sully), H. P. met a couple of other native Vermonters. One of them, Miss Walter's aunt, turned out to be the lady who had been writing letters to the Providence *Journal* advocating that all roving cats be belled or done away with altogether because they killed the wild birds. Feeling like a spy in the enemy camp, H. P. claimed he had pressing work to do and beat a hasty retreat back to College Street!

One item of real work that H. P. had to do, as opposed to letter-writing, was revising a horror story for a client who lived outside Boston. This individual was a reliable client for whom he had already "touched up" several tales, including one I had read in *Weird Tales*, "The Horror in the Museum." When he finished his editing, he gave me the text to type. I saw then that the story was ninety-nine percent H. P.'s, as barely a word or a phrase let alone a sentence survived from the crude original.

Entitled "The Horror in the Burying-Ground," the story struck me as pretty routine compared to his own work. When I asked him for his opinion, H. P. said that he was indifferent to the tale's quality because officially no one would ever know he had a hand in it. Since I was to meet her later, I had reason to remember the nominal author's name—Hazel Heald.

When I asked if he was writing any stories for himself, H. P. said that he was contemplating a novelette in his so-called "Arkham cycle." What prevented him from buckling down to the job was evidently another crisis of confidence. The surge of optimism that had produced "The Thing on the Doorstep," "The Book," and "The Wicked Clergyman" in quick succession the previous fall had given way to self-doubt. What if even that portion of the reading public sensitive to the weird spurned his story collection? What if the reviewers noticed the cheap magazine influence that he had subconsciously subsumed into his style? The critical and commercial failure of the book would be devastating.

In my role as cheerleader, I did my best to encourage H. P. At the time I knew nothing about his early childhood, but I could guess that the root of his insecurity lay in his upbringing. One afternoon when H. P. was still in bed and I had to wait in the living room, I asked Aunt Annie about the Lovecraft side of the family. She had barely known Winfield Lovecraft, H. P.'s father, whose health had completely broken down due to overwork when H. P. was a toddler. He had lived out his few remaining years in an institution.

"What did the senior Mr. Lovecraft do for a living, Aunt Annie?" I said, eager to hear more about the poor man.

"He was employed by the Gorham Silver people, dear," she said. "A fine old company."

"As what?"

"His position was that of commercial traveler, I think."

"You mean he was a traveling salesman?"

"Yes."

"Is that more respectable than being a tradesman?"

Aunt Annie had to think a moment before she answered this one.

"The important thing, dear," she said primly, "is that Howard's father came from a good family, of British stock. I do remember that he spoke with a slight English accent and was always impeccably dressed."

When I asked Aunt Annie if H. P. had been in touch with anyone on the Lovecraft side of his family in later years, she said that there may have been an aunt who used to send him information on his paternal ancestry. To her knowledge the grandparents, assuming they were alive, never made any effort to communicate with the boy after their son's breakdown and confinement. It all sounded rather sad.

The prevailing mood of the present Lovecraft household was, as I say, mostly happy. If H. P. was worried about the reception of *The Call of Cthulhu and Other Weird Stories*, he was doing his utmost to ensure that the book was as presentable as possible. He must have read page proofs at least three times, and he even had me take a look just in case he missed anything. He was particularly pleased when Mr. Ullman solicited and then accepted his input on the dust-jacket design. Permission to use several Clark Ashton Smith sculptures of monstrous alien beings on the front cover came cheap compared to what a professional artist would have cost.

For the inside of the jacket H. P. had to supply a photograph. When I looked over the meager collection of snapshots of himself he had on hand, I decided none of them did him justice. H. P. said he had an old Brownie which I could use to take a new one, but I told him I was sure I could borrow my father's Leica. We waited for a sunny and not too cold winter's day when, with the Leica, I photographed the distinguished author standing in front of his fanlighted doorway. Getting him to smile was the chief challenge. In the end I got a couple pictures that showed his cadaverous face to best advantage.

When the Knopf publicity department requested an autobiographical sketch, I agreed with H. P. that "Some Notes on a Nonentity" would do, though I insisted on retyping the first page without the overly modest title. Rereading this piece of self-history, I was again struck by its underlying melancholy. It was a real shame that "ill health" had prevented H. P. from attending college.

"Where were you hoping to go to college, H. P.?" I asked as I handed him back the essay.

"It was my earnest desire to matriculate at Brown, where my learned uncle-in-law had received his degree."

"I'm sorry. You must have been very sick." I remembered that Aunt Annie had told me that H. P. had suffered from "nervous trouble," but I wasn't about to let on that I was aware his problems had been primarily psychological.

"I was indeed quite ill," said H. P. He folded the essay into thirds and stuck it into one of his obsolete George Kirk Bookseller envelopes. Investing in personal stationery was still a luxury for this thrifty New Englander.

"Still, I suppose you could've waited until you were better and gone to Brown a year or two after you graduated from high school." Somehow I knew that H. P. had gone to a public high school, not to a private school such as Moses Brown, like the hero of *The Case of Charles Dexter Ward*.

"Miss Stone…Clarissa," said H. P., sounding more weary than angry. "No one appreciates better than I do all that you have done for both me and my aunt since last summer. As a typist you have proven yourself to be of infinite value. And yet you also have an uncanny knack of touching on some very sensitive matters."

"Oh, H. P., I don't mean to. I just want to understand."

"Well, understand this, young lady. I never graduated from Hope Street High. Attending Brown was never more than a pipe dream."

"I'm sorry, H. P."

"I trust you now understand why I chose not to be fully honest about my schooling," he said, as he scribbled the Knopf address on the envelope. "Would you be kind enough to mail this letter on your way home?"

"Of course, H. P."

"I have never ceased to be ashamed of my lack of a university education," he said in a low voice. "But I am even more ashamed not to have earned my high school diploma."

And what of my own schooling? As an honors student who was as healthy as a horse, I was confident that I would graduate from Miss Abbot's and go on to college—maybe Barnard (certainly not Pembroke). In my junior year I was fitting in well enough, having made a few friends and become active in the drama club, though I never let rehearsals interfere with my duties at 66 College Street. Once in a while H. P. and I discussed the theater. He said that at age seven he had seen his first Shakespeare play, *Cymbeline*, at the Providence Opera House. As an older child he had composed short plays and acted out all the parts. I would tell him about favorite Broadway shows, seen with my parents on trips back to New York, as well as the student productions I was involved in at school. I mentioned that certain performances were open to parents and friends, but he failed to take the hint. I hesitated to invite H. P. directly, not because I was afraid he would refuse but because I didn't want to put him in the position of having to accept only to be polite.

Now I was the one feeling insecure, though I will say that one relatively mild winter afternoon he did ask me to accompany him and Aunt Annie to the movies. Afterwards I was hesitant to say how much I liked *The Invisible Man*, fearing H. P. would dismiss it as he had *Frankenstein* and *Dracula*. But as soon as he declared that he had found the film surprisingly good—what might easily have been absurd succeeded in being genuinely sinister—I said I agreed entirely.

With the arrival of spring and the approach of the publication date of *The Call of Cthulhu*, H. P. was feeling increasingly anxious. A report from Mr. Ullman that higher than expected advance orders had prompted Knopf to increase the first printing did little to allay his fears. He did his best to focus on revision work, but on more than one occasion he threw down his pen and announced that he could no longer concentrate on such drivel and had to go out for a walk. One afternoon I arrived at 66 College Street to find him out. Aunt Annie informed me that he had gone on one of his ever more frequent and lengthy walks around Providence and beyond.

I took advantage of H. P.'s absence to plot a surprise party to celebrate the publication of his book. Aunt Annie was a willing conspirator, and between us we worked out a guest list. Besides Harry Brobst, there was Mr. and Mrs. Eddy, who lived in East Providence; Miss Bonner, a fellow cat aficionado; Mrs. Morrish, a second cousin; and Hazel Heald, his revision client from the Boston area. I was sure my parents would want to be included too. We considered inviting some of H. P.'s New York friends, but decided that potentially it would make the party too big. No doubt "the gang" would fête him royally the next time he visited the "pest zone."

We later settled on a Friday in April, close to the official publication date. Aunt Annie had learned that her nephew planned to attend a psychology lecture at Brown that evening. Since these lectures usually ran an hour, my parents and I would have plenty of time to drive over from our house with the party supplies and set everything up.

I too, as it turned out, was in for a surprise. The Thursday afternoon before the party I found *The Call of Cthulhu and Other Weird Stories*, by H. P. Lovecraft, propped up in front of the typewriter. H. P. had greeted me from his work table in his usual understated way when I entered the study, but now he was grinning like a ghoul!

"Congratulations, H. P.!" I exclaimed. This time I opened the book and looked for the inscription, which started: "To my favourite adopted granddaughter…" No matter that it was essentially the same as the one he had written in my Christmas present. I was thrilled. Unable to restrain myself, I rushed over and give him a big hug. This time he even stood up from his chair and returned the hug! Happy day!

In the next moment H. P. was explaining how his six author copies had arrived that morning in the mail. To hold in his hand a handsomely bound collection of his stories, issued by a proper publisher, was something he never dreamed he would live to see. He felt overwhelmed and humble in the face of the wonder.

As much as I shared his enthusiasm, I have to say that I was kind of disappointed by the dust jacket. Those Clark Ashton Smith

stone figures on the front cover, I now noticed, had a peculi-
arly *phallic* look. Suspecting that H. P. would be highly offended,
not to mention embarrassed by an innocent girl raising such an
indelicate subject, I decided not to remark on this resemblance
to him.

The next day all went according to plan. My parents and I arrived at 66 College Street soon after six. Aunt Annie said that H. P.
had gone off to his lecture shortly before the hour. We set up the
party things in the living room—lots of cheddar cheese and crackers, plus a platter of raw carrots and broccoli. Aunt Annie had said
that her nephew was eating a bit more fresh fruit and vegetables
since consuming the goodies I gave them for Christmas. Despite
H. P.'s disapproval of alcoholic beverages, we brought a bottle of
champagne. How could he object? Otherwise there was ginger ale,
coffee, and tea to drink. We displayed a copy of *The Call of Cthulhu*
on the fireplace mantel.

The first guest to arrive was Harry Brobst, bearing a couple of
bottles of beer. Miss Bonner, the Eddys, Mrs. Morrish and her husband soon followed. People put their hats and coats in Aunt Annie's
bedroom. The last to arrive was Hazel Heald, who greeted Mrs. Eddy
with a kiss on the cheek. Everyone seemed to know at least one other
person present, and we were soon all chatting away about the unsus-
pecting guest of honor and his new book.

Around seven, at Aunt Annie's suggestion, we each took our hiding places and turned off all but a little side lamp. Within minutes
we heard the front door open and then the steady tread on the stairs.
Aunt Annie called out to her nephew to join her in the living room.
She wanted to hear all about the lecture.

A moment or two later H. P.'s tall, lean form appeared silhouetted in the doorway. Then Harry switched on the overheard light
and we all shouted "Surprise!"

"Good Lord!" cried H. P.

In the next instant he was engulfed by his fans, offering their
congratulations and saying how swell the book looked. No one,
though, specifically commented on the dust-jacket design. Earlier I
had overheard my father make some quip about Smith's artwork to
my mother as they admired the volume on the mantel.

Harry popped the cork of the champagne bottle and Aunt Annie produced a tray of tiny crystal glasses, evidently reserved for special occasions. Harry filled the glasses with champagne and we each took one, except H. P.

"To Howard," said Harry, raising his glass. "Long may he live and long may he write stories like 'The Call of Cthulhu'!"

"You mean *Klu-hloo*," said H. P. in a thick, guttural voice. "It's an absolutely non-human word and hence can never be uttered perfectly by human throats."

Everyone drank H. P.'s health and toasted his success. Aunt Annie handed him a glass of ginger ale. He in turn raised his glass and briefly thanked everybody for coming. By now he seemed to have recovered from his initial shock and to be almost enjoying all the attention.

The person most paying court to H. P., I noticed, was Hazel Heald. A little woman of about forty with too much rouge on her face and dressed in expensive clothes a few seasons out of fashion, she simpered or cooed at the great author's every word.

At the edge of the crowd, viewing this sickening display with approval, was Mrs. Eddy. I made a point of drawing her into a tête à tête and asking about Hazel's relationship to H. P.

"Howard has been such a help to Hazel with her writing," she confided. "I hope they'll see more of each other now that Howard's an established writer."

"Did they use to see each other a lot?" I whispered.

"Oh, yes, when she first became his client a couple of years ago they used to meet regularly in Boston. Early on she treated him to a candlelit supper at her house with all the foods he liked best on the menu. He was greatly impressed by her thoughtfulness in not having a houseful of people to greet him." Mrs. Eddy chuckled. "Men can be so naïve sometimes."

I decided then and there that Mrs. Eddy was a rather vulgar woman. How did H. P. ever become friendly with her and her dolt of a husband, I had to wonder.

"Hazel is also divorced, you know," Mrs. Eddy continued, lowering her voice. "Just between us, I believe Hazel would be far more suitable for Howard than that first wife of his. She wasn't at all from his sort of background, if you know what I mean."

I did know what Mrs. Eddy meant and I didn't like the implication. Worse was to come. By nine o'clock the cheese and crackers and vegetables were gone and so were most of the guests. My parents were ready to leave, but I wasn't—not until I saw Hazel go out the door first. I was relieved to see her finally get her hat and coat. Having retired to his study, H. P. reappeared with his hat and coat and announced that he was walking Hazel to the Biltmore. Turning to Aunt Annie, he said that he might join Hazel for a light supper at the hotel restaurant. Hazel breezily explained that she had decided to stay overnight at the Biltmore rather than worry about returning late to Boston. Mother and Dad offered to help with the cleaning up, but Aunt Annie wouldn't hear of it. There was nothing to do.

I tried to pretend my tears were tears of joy when I gave H. P. a goodnight hug and once more wished him happy publication day.

Chapter 13

That weekend there was no hiding my bad mood. Irritatingly enough, my parents didn't hesitate to show their concern. Mother suggested that maybe I needed to see less of H. P., while Dad bluntly told me that even a repressed New England bachelor might like some mature female company once in a while. In Dad's view, H. P.'s taking Hazel out to dinner was a reassuring sign that his instincts were normal.

I admit I had mixed feelings about going over to College Street for my next typing session. I was dying to hear what H. P. had to say—or not say—about the aftermath of the surprise party. But I dreaded it too.

When I arrived for work H. P. was using a penknife to cut something out of the newspaper.

"Good day, Clarissa," said H. P.

"Hi, H. P.," I said, trying to sound as cheerful as he did.

"Have a look at this cutting, young lady." He handed me a substantial column of print. It was a book review—of *The Call of Cthulhu*!

"Oh, boy! Your first review!"

"I have to hand it to those Knopf publicity bimbos," he said. "They promised to target the local press and look at the almost instant result!"

When I finished reading the review, I handed it back to him. "That's terrific, H. P.!"

The review was indeed positive, apart from a patronizing comment at the start about scaring the reader ranking low as an aim in literature. Worthier was H. P.'s New England regionalism, as reflected in the title story, which pleased the reviewer in particular on account of its Providence setting. The piece was signed "W. T. Scott."

"Winfield Townley Scott is the literary editor of the *Journal*," said H. P. "It is truly an honor to receive such notice from so eminent a critic. I shall have to write him a personal note expressing my gratitude."

I had completed my own reading of *The Call of Cthulhu and Other Weird Stories* over the weekend. The two tales that impressed me the most were "The Outsider" and "The Rats in the Walls," maybe because they each reflected some strong human emotion other than fear, like loneliness or grief. On the whole, I thought the collection, which was arranged chronologically, improved as it went along. Some of the earlier tales seemed overwritten, with too many adjectives or strings of words that didn't make a lot of sense.

"H. P., I have a question," I said. I wanted to show that I too was capable of being a perceptive critic. "In one of your stories"—I didn't dare try to pronounce the name of it—"you mention 'the revolving graveyard of the universe.' That's very poetic, but what does it mean?"

"Did you say *revolving* graveyard?"

I nodded. H. P. picked up a copy of the book and started to thumb through it.

"Are you saying the universe is like a merry-go-round—"

"Yes, here it is." H. P. groaned. "At the end of 'Nyarlathotep.' Confound it, that know-it-all copy-editor must have ignored my correction in the page proofs. It should be the *revolting* graveyard of the universe, not *revolving*. Bah!"

"*Revolting* does make more sense," I said, though I wasn't sure it did.

"This is most embarrassing," said H. P. "How fortunate that I have yet to mail out presentation copies."

From my seat at the typing desk, I observed H. P. take each copy of *The Call of Cthulhu*, scratch out the second "v" in the word *revolving* with his penknife, and with black ink put a "t" in its place. I complimented him on his handiwork when he showed me one of the corrected copies. Privately I thought this was a little much. After all, the error could always be fixed in the second printing.

When H. P. asked me to compose a brief note to Mr. Ullman requesting just that, that "revolving" be changed to "revolting" in the next printing, I suggested that maybe it would be better to wait in case more typos turned up. The proud author, however, was confident that no other errors would be uncovered.

As soon as I had finished typing this missive, H. P. handed me the penciled draft of a slightly longer note—to the president of the National Amateur Press Association—tendering his resignation from the Bureau of Critics.

"As you can see, Clarissa," he said, "I am heeding your advice to cut back on certain unremunerative commitments."

"Good for you, H. P.," I replied. How nice that I didn't always have to nag him to do what he ought to do.

When I handed him this letter to sign, I said, "By the way, H. P., how did you get to know the Eddys?" By this point I had summoned enough nerve to take an indirect approach to the subject of Hazel.

"Mrs. Eddy's mother and my mother met at a suffragette meeting, in 1919, I believe," he said in his professorial voice. "When they discovered that they both had offspring with an interest in writing, they arranged an epistolary introduction. I recognized at once that both Muriel and her husband, Cliff, could benefit from joining the amateur journalism movement, and duly recruited them to the cause. After an agreeable if desultory correspondence, we finally met face to face in 1922."

"H. P., if you don't mind my saying so, the Eddys don't strike me as your type."

"Clarissa, I grant that Muriel and Cliff are what one might call the traditional salt of the earth."

"Still—"

"The Eddys have shown me great hospitality in the past. Cliff was once a steady revision client. I will admit, though, that in recent years I have not seen them as often as formerly."

"And what about Hazel?"

"I have the Eddys to thank for introducing me to Mrs. Heald."

"Did she get home to Boston all right?"

"A thank you note in this morning's post confirmed her safe return to the Bay State."

"I bet you treated her to a swell dinner at the Biltmore."

"Mrs. Heald did seem to enjoy the simple repast served by the gracious staff of the hotel restaurant."

"And how about you, H. P.?"

"Having earlier consumed plentiful quantities of cheese and crackers, I was content with a slice of the Biltmore's excellent lemon chiffon pie. In all honesty I had no need of another meal. But when Mrs. Heald suggested that she would prefer not to dine alone at the hotel, I felt that I had no choice but to act as her escort. I returned home as soon as I politely could."

This didn't sound like a man talking about a woman to whom he was attracted. Or was H. P. deliberately leading me off the scent?

"H. P., may I ask you a personal question?"

He gave me that wary look of his, then said with sigh, "Yes, if you must, Clarissa."

"Do you think you'll ever get married again?"

"I am very much in favor of an harmonious married state," he answered after some reflection, "but do not relish resuming at any-time soon the old ball and chain."

"Why did you and your wife divorce?"

"For reasons ninety-eight percent financial."

"What about the other two percent?"

"Clarissa, really—"

"Don't you miss being married?"

"If one expects to be a man of letters one has to sacrifice some-thing—"

"No you don't!"

"—and for anybody of reasonably ascetic temperament the in-terests and freedoms of imaginative life more than overbalance the advantages of domesticity."

"What about sex, H. P.?" I blurted.

"Miss Stone!" declared Howard P. Lovecraft, turning crimson. "A proper young lady does not ask a conservative old gentleman such a question!"

"I'm sorry, H. P." I bowed my head, startled and ashamed by my boldness. I had really crossed the line now.

"In these transitional days," I finally heard him mutter, "the luckiest persons are those of sluggish eroticism who can cast aside the whole muddled business and watch the squirming of the primitive majority from the sidelines with ironic detachment."

"Oh."

"And that, my dear Miss Stone, is all I have to say to you on *that* subject."

"If you say so, Mr. Lovecraft," I replied, still not daring to look him in the face.

After this embarrassing exchange, I couldn't imagine doing any further typing. I was sure that if H. P. didn't dismiss me for the day he would be relieved to see me go. But when I stood up and announced I was getting my coat, he said that he had something important to tell me. His face had resumed its normal corpse-like pallor.

"Yes, H. P.?"

"Before you leave, Clarissa," he said, his Yankee dignity restored, "you should know that I shall be departing shortly on an extended trip."

"Where to? Quebec?"

"No, to Florida. Robert H. Barlow has invited me to stay with him and his family at their home in De Land near the Ocala swamp country."

I recognized the name as that of one of H. P.'s more persistent correspondents, but that was about it. H. P. said that his friend had recently done him the honor of binding up several sets of proof pages of a story of his, "The Shunned House." *The Shunned House*, originally supposed to be published by his amateur associate Mr. W. Paul Cook, thus stood as his first appearance between cloth covers.

"Is Mr. Barlow married with children?" I asked.

H. P. laughed. "My prospective host is a delightful young fellow, who lives with his parents, five cats, and six infant opossums."

"So he's just a boy. Do you know how old he is exactly?"

"I have never inquired, but I dare say the kid must be in either his seventeenth or eighteenth year."

"And what's so special about Master Barlow?"

H. P. explained. Besides being an embryonic weird author, the lad was a marionette maker, landscape gardener, tennis champion, chess expert, crack rifleshot, book and manuscript collector, and heavens knew what else.

"And how long will you be visiting this prodigy?"

"Several weeks I should imagine."

"Several months sounds more like it, what with all this guy's hobbies."

H. P. laughed again. He didn't seem to notice my sarcasm. "Just how long I stay depends largely on finances. As soon as I receive the five-hundred berries due me from Knopf on book publication, I hop the bus for New York and points south."

"Swell, H. P."

"Clarissa," he said, shifting to his serious voice, "I hope I can count on you to act as my secretary in my absence—answer any correspondence from Knopf, forward personal letters to my Florida address, and generally deal with any business that might arise. I have full confidence in your abilities, young lady."

Well, this was some comfort. At least I still had a job. "Okay, H. P.," I said. "Do you want me to open all your mail first?"

"I trust you to use your judgment, Clarissa."

"Thanks, H. P."

"Farewell, then, if we do not meet again before I go." H. P. rose from behind his writing table and made a jerky motion that I took for an attempt at a bow. The earlier awkwardness was back.

"See ya," I said at the door, pretending I was playing the tough, Betty Davis broad.

Chapter 14

Ididn't see or speak to H. P. again before he left on his travels. The next time I stopped by 66 College Street, I found an envelope propped on the typewriter labeled "C. S." Inside was a big check, along with a note saying that he hoped this recompense was sufficient to cover my needs in his absence. The money was more than ample. If work was slow, he added in a P.S., I could always try to type the manuscript of yet another novel-length work of fiction, *The Dream-Quest of Unknown Kadath*, which he had left out in its file folder on his table.

It wasn't the same, I have to admit, without H. P. around. Without the smidgen of attention his presence guaranteed, I didn't have a lot of desire to type what I soon discovered was a nearly undecipherable manuscript, with long paragraphs, lots of funny made-up names, no dialogue, and no chapter breaks. *The Dream-Quest of Unknown Kadath* had no plot to speak of either. A total mishmash, it should have remained buried in whatever crypt H. P. kept the bodies of his inferior fictions.

The personal mail from those correspondents familiar to me I simply forwarded to H. P. c/o R. H. Barlow, Box 88, De Land, Florida—without opening. What did I care what a bunch of immature fans had to say to H. P., or amateur journalists who would never earn a dime from their pathetic attempts at writing? In consolation I was now receiving mail from H. P. again, addressed to me at home, postcards mostly, which tracked his progress down the East Coast: New York, Charleston, Savannah, Jacksonville. These were all picture postcards showing one or another old house of architectural or historical significance. Their contents were full of his usual antiquarian ravings, but now he could boast of a new, more personal thrill: spotting copies of his book in bookstores. Modesty, of course, prevented him from identifying himself as the author of that latest Knopf sensation, *The Call of Cthulhu and Other Weird Stories*.

As for accommodation, H. P. was staying almost exclusively at Y.M.C.A.s. At this point he could have afforded hotels, or so my parents said when I asked their opinion, but frugal habits die hard. That he was staying at Y.M.C.A.s prompted Dad at the dinner table one evening to quip that he hoped H. P. knew enough to watch his behind in the men's shower. Mother's "That's enough, Henry!" put an end to that line of conversation.

I knew what Dad was suggesting, though. And I will say I had to wonder why H. P. was traveling a thousand miles to visit a teenage boy he had never met. The reports in the postcards he sent from De Land, after he was settled with the Barlows, were rather ho-hum. The letters to Aunt Annie that she shared with me added little to the picture. H. P. didn't play chess or tennis, make marionettes, or shoot guns. Apart from reading and letter-writing and playing with the family cats, he and young Bobby mainly sat around outdoors talking about books and authors. (Barlow didn't seem to have to go to school—was he too a high school drop-out?) Once H. P. went berry picking and fell into a creek, losing the berries. That was about as exciting as things got in De Land. One of his host's kittens, possessed of an erudite visage wise beyond its years, he named Alfred A. Knopf.

I did open mail from H. P.'s publisher. The most interesting item during those first weeks on my own was a letter from Mr. Ullman containing a detailed critique of *The Case of Charles Dexter Ward*. Most of his objections were pretty picayune, but one major point sticks in my mind. More than one character urges the hero, Dr. Willett, to dissolve the body of the villain, Joseph Curwen, in acid. But in the end a magic spell reduces Curwen to a pile of gray dust that blows away. For the sake of consistency, the Knopf editor argued, H. P. had either to eliminate or alter these early warnings or else have Willett dispose of Curwen by dunking him in an acid bath. The dialogue between the two during their climactic confrontation needed work anyway. Why not simply rewrite the last few pages? Since I never read the published version of the novel, and H. P. never remarked on the matter to me, I can't say whether he accepted these suggested alterations or not—and if he did, whether they improved the book.

Another notable letter arrived from Winfield Townley Scott, who took some pains to answer H. P.'s defense of the weird tale. Evidently in thanking Mr. Scott for his review of *The Call of Cthulhu*, H. P. had made a case that the genre, humble though it was, deserved at least a little literary respect. In closing Mr. Scott said he would like to meet H. P. sometime. Bertrand K. Hart, who wrote a literary column for the Providence *Journal*, sent a congratulatory note in which he expressed delight at a collection whose title story featured a former College Hill residence of his. When I later asked Aunt Annie about this, she said that Mr. Hart, after reading "The Call of Cthulhu," had playfully threatened in his column to send a ghoul to her nephew's door in retribution for H. P.'s using his address on Thomas St. as a ghostly locale.

In another category altogether was a fan letter, postmarked Paris, France, from a guy named Henry Miller. Yes, that Henry Miller, author of *Tropic of Cancer*, due to appear in its first Obelisk Press edition later in the year. Miller would, of course, eventually become in his way almost as famous as H. P. as a defiantly off-beat writer with a specialized appeal. A friend from the States had given him a copy of *The Call of Cthulhu*, which had evidently struck a slimy and chaotic chord with the expatriate bohemian, who compared the book favorably to the work of Arthur Machen. Miller was so enthusiastic, he even suggested that he and H. P. collaborate on a tale, "Tropic of Cthulhu." It was hard to tell whether the man was serious or not. In any event, as far as I know, H. P. never pursued this bizarre proposal.

My father got into the act by recommending possible magazines for H. P.'s essays. I submitted "Some Repetitions on the Times" to the *New Republic* and "Cats and Dogs" to *Scribner's*, each with an appropriate cover letter. The first essay soon came back with a polite note stating that it wouldn't do for them because the author lacked the proper credentials, but after a few weeks a provisional acceptance arrived from *Scribner's* for "Cats and Dogs." The editor wrote that if the author would permit the more obscure personal and topical references to be cut, they could use the piece. I duly forwarded this offer to H. P., who I assume must have agreed to the requested changes—and a new title. "Something About Cats" appeared in the October issue, complete with distinction between human beings and tradesmen.

As May turned into June and I neared the end of another school year, I became increasingly anxious about H. P.'s return home. Nothing in his letters indicated that he was growing tired of the Barlow family's seemingly boundless hospitality or that he had better things to do elsewhere. Then one day the buzzer sounded. At Aunt Annie's request I went downstairs to see who was at the door. It was a delivery boy from Western Union with a telegram addressed to Mrs. A.E.P. Gamwell.

Back upstairs I gave it to Aunt Annie, who was listening to the radio in the living room. I could guess who it was from—but why a telegram? Aunt Annie opened it while I stood at a respectful distance.

"Oh my stars!" the old lady exclaimed. "I can't believe it."

"What is it?" I asked. "What is it?"

Wordlessly Aunt Annie handed me the telegram. It read:

"DEAR AUNT, AM OFF TO HOLLYWOOD. KNOPF HAS SOLD FILM RIGHTS TO HERBERT WEST. FULL DETAILS TO FOLLOW. IA! IA! HPL."

Chapter 15

I was wondering if I was going to have to rely on Aunt Annie to tell me the full story of H. P.'s latest triumph, but in fact I received a postcard a day or two later. In his miniscule script H. P. outlined the essentials: after receiving this extraordinary offer, he only had to think a moment or two before authorizing Knopf to accept. He could justify the sale of "Herbert West" to the movies because the tale represented his poorest work, written to order for a vulgar magazine. How could Hollywood ruin what was refuse in the first place? The important thing was that the money would allow him to extend his trip. The head of the studio who had bought the rights, evidently with the idea of making a film to rival Warner Brothers' *Frankenstein*, wanted to meet him. Hence the Old Gentleman was headed for Hollywood, with an intermediate stop in Texas, to visit "Two-Gun Bob" Howard.

The news of this coup must have traveled fast, for the volume of H. P.'s correspondence soon picked up. At his instructions I forwarded important mail to Robert E. Howard's address in Cross Plains, Texas. Though he intended to linger there awhile, he left after only a few days, realizing that Dr. and Mrs. Howard, the barbarian-author's parents, didn't have the resources to be as accommodating as the senior Barlows had been. Reading between the lines, it would seem that Two-Gun, unlike little Bobby, was a grownup with some real work to do and only limited time to spare on entertaining a guest. The steady stream of fan letters sent in care of Knopf I put on his study table for his later perusal.

By the end of June, H. P. had reached California—and here my account of the private man must give way to the story of the public figure that he was so rapidly becoming. Since H. P.'s adventures in Hollywood have been adequately chronicled elsewhere, I will touch on only some of the highlights. Right off the bat he made an impression when, instead of taking a taxi from the downtown bus terminal, he rode the trolley car to a scheduled meeting at the Hal Roach Studio, arriving more than an hour late. Ever the thrifty Yankee!

It was fortunate that Mr. Hal Roach Sr., whose company of course specialized in making comedies, had a sense of humor. Mr. Roach seems originally to have had the idea of signing up H. P. as a scriptwriter, but on seeing the author in the flesh decided that the lantern-jawed New Englander would be perfect for another job—a role in *Reanimator*, as he had already titled his projected feature-length adaptation of "Herbert West." I can well imagine H. P. at first protesting his unfitness, elaborating on his lack of acting ability, but by the end of the interview agreeing to take a screen test. The rest, as they say in show biz, is history.

Because it mixed humor with horror, *Reanimator* didn't do all that well at the box office. There would be no *Return of Reanimator* or *Bride of Reanimator*. Nonetheless, H. P. had a memorable ten minutes or so on screen playing a reanimated corpse. Bearing more than a passing resemblance to the Frankenstein monster, H. P. mostly just had to grunt and growl as he terrorized the students and professors of Miskatonic U., played by such Roach regulars as James Finlayson and Edgar Kennedy. Laurel and Hardy were perfect as a pair of bumbling grave robbers. When H. P.'s character did speak intelligible words, his high-pitched voice contrasted amusingly with his sinister appearance. In contrast to Boris Karloff, he didn't need a lot of makeup to look really scary!

After the filming of *Reanimator*, Mr. Roach thought well enough of H. P.'s performance to offer him a six-month contract with the studio. H. P. had to consult with Aunt Annie first, even making a long-distance phone call to Providence to discuss the matter. Her assurance that she was doing fine on her own was enough to persuade him to stay on in California. She was so happy for her dear nephew, first a book author, now a movie actor with the guarantee of a steady job! Given their dire circumstances only the year before when they had to consolidate living quarters, how wonderful it was that Howard could now afford to pay rent on two places at once, on opposite sides of the country no less!

In order to be within reasonable commuting range of the "Lot of Fun," as those who worked at the Hal Roach Studio fondly called it, H. P. rented a couple of furnished rooms at the Oxford Arms, a mock Tudor apartment building in Hancock Park, a residential neighborhood south of Hollywood. He took pride in avoiding the L.A. suburbs farther to the west near the ocean favored by most people in the acting community. Among the solid citizens of Hancock Park, with their two-car garages, he quickly gained a reputation as an eccentric for walking everywhere. Later he bought a second-hand bicycle, resuming one of the favorite pastimes of his youth. Since only kids rode bikes, this only made him seem more an oddball, especially as he often wore a jacket and tie while pedaling the streets of L.A. Or so he boasted in his letters.

In other letters he commented on the pleasure he took patronizing the local farmer's market, which offered a profusion of fresh fruit and vegetables like nothing he had ever seen in the East. Such hitherto unknown delights as avocados and artichokes might have come from another planet. Truly the food of the gods! Spicy Mexican dishes— enchiladas, tamales, and tacos—he particularly came to relish, while in the sweets department he developed a fondness for Vandekamp's sugar cookies and Mrs. See's candies. Aunt Annie was kind enough to share with me the box of assorted See's chocolates that he sent her as a birthday present.

Energized by the hot sunshine even more so than in Florida, H. P. didn't mind rising early for work. As a contract player at Roach, he mostly did bit roles as heavies in the "Our Gang" and "Laurel and Hardy" two-reelers. In the idle hours that are inevitable on any set, he occupied himself with—some habits never die—letter-writing. My impression is that he didn't mix much with the other actors (he was evidently put off by Laurel and Hardy's real-life marital woes), though he was on friendly terms with Marvin Hatley and Leroy Shield, who composed the incidental music for the Hal Roach shorts. Their simple, catchy melodies held an irresistible appeal, reminding him of the popular songs of his youth.

H. P. also met a more serious composer living in Los Angeles, Harold S. Farnese, who had once written him a fan letter asking permission to set two of his *Fungi from Yuggoth* sonnets to music.

Mr. Farnese now wanted the pulp-writer-turned-actor to try his hand at writing the libretto of a light opera based on the *Fungi* cycle. H. P. begged off, telling the man in consolation that he was welcome to set the rest of the *Fungi* to music. With no experience in writing drama, he was unfit to play W. S. Gilbert to Mr. Farnese's Sir Arthur Sullivan.

If H. P. was meeting any beautiful starlets he didn't say, at least not in his letters to me. Aunt Annie didn't always show me the much more detailed and frequent letters he wrote her, but those I was privileged to read said nothing on the subject of the fair sex.

An outing to the La Brea tar pits, not to mention the ubiquitous palm trees and other exotic subtropical vegetation, helped inspire a new story, set largely in Earth's prehistoric past when the climate worldwide was as warm as Southern California's. This was to be another mind-swapping yarn, but on a far more ambitious scale than "The Thing on the Doorstep." H. P. would make several false starts and tear up more than one draft over several months before he was finally satisfied with the results. The finished tale, "The Shadow Out of Time," was one of his finest with its undercurrent of loneliness and family tragedy. I felt I was still in his good graces when he took the trouble to send me the handwritten manuscript for typing instead of hiring a secretary locally. By this stage there wasn't much for me to do, other than to forward mail.

I know that he was engaged with one other literary project at this time—revising and expanding a study called *Supernatural Horror in Literature*. The discovery that summer of a hitherto unknown British author of the weird, William Hope Hodgson, who died in the Great War, had inspired him to resume work on it again, as he explained at considerable length in a letter to Aunt Annie. This he didn't ask me to type, perhaps because it was only a small job.

H. P. toyed with the idea of returning to Providence for Christmas, but wrote to Aunt Annie that, having grown accustomed to California weather, he just wasn't ready to face a New England winter. Instead he accepted an invitation to spend Christmas with Clark Ashton Smith in the northern part of the state. Smith's frail and elderly parents, who also lived in the small town of Auburn (you have to give Smith credit for at least not living under the same roof with his folks), joined them, along with Helen and her mother, in a festive turkey dinner at a local boarding house. (Since the cottage that Smith inhabited was rather primitive, with no running water, entertaining there wasn't practical.) Helen, according to H. P., had had a rough time of it emotionally since her Providence visit, so while in Auburn he did his best to try to cheer her up.

Back in Hollywood after the new year, H. P. resumed work as a bartender in the Laurel and Hardy short "The Fixer-Uppers"—an ironic role for the still confirmed teetotaler! This, however, would be his last acting job. Mr. Roach, under pressure to cut costs and compete with the major studios, was getting out of the two-reeler business. He made it clear that he wouldn't be renewing H. P.'s screen contract, though he was prepared to keep him on as a scriptwriter. While H. P. was tempted to accept, an experimental attempt at a screenplay convinced him that he simply had no gift for dialogue. He might be the author of a short-story collection published by a noted New York house—impressive credentials in Hollywood where few people actually read books—but he knew his own limits all too well.

With the arrival around this time of a substantial check, mainly from the sale of British rights to *The Call of Cthulhu*, H. P. decided he was ready to move on. Despite the salubrious climate, Southern California's initial charm was starting to fade. He couldn't stay forever in a place where the oldest buildings dated only as far back as the end of the last century. The native Spanish stucco and bungalow styles he viewed as natural outgrowths of the semi-arid landscape, but much of California architecture was unspeakably grotesque. You would never catch him inside a monstrosity like the Brown Derby restaurant!

The truth is he was homesick for New England and the familiar surroundings of his College Hill eyrie. In late February, soon after completing "The Shadow Out of Time," he left Hollywood. As with his journey westward across the country, he went out of his way to see friends. First he called on Ed, who by then was living in San Diego. Postcards tell the rest of the story. A second stay with Clark Ashton Smith in Auburn was followed by visits to two teenage fans, F. Lee Baldwin and Duane Rimel, in Washington state. He then rode a train (not a bus!) across the Northern Plains to

Milwaukee, Wisconsin, where he was the guest of yet another teenage admirer, Robert Bloch. August Derleth spent several days with them in Milwaukee.

In Chicago he met *Weird Tales* editor Farnsworth Wright, who since the publication of *The Call of Cthulhu* had been busy reprinting early Lovecraft stories. Since H. P. had sold all rights to these stories to the magazine back when he didn't know any better, he didn't receive a cent for them now. Wright was eager to get his hands on a new tale from his celebrity author, but he had to concede when he read the typed manuscript, which I mailed him from Providence, that "The Shadow Out of Time" would be way over the head of his average reader. This tale wouldn't see the light of print until Knopf saw fit to combine it in a book with the novel whose original rejection H. P. had taken so hard, *At the Mountains of Madness*.

Forgive me if much of the above is familiar, but I can't be sure that everyone of you is a diehard Lovecraftian who already knows H. P.'s basic biography. Don't worry, those of you who are impatient; I'm almost finished.

Chapter 16

Like Charles Dexter Ward after his sojourn abroad, H. P. at last came home in the spring, at sunset. Or so I like to think. Only Aunt Annie was at 66 College Street to greet him, and I never did learn at what hour or even what day he returned. As president of the drama club my senior year, I had plenty to do after school and on weekends, and was dropping by the apartment only now and then since typing "The Shadow Out of Time." Having been accepted by my first-choice college, Barnard, I was looking forward to returning to New York in the fall.

I was nervous, I admit, at the prospect of seeing H. P. again after so long a time. I wasn't sure whether I should just stop in or wait for his summons. Then one evening he phoned. While he did ask how I was doing and offer his congratulations on my college acceptance (even if it did mean residing in the "pest zone"), he deflected my questions about himself by saying we could go into all that in person. When was I next available to come over? I said I would be free the following afternoon. He said that would be fine. After a final pleasantry or two, he hung up. This brusque and business-like conversation did nothing to relieve me of my anxiety.

As it turned out, this time I wasn't being oversensitive. When I entered his study, I couldn't help noticing the fleeting look of surprise and fear that crossed his face before he stood up from behind his work table and gave me one of his formal bows. There would be no welcoming hug for his "favorite adopted granddaughter." Always mature for my age, I knew that I had grown up a lot since the year before, while he was still the reserved gentleman, ill at ease with members of the opposite sex, unless they were elderly aunts.

I will say that H. P. looked healthier than at any time I could remember in the past. His skin had almost a ruddy glow, perhaps the remnants of a California tan, and he wasn't quite so gaunt and lean, due I'm sure to an improved diet. He quickly recovered from his initial alarm, and spoke of his travels not only with enthusiasm but with confidence. The old self-deprecating modesty was still there, but he was no longer the diffident, defensive "Grandpa." Here at last was a man used to success.

Whatever role I had in the life of the successful writer would soon be coming to an end, I sensed, even if I wasn't leaving Providence for college. For the moment, though, H. P. still needed me to deal with his mail and do his typing. He could afford to give me a raise—to fifty cents an hour. Preparing his taxes on his own this year, what with his complicated income situation, had been a hellish experience. Might my father know of a good accountant? I said I would ask. The interview was over.

Later Dad did refer an accountant to H. P., plus he was instrumental in getting the Brown English department to sponsor a reading at the Providence Atheneum. For H. P. this was a high honor, to speak in the same learned institution where his god of fiction, Edgar Allan Poe, had held forth a century or so earlier. H. P. read the opening sections of "The Shunned House" and "The Call of Cthulhu," as well as from the eighteenth-century part of *The Case of Charles Dexter Ward*, which had just been published. The lecture hall was full, mostly with college students, though there were a few genteel East Side types. People I knew included Aunt Annie, Harry Brobst (with new girl friend), Mr. and Mrs. Eddy, my parents, and several of my father's Brown colleagues. (I didn't notice Hazel, not that I would have minded her presence.) As an experienced actor, H. P. read with real effect, modulating his voice to indicate a shift in mood. When he finished, everyone applauded warmly.

At the reception afterwards, I stood close enough to H. P. to overhear him talking to his admirers. Among them were Winfield Townley Scott and Bertrand K. Hart, who promised to write up the occasion for the *Journal*. There was also a pushy high school kid, Ken Sterling, who that summer would become a frequent visitor at 66 College Street. What was it with these teenage boys? At least H. P. had the sense to turn down Kid Barlow's repeated requests to come to Florida for a second extended stay.

Bertrand K. Hart published an account of the reading in his "Side Show" column, playfully suggesting that H. P. resembled (shades of *Reanimator*) one of his own fantastic creatures. In his book review Winfield Townley Scott praised H. P.'s use of Providence history in *The Case of Charles Dexter Ward* while expressing his usual reservations about the literary value of such fiction. H. P. took this criticism with good humor, but not so an essay-review that later appeared in the *New Yorker*, by Edmund Wilson. Surveying *The Call of Cthulhu* and *The Case of Charles Dexter Ward*, as well as *Supernatural Horror in Literature* (released by Knopf a month after the novel), Wilson had few kind things to say about individual stories. Most devastating, though, was his attack on H. P.'s style, in particular H. P.'s overuse of adjectives. When the subject inadvertently came up, H. P. admitted that it hurt to have the dean of American critics damn him as a bad writer.

Fortunately, there was plenty of good news to offset this blow. The publication of the Gollancz edition of *The Call of Cthulhu* was bringing him a load of fan mail from England, including appreciative notes from such admired writers as Arthur Machen, Lord Dunsany, and Algernon Blackwood, author of the greatest horror tale ever written, "The Willows." A somewhat less complimentary letter came from M. R. James, the ghost-story writer, asking about the origin of Asenath in "The Thing on the Doorstep." It seems Dr. James had done some research into the subject in his youth.

A highly pleasant surprise was receiving word of the acceptance by the *Saturday Evening Post* of "The Shadow Over Innsmouth." August Derleth had submitted this lengthy, unpublished tale behind his back, and while H. P. hardly agreed with the boosterish, main-street values espoused by the *Post*, who was he to turn up his nose at their extremely handsome offer of payment? The legendary *Post* editor, George Horace Lorimer, was candid about their taking a risk with "The Shadow Over Innsmouth," but favorable reviews of H. P.'s books (this was before the blast in the *New Yorker*) had convinced him to try something a little different. The two-part serial, as it turned out, provoked strong responses from readers in the magazine's letters column, running the gamut from bewilderment to outrage. Soon after Lorimer announced his retirement. In consolation, H. P. was gratified to receive a bemused letter of inquiry from fellow New Englander and regular *Post* contributor, J. P. Marquand. The popular mainstream author was curious to confirm his suspicion that his native Newburyport, Massachusetts, had served as the model for decadent Innsmouth.

Meanwhile, a revised version of "Some Repetitions on the Times" had finally found a home, thanks to Dad's continued efforts, with a leftwing journal called *The New Leader*. A glowing capsule biography accompanied the piece, explaining that Mr. Lovecraft, notwithstanding his cogent proposals for dealing with the Depression, was principally an author of the weird.

After graduating from Miss Abbot's in June, I went on a trip abroad with my parents. From France and Italy I sent H. P. a stream of postcards. Two could play at this game! We returned to Providence in early August. My first task, on resuming work for H. P., was to sort through the stacks of mail that had accumulated in my absence. How was he going to fend without me? H. P. had managed to retrieve the letters from his most important friends, but unopened correspondence lay everywhere in piles around the study. It was in going through these that I discovered a letter, on heavy cream stationery, with the return address of…The White House, 1600 Pennsylvania Avenue, Washington, D.C.!

"Good heavens, H. P.!" I cried. "You better open this quick!"

"What is it, Clarissa?" he said, not looking up from the letter he was scribbling on his writing table.

"It's from the White House!" I yelled, handing him the envelope.

"Egads, a message from Olympus!"

"I better go get Aunt Annie!" But as I turned around to leave, she appeared in the doorway.

"Is everything all right?" she said, looking worriedly at each of us.

By this time H. P. had opened the letter.

"My dear aunt," he croaked. "I have received a personal letter from President Roosevelt!"

"What does he say? What does he say?" I said, sounding I'm sure like a silly schoolgirl half my age.

"Mr. Roosevelt compliments me on my article in *The New Leader*, then goes on to…to express his thoughts on…*on the weird tale*!"

Well, after this accolade anything else would have to be a letdown. A week or so later H. P. announced that he was shortly to leave on a trip—to England. I was upset that he didn't give me more warning, that he was leaving before his birthday, and a hundred other things besides. But he reminded me that I was soon headed for college, that we must all move on in life. He was arranging for August Derleth to act as his literary agent and deal with many of the clerical matters that were presently my responsibility. And while I knew we would write each other and possibly even cross paths in the future, I felt that this was the end, that the old intimacy, such as it was, was over. I would have one more indirect part to play in H. P.'s life in later years, but that's another story, one I'm not sure I'll ever share. I've said enough for now, except to confess that our farewell, on the stoop of 66 College Street, on a sweltering August afternoon, ended in anticlimax—a jerky handshake and a muttered, "I cannot tell you how much I have appreciated you."

By the time I had reached the sidewalk and turned to wave goodbye, he was already back inside the house.

Leonora

Chapter 1

A single woman on the wrong side of thirty should never give up hope of finding a man. So it was that shortly after a six months' flirtation with an assistant curate came to nothing, I decided to work for my friend Jane's private secretarial service. Jane had been urging me for years to join the firm, which she assured me had an excellent placement record. Several of her girls had ended up marrying their employers, and while it was also the case that more than a few had suffered heartbreak, they really had only themselves to blame. Falling in love with married men was not recommended company policy.

Jane, however, promised me that my first client would be entirely suitable, a bachelor gentleman from America—to be exact, from Providence, Rhode Island, one of the original thirteen United States. Yes, he was a trifle on the old side, and you wouldn't exactly call him handsome, but he was the best that was available at the moment. One point in his favour was his being of British stock, with the most unusual family name—Lovecraft.

Since Mr. Howard P. Lovecraft lived in Highbury, in North London, on the appointed day I took a bus from my home near Victoria and changed at the lower end of Upper Street to a second bus, per Jane's instructions. At Highbury Corner I got off and walked up a straight road past a neglected-looking Boer War memorial and a rather ugly public wading pool, in which a small boy was splashing merrily about, despite the lateness of the season. On the left was a none too tidy park and on the right a row of drab Georgian terrace houses. Clearly the neighbourhood had seen better days.

At the first corner I turned on to a side road and a few houses down found number 7A. I rang the bell and waited. After about a minute I rang again. Still no response. My watch showed half two. I was right on time.

I did have Mr. Lovecraft's telephone number, and was debating with myself whether to go in search of a phone box, when an older woman dressed in soiled overalls emerged from a nearby door.

"Can I help you, dear?" she asked.

"I was supposed to meet Mr. Lovecraft," I explained. "Do you by chance know him?"

"Indeed I do. I'm his landlady, Joan Angel."

"Have you any idea where he might be, Mrs. Angel?"

"I thought I saw him go out this morning, and I'm sure I would have heard him return, though of course I have been working in the garden and it's always possible he slipped in without my noticing."

"What do you suggest I do?"

"I know it's a mite early, but why don't you come in for a cup of tea, Miss…"

"Miss Lathbury. Leonora Lathbury," I answered, warming to the woman's easy manner.

"You mustn't think me a busybody, Miss Lathbury," she said, leading the way into her house. "But since Mr. Lovecraft has the up-stairs flat—the maisonette, we call it—and we're home most of the time, it's hard not to observe his comings and goings."

Mrs. Angel showed me into an airy drawing-room, with floor-to-ceiling bookshelves along one wall and exotically coloured rugs, North African perhaps, hanging everywhere else. On a divan, listening to a wireless, sat a lean elderly man wearing thick spectacles, whom she introduced as her husband, Edward. Mr. Angel greeted me in that vague unfocussed way I've noticed the blind often have when they speak.

We continued into the kitchen, where Mrs. Angel went about preparing the tea while at her insistence I took a seat at the large table which almost filled the room. Through the window I had a good view of the back garden, which was full of luxuriant, growing green things, for all it was late September.

"Do you like to garden, Miss Lathbury?" asked my hostess.

"I live in a flat without a garden, Mrs. Angel," I said, almost as if I needed to apologise for the fact. "I do, though, enjoy arranging flowers for the altar at our church. And then there's the annual plant sale." Somehow I felt this wasn't very adequate.

"Well, you should get along with Mr. Lovecraft then," she said. "He hasn't the slightest interest in gardening either, despite his claims of being a great Anglophile."

"Mr. Lovecraft's an American, I understand."

"Quite. On the other hand, he's taken quickly to English ways."

Mrs. Angel set the tea things on the table, along with a plate of biscuits. I poured a little milk into my cup, while Mrs. Angel reached for a biscuit.

"Mr. Lovecraft does enjoy his sweets, especially chocolate," she said between bites. "He sometimes joins Edward and me for a spot of Ovaltine at bedtime."

"I'm glad you get along so well with your tenant, Mrs. Angel," I said.

"Oh, yes. Mr. Lovecraft is a perfect gentleman. He's especially good with Edward. Talks to him about politics and economics, the kinds of serious subjects men seem to like. Since Edward so rarely gets out these days, what with his infirmities, Mr. Lovecraft's company is a real blessing."

"Mr. Lovecraft's a writer, is he not?" I didn't wish to appear overly curious, but I could hardly resist taking advantage of this unexpected opportunity to learn what my prospective employer was really like.

"Yes, he's a *published* author, with several books to his name. He's too modest to talk about his profession, although I believe he writes fiction of some sort."

"Forgive me for prying, Mrs. Angel," I continued, excited to think that Mr. Lovecraft might be a true man of letters, a fellow lover of literature, not some boring businessman or entrepreneur.

"Not at all, dear," the older woman answered, patting my hand. "Feel free to ask what you like."

"I should explain I'm here on a professional matter. I'm told Mr. Lovecraft is in need of a typist."

"Indeed, he is. He let us know in no uncertain terms that he detested doing his own typing."

"Does any man care to type, one has to wonder?"

At that point Edward called from the drawing-room to say he thought there was a commotion going on out front. Mrs. Angel and I rose from the kitchen table and hurried into the drawing-room.

Through the window that overlooked the road we could see two men arguing, evidently more in exasperation than in anger. One was very tall and had the worn, lined face of a martyred saint. The other man, who had his back to us, was on crutches. A taxi waited at the kerb.

"That's your Mr. Lovecraft," said Mrs. Angel, pointing. "The one on crutches. He seems to have hurt himself."

"Oh, dear. We must help him," was all I could think to say.

By the time we got out the door, only Mr. Lovecraft was left on the pavement, waving to his companion in the departing taxi. He was of good height and broad-shouldered, but when he turned towards us, I have to say I received a real jolt. Not handsome was putting it mildly, given that long face and lantern jaw!

"Are you all right, Mr. Lovecraft?" exclaimed Mrs. Angel. We could both now see that one of his feet was wrapped in bandages. In one hand he clasped a boot. He was attired in what might be considered casual riding clothes.

"I am afraid I fell off a horse," he answered in a peculiar American accent. "I have just come from the hospital. Or rather, I have just come from hospital." Mr. Lovecraft smiled, and for a moment or two his gargoyle-like visage looked almost human.

"Is it serious?" asked Mrs. Angel.

"Just a sprain, thank you. Three years ago my aunt suffered a broken ankle and was laid up for weeks. Fortunately, the steed I was attempting to tame a short while ago proved far less lethal than the stairs at our then new home on College Street."

I had been standing somewhat behind Mrs. Angel, trying not to draw attention to myself, but at last I had to say something.

"Mr. Lovecraft," I began, "I..."

"I am so sorry," he interrupted, "you must be Miss Lathbury. I apologise for my lateness." We shook hands somewhat awkwardly, on account of the crutches and the boot.

"If you would prefer not to talk with me today," I said, "I could..."

"Please, Miss Lathbury. My accident has in no way affected my vocal cords. I always honour my obligations, especially to a lady. But first I hope you and Mrs. Angel will oblige me by ensuring that I can make it upstairs on my own steam."

Mrs. Angel unlocked the door to 7A, which opened on to a narrow hall, then offered to hold his boot. Mr. Lovecraft muttered his thanks as he handed it to her. Half way down on the left was a set of stairs. At the end of the hall was a door that Mrs. Angel said connected to their flat.

Mr. Lovecraft took each step slowly and deliberately, explaining as he did so how the friend who had taken him riding had insisted on paying for the cab, something of course he couldn't allow. In the end this friend had reluctantly accepted a half crown. At the top of the stairs we followed him down a short hall into a sparsely furnished drawing-room facing the street. After asking if there was anything further she could do and receiving Mr. Lovecraft's assurances that there was not, Mrs. Angel gave him back his boot and returned downstairs. All of a sudden I felt terribly shy.

"Do take a seat, Miss Lathbury," said my host, gesturing to a sofa with a white slipcover by the window. "May I get you some tea or coffee?"

"No thank you, Mr. Lovecraft. Mrs. Angel has already given me a cup of tea."

"Well then, please excuse me while I go to the kitchen and fix myself a coffee."

"Are you sure you don't need some help?"

"I can manage, thank you, Miss Lathbury."

After Mr. Lovecraft disappeared back down the hall on his crutches, I studied the drawing-room. Compared to the Angels' it didn't look very lived in. There was a single framed print above the fireplace and a lot of empty bookshelves. A shaggy orange and brown rug, akin to those in the Angels' flat, lent the only colour.

I began to worry when Mr. Lovecraft didn't return after several minutes, then I heard a muffled crash as of breaking crockery. I leapt from the sofa and was on the verge of rushing in the direction of the kitchen when my host appeared in the door, rather red faced, and said in a breathless way that he had changed his mind: he wouldn't be having coffee after all.

I resumed my seat on the sofa, while Mr. Lovecraft hobbled over to a wing chair by the fireplace. As he gingerly arranged himself and his crutches, I noticed that the bandage on his injured foot was splattered with a brown stain. The poor man, I thought, but decided it was best not to make a fuss and asked instead what had brought him to England.

"Ah, Miss Lathbury, where to begin!" he exclaimed. "It had long been a dream of mine to view the ancient glories and monuments of my race, and in the summer of '35 I at last had the means to do so. Altogether I spent nearly two months in Old England, drinking in its venerable oaks and abbeys, manor-houses and rose gardens, lanes and hedges, meadows and mediaeval villages. But it was *London*, with its classical landmarks and Georgian architecture, magnificent parks and drowsy Thames, as well as rich, continuous history stretching back to Roman times and beyond, that packed the greatest aesthetic kick. God Save the King!

"I once accounted my first view of colonial Marblehead, Massachusetts, late one winter's afternoon the supreme emotional experience of my life, but now, having gazed at St. Paul's in the light of a setting sun glittering on its massive dome, I have known true ecstasy! Now that I have seen London, Miss Lathbury, I can die content!"

Well, it was hard to know how to respond to this, although his enthusiasm for English landscape and architecture was certainly to his credit. Mr. Lovecraft's rhetoric, too, was impressive. Here was no typical American tourist—or typical American for that matter.

"May I ask, Mr. Lovecraft, what has brought you to London this year? If I may say so, you appear to be settling in for a lengthy stay."

"That is correct, Miss Lathbury. I have signed a year's lease with Mrs. Angel. After my first trip I vowed that I would return for an extended sojourn as soon as commitments, both professional and personal, allowed. Of most concern was my dear aunt, who was seriously ill earlier this year, though I am happy to say she has made a full recovery."

"I think it wonderful that you can so travel so easily," I said. It occurred to me that a man with a sweetheart would be unlikely to have such freedom. The existence of a beloved aunt was also auspicious.

"Indeed, I am in a most fortunate position. This time, however, I intend to be more than a simple sightseer. Last trip I made some important connections in the London literary world, who have been urging me to try my hand at professional journalism over here."

"How exciting," I said, though I suppose it depended on what kind of journalism one did.

"I should say, Miss Lathbury, that I have a certain financial cushion," he continued as if confiding a shameful secret. "Earnings from books of mine published in Britain. If I fail at this new endeavour, I shall not starve. My biggest worry is surviving a winter without central heating!"

"What sorts of books do you write, Mr. Lovecraft?" I inquired, more interested in this subject than the heating issue.

Here he looked at me strangely, again as if he were ashamed or possibly embarrassed to be frank. Might he be one of these voguish writers who deliberately set out to shock or provoke while pushing decency to its limit? At last he spoke:

"Miss Lathbury, I am the author of tales of supernatural dread, the fiction of cosmic fear. For years I contributed to the cheap magazines with middling success. Then a miracle happened: I finally placed a collection of my stories with a reputable American house, who in turn sold British and Commonwealth rights to one of your distinguished London publishers."

"Which one?"

"Victor Gollancz."

"I thought Gollancz specialised in political books."

"They do. Their accepting my weird work was another fortunate fluke. The fact is, Miss Lathbury, I have been shifting my focus, away from imaginary horrors to the horrors of real life and what we as a society can do to alleviate them."

"How noble of you, Mr. Lovecraft," I said. I was pleased to learn he had a social conscience.

"One of my fellow Gollancz authors has been a tremendous influence on me politically. Have you read George Orwell's *Down and Out in London and Paris*, Miss Lathbury?"

"No, I have not. Is he by chance the same Mr. Orwell who wrote *A Clergyman's Daughter*?" As the daughter of a clergyman myself, I had made the mistake of picking up this novel the previous year. It was not at all true to life, or maybe I just had an overly sheltered upbringing. At any rate, I abandoned it well before the end.

"Yes, but I do not believe it is a book he is proud of."

"You're acquainted with Mr. Orwell?"

"Yes, as a matter of fact, he is the friend who took me riding earlier today. We met in London last year, following a brief trans-Atlantic exchange. As a ghost story aficionado, Orwell paid me the compliment of saying my tale 'The Rats in the Walls' was one of the most horrible things he had ever read. He has a particular dread of rats. Through his aunt he's acquainted with M. P. Shiel, author of that hideously noxious fragment 'Xélucha.' Thanks to his political instruction, I am now a firm supporter of Indian independence and of democratic Socialism, not Fascistic Socialism, a system I once naïvely advocated."

These terms meaning nothing to me, I said nothing. I was far more interested in literature than politics. Mr. Lovecraft added that Mr. Orwell, though an astute thinker on many subjects, could let emotion cloud his reason, as shown by certain dark hints of a troubling "occult" experience his first year at Eton.

"While in England I hope to contribute articles to such journals as *The New English Weekly*, *Time and Tide*, and *New Statesman & Nation*. Bring the liberal American perspective to the vital issues of the day. But—and here is where you come in, Miss Lathbury—I need someone to do my typing and attend to general secretarial duties."

"Yes, I suppose we ought to talk business, Mr. Lovecraft."

"I hired a regular typist once before, a high school student who eventually went off to college. She was a bit of a handful—kept giving me advice. More than half the time she was right, though." Mr. Lovecraft smiled, but I wasn't sure from his tone just how fondly he remembered this girl.

"Your agency highly recommended you, Miss Lathbury," he continued, "but as a formality could you please tell me something of your background? Where you were educated, for instance?"

I told him that I had attended the Francis Holland School, near Baker Street. I admitted that my father had been a vicar. Both parents were now deceased. I devoted my mornings to a church organisation that looked after impoverished gentlewomen.

"There is a vast satisfaction in alleviating the misfortunes of others," said Mr. Lovecraft warmly.

"Yes, even if they are of one's own class, they are no less needy and deserving than the working poor," I answered, hoping I didn't sound too defensive. Mr. Lovecraft nodded, seemingly in approval, then asked:

"You are free to come afternoons, say twice a week to start?"

"Whatever would suit you."

"Can you come tomorrow at two o'clock?"

"Yes."

Since Jane's agency set the fee scale, we were spared the unpleasantness of discussing money. When I rose to leave, Mr. Lovecraft had to struggle to get out of his own seat. I couldn't bare to watch, and on impulse moved to lend him a hand. Before I could touch him, however, he gave me an imploring look that suggested I should keep my distance.

"One last thing, Miss Lathbury," he said, as he finally hoisted himself, with flushed face, on to his crutches. "I trust you realise that you won't be alone here? That is, alone with me."

"I understand, Mr. Lovecraft."

"Mr. and Mrs. Angel will be just downstairs. The connecting door is always left unlocked."

"Yes, Mrs. Angel pointed that out earlier." Perhaps it was a bit ridiculous, but I couldn't help admiring a man who was mindful of observing the proprieties.

"Good-bye, then, Miss Lathbury, and please forgive me for not seeing you to the door." He made a little bow and an attempt at a smile.

"Until tomorrow, Mr. Lovecraft," I replied.

Chapter 2

That evening at home I was very restless. I couldn't stop thinking about Mr. Lovecraft, what an unusual if not extraordinary man. Like a traditional English gentleman in some ways, and yet so different. Could a man who wrote supernatural horror be trusted? Could he be loved? And then there was his person. I won't deny that I felt both attracted and repulsed.

The next day I worried that the distressed gentlewomen I attended to would notice my air of abstraction, but the morning passed uneventfully. By the time I was back in Highbury, I like to think I had convinced myself I was worked up over nothing—Mr. Lovecraft was a human being like anyone else, wasn't he?

On the door of 7A was a note stating that visitors should ring the bell of number 7. When I did so, Mrs. Angel opened the door, greeting me with the same easy warmth of the previous day. As she ushered me through the drawing-room, where again Mr. Angel sat listening to the wireless, she explained that of course with his injured foot Mr. Lovecraft was in no condition to answer the bell himself. She pointed the way through the connecting door, and shortly I found myself in my employer's first-floor drawing-room, where there was now a table with a typewriter set up near the fireplace. A slow clumping sound on the stairs from the second floor announced Mr. Lovecraft's arrival.

"Good afternoon, Miss Lathbury," he said. I had half-expected the invalid to be wearing his dressing gown, but instead he was attired in a tasteful if not stylish dark suit, which put me in mind of someone engaged in dull and respectable work, like a City clerk. One foot was conventionally shod, while the other was bandaged, the coffee stains still evident. Didn't the poor fellow have a fresh bandage?

"Good afternoon, Mr. Lovecraft," I replied. "I hope you're feeling better today."

"An uninterrupted twelve-hour sleep has done much to restore the old man, both in body and spirit, thank you."

To refer to himself in this manner struck me as odd, even amusing, and I had a hard time repressing a smile. For a moment he looked almost alarmed, but then he smiled too, as if pleased that he had impressed me in some fashion.

Fearing I was in danger of not appearing sufficiently serious my first day on the job, I decided to shift to the business at hand and asked whether he had a political article in need of typing. His answer surprised me:

"Miss Lathbury, I confess I have decided to give you something more literary to begin with…a memoir."

"A memoir?"

"I promised a friend of mine that I would help edit his wife's account of her family and her career as a strolling player. Have you by chance heard of Arthur Machen?"

Such a light came into Mr. Lovecraft's eye that I hated to disappoint him by saying no.

"Is he a politician?" I ventured.

"He may sound like one at times," said Mr. Lovecraft, "but, no, he is something far finer than that—a general man of letters and a master of an exquisitely lyrical and expressive prose style. His horror fiction of the 'nineties and early nineteen-hundreds stands alone in its class. No one can so well as Mr. Machen suggest dim regions of terror whose very existence is an affront to creation."

I listened patiently for who knows how long while Mr. Lovecraft held forth on the great man and his work. As with Mr. Orwell, he had first become acquainted with "the venerable Welsh mystic" through correspondence. An admirer of both his and Mr. Machen's work, an Ohio journalist named Howard Wolf, had helped him overcome any scruples about imposing on the Welsh writer on his initial English tour. So, after first making a trip to Mr. Machen's native Gwent, he had visited his hero at his present home in Amersham and, notwithstanding certain aesthetic and philosophical differences, they had established a genuine bond. More to the point, his having sung Mr. Machen's praises in a treatise of his on supernatural horror in literature had set the right tone from the start.

In due course Mr. Lovecraft produced a stack of manuscript pages: the first several chapters from Mrs. Machen's pen, with extensive changes and corrections in pencil in a different hand, presumably his. Neither handwriting, I have to say, was terribly legible. My employer instructed me to call him if I had any trouble. He would be working in his second-floor study.

For an hour I struggled as best I could at the typewriter. At last, though, I got up, walked into the hall, and shouted up the stairs as loudly as I dared that I needed help. I hated for him to make an unnecessary trip, but there was nothing for it.

Mr. Lovecraft seemed a bit puzzled at first when I pointed out my difficulties, which I suppose a truly professional typist would not have found as formidable as I did. For a moment I felt as if I were a dull schoolgirl back at Francis Holland, and he the stern master hovering by my desk about to rebuke me for an unsatisfactory lesson. Instead Mr. Lovecraft was ever so patient in going over the manuscript pages and deciphering the thornier hieroglyphics. I will say his close presence made me self-conscious, while as before I sensed an awkwardness on his part that may have been more than just a result of his being on crutches.

I think both of us welcomed the arrival at four o'clock of Mrs. Angel bearing a tray of tea things. Mr. Lovecraft invited her to join us, but after pouring the tea and seeing her tenant settled comfortably in the wing chair she insisted on returning downstairs to look after Edward. I had in the meantime slipped from my chair at the typing table to the sofa by the window. The work day was evidently over, and I intended to take advantage of it.

To get the conversation rolling, I inquired what he as an American thought of the recent Arsenal football match that was in the headlines. All men of whatever nationality were interested in sport, were they not?

"I am afraid, Miss Lathbury, that I do not follow the sports pages, in either your old or my New England. I have not the least trace of sporting blood in me."

"But you do ride, Mr. Lovecraft."

"Yesterday was my first time on a horse."

"How so?"

"A gent must ride."

"Oh?"

"And fence."

"You don't say."

"And play chess."

"And know Latin and Greek?" I said, finally answering his banter in a similar spirit. For a man with a naturally grave demeanor, Mr. Lovecraft certainly had his exuberant side. After some discussion of the Classical languages (he had studied both Latin and Greek in high school), my curiosity got the better of me and I asked what had induced him to go riding in the first place, especially for the first time.

"Orwell thought I might find it of practical use some day," he replied. "He was most persuasive." Here followed a digression on the value of riding to Mr. Orwell whilst serving with the Indian Imperial Police in Burma. This in turn led to comment on Mr. Orwell's high principles as well as willingness to take risks for those principles.

"You know, Miss Lathbury," he continued, "I used to be quite set in my ways. Though I am an enthusiastic traveller, until recently my peregrinations were of necessity limited. With increased earnings, however, I have expanded my horizons. I find myself yearning to try new and different experiences—like riding a horse." He laughed. "You never know what a guy like me is going to do next!"

"Take up fencing perhaps?"

"I dare say chess would be safer, though I am no good at it and cannot keep awake over it."

"When your ankle is healed do you think you'll try riding again?"

"Not likely, Miss Lathbury. I may, though, once fully bipedal again, attempt a more reliable, mechanical means of transport—bicycle-riding. In my youth it was my greatest exercise."

I listened attentively while he explained how by cultivating high speeds he managed to cover a large and picturesque area of countryside, thus forming a close acquaintance with rural New England which ultimately turned him into a local antiquarian. He made most of his cycle trips in quest of new and surprising landscape vistas.

"I always sought the element of surprise," he asserted, "the unfolding—the unexpected—the edge of the unreal, where anything is possible…"

By this time I had finished my tea, and though Mr. Lovecraft was a fascinating conversationalist, I had to go if I didn't want to miss the start of the meeting to discuss the annual church whist drive. While I had a fleeting thought of inviting my employer to this worthy charity event, I suspected Mr. Lovecraft was no more fond of cards than he was of chess, so I didn't mention it as I took my leave. Besides, he was surely involved with a church in Highbury, or soon about to be. How wrong I would be proved on that score!

After this first afternoon as Mr. Lovecraft's typist I came almost to expect the unexpected, not that my duties weren't routine enough. Before long I had mastered his unusual scrawl and thus the act of typing became a lot less onerous. While Mrs. Machen's memoirs remained a steady and on the whole agreeable task, he began to supply me, as promised, with the texts of political articles. Unlike Mrs. Machen, he was a natural writer, his paragraphs long, his sentences complex, his vocabulary learned. And yet there was nothing stuffy about his prose, which for all the seriousness of his subjects never lacked for light or humorous touches. I've forgotten their titles now, but these articles treated such topics as the forthcoming elections in America (he was a fervid supporter of President Roosevelt and the New Deal), Hitler and his racial policies (he wasn't wholly critical), and the civil war in Spain.

As always Mr. Lovecraft worked in his second-floor study while I performed my typing chores at the drawing-room table. Punctually at four o'clock Mrs. Angel brought up tea. I never did find out who was originally responsible for this amenity, but it made for a pleasant and sociable break. Mr. Lovecraft didn't always join me if he was busy, though more often than not he did. Thankfully, within days he was able to substitute a cane for his crutches and could get up and down the stairs with comparative ease. Within a fortnight he was walking without artificial aid.

And walk he did! A chief topic of conversation over tea was the pleasure he took in exploring the surrounding neighbourhoods. He was enchanted with the lovely Canonbury area, with its leafy trees and hidden stream. Sixteenth-century Canonbury Tower was a potent relic of monastic times. Suburban Barnsbury, prosaic as it was, was the seat of ineffable mystery. Even the less savoury districts of Green Lanes and Hackney fascinated him. Highgate and Hampstead were veritable fairy lands.

After reading a new story collection by his literary hero, Arthur Machen, he made a special expedition to Stoke Newington, for one of the stranger stories was set there. Stoke Newington also was the site of a school attended by his principal literary hero of the past, Edgar Allan Poe. Alas, the school building had long since been torn down.

In the nearby Holloway Road he discovered a second-hand bookshop which happened to offer a large stock of ghostly titles. He soon became friendly with the co-owners, who went out of their way to cater to his taste for macabre fiction. The empty bookshelves started to fill up, giving the drawing-room a cosy air hitherto lacking. More than once Mr. Lovecraft despaired at the prospect of having to consolidate his new books with his existing library when he returned to Providence.

One author high on his collecting list was Algernon Blackwood, who he told me had produced some of the finest spectral literature of this or any age amidst incredible amounts of insufferable namby-pamby. One day Mr. Lovecraft casually mentioned that he would be having lunch in Soho with Mr. Blackwood, who had just spoken on the new BBC television, but after the event he declared he never wished to repeat the experience. Blackwood's genius was indisputable, his mastery of weird atmosphere absolute and unquestioned, but his cranky devotion to modern "occultism" put the man beyond the pale.

One afternoon I arrived for work to find hanging on a formerly bare patch of wall a period print showing Canonbury Tower. When I complimented him on it, Mr. Lovecraft said that he had bought the print at an antique shop in Camden Passage, at the lower end of Upper Street. I had often wondered about the watercolour print of relatively recent vintage above the fireplace, titled "On the Old Roman Road, Caerleon," and now asked if this too was a Camden Passage find.

"No, Miss Lathbury, I acquired that print in Newport, South Wales, last summer," he answered. "Its serene townscape, I confess, evokes little of the wild domed hills, archaic forests, and cryptical Roman ruins of the Gwent countryside associated with Arthur Machen, but the road depicted at least *leads* to true Machen territory. The *suggestion* was enough for me to make the purchase."

"Your Mr. Machen sounds as if he's a bit of a pagan, Mr. Lovecraft," I observed. "Is he?"

"Like myself, he has yielded to the spell of the Britanno-Roman life which once surged over his native region. Unlike myself, he is also a champion of the Middle Ages in all things—including the Catholic faith."

"I remember your saying you and he had certain…differences."

"Religion is one of them."

"Yet it is no impediment to your friendship."

"Indeed not. The old boy is remarkably tolerant of my materialist views."

Had Mr. Lovecraft said my "Mohammedan" or "Hindoo" views I could not have been more taken aback. "You don't consider yourself a Christian, then, Mr. Lovecraft?" I said in as even a tone as I could muster.

"My theological beliefs are likely to startle anyone who has imagined me an orthodox adherent of the Anglican Church, Miss Lathbury. My father was of the Episcopal faith, as we call it in America, and he and my mother were married by its rites, though she was of Yankee Baptist background." Here followed a disquisition on his religious disillusionment at Baptist Sunday school, his fondness for Greco-Roman mythology, and his declaration at age eight, much to his family's astonishment, that he was a Roman pagan!

He must have sensed my discomfort, for he abruptly shifted his ground and stammered that he had the greatest respect for the Church of England as a venerable and estimable institution. He valued its rich history, in particular its close association with the monarchy. In fact, he himself had insisted on being wed by its rituals.

"Are you married, Mr. Lovecraft?" This time the distress in my voice must have been all too evident.

"I am divorced, Miss Lathbury," he said quietly.

After this admission I didn't know what to say. I was dying to learn more about his former wife, but of course I could hardly pursue the matter, especially as my relief at hearing of his divorce seemed at the moment so embarrassingly palpable.

"I think, Miss Lathbury," said Mr. Lovecraft at last, "I just heard the afternoon post drop through the front door slot. Please excuse me while I go collect it."

I usually picked up the afternoon post, being only one floor away to his two, but this time I demurred. The volume of his correspondence I should say was enormous, much of it from America, and my duties soon expanded to typing letters. A letter, too, was the source of a later conversation concerning another sensitive personal matter.

I remember the date was late October, because I was startled to find on arrival a gourd with an evil-looking face cut into it set on the fireplace mantel. When I asked him about this peculiar ornament, Mr. Lovecraft explained in his half-jocular, half-sinister way that it was an American tradition to carve pumpkins for All Hallow's Eve, popularly known as Halloween.

Since the morning post was still lying in the front hall, I had brought it up with me and given it him while we discussed pumpkins and Halloween. One envelope seems to have caught his eye, a letter postmarked New York City, which he proceeded to open and scan. He was speaking of the pagan significance of the Feast of All Saints when his voice faltered and stopped.

"Are you all right, Mr. Lovecraft?" I asked. Judging from his beetroot red colour, I feared he was having an apoplectic fit.

"Good Lord!" he finally exploded. "My favourite adopted grandson! That bushy-haired, pipe-smoking, pint-sized Romeo has really done it this time!"

Mr. Lovecraft was obviously upset, though mention of a grandson, even if adopted, was what mainly disconcerted me. Was he so old that he could have children from his marriage of an age to have grown children of their own? I wanted to offer him some comforting words but knew not where to begin, while he remained practically speechless in his agitation.

"Miss Lathbury, pray forgive me, but I have just received some terrible news from my closest friend."

"You don't mean your grandson?"

"No, no, 'grandson' is a purely honorific title. Belknap is my junior by a mere twelve years."

"Don't you think you had better sit down?"

"Yes, thank you."

I resisted an impulse to take his arm and guide him to his accustomed wing chair. On his own he sat down and read more of the offending letter before tossing it aside with a groan. I waited on the sofa for him to say more. Whatever he had to say was clearly not easy for him.

"Mr. Lovecraft, can I help in any way? Get you a cup of tea perhaps? If you like, I can ring for Mrs. Angel."

"Miss Lathbury, you are very kind, but I am in no need of liquid sustenance. The fact of the matter is, at the risk of raising an indelicate subject in front of a lady, I have just received word from my friend and protégé, Frank Belknap Long, Junior, that he has become romantically entangled with…with…"

"Yes, Mr. Lovecraft?"

"*…with my former secretary, Clarissa Stone!*"

Chapter 3

Well, that one's best friend had become involved with one's former secretary didn't strike me as so objectionable on the face of it. After saying I was sorry, I couldn't help asking what in particular troubled him about the match. "I can assure you it is totally unsuitable."

"Is there a wide disparity in age?"

"I should say! Clarissa is a sophomore in college, not yet nineteen, whilst Belknap is a grown man of thirty-four!" I did a quick calculation. Adding twelve to thirty-four made forty-six.

"Is he really too old for her?" Fifteen years, I was now acutely aware, represented the same age difference between me and Mr. Lovecraft.

"It is difficult for me to explain, Miss Lathbury. The real problem lies in their opposing personalities. In self-reliance and practical affairs Belknap is greatly retarded because of his coddled existence. Born with certain organic weaknesses which arrested his development, he is still living at home with momma and papa!

"Clarissa, on the other hand, is a vigorous, independent, strong-willed young lady. Her figure is what one might call Juno-esque. Belknap is small of stature. She is sure to overwhelm him, emotionally as well as physically."

"Perhaps Mr. Long could benefit from a relationship with such a woman," I said boldly. "Opposites do after all attract."

Mr. Lovecraft frowned and said in a tone that discouraged further debate, "Let us hope, Miss Lathbury, that this infatuation will quickly pass."

More was soon to follow, however. In the afternoon post, I couldn't help noticing that among the several personal letters was a picture postcard, from America, showing Barnard College. On the reverse side was a densely written message signed "Clarissa."

I routinely left the post on the stairs leading to the second floor, but on this occasion I encountered my employer as he was emerging from the kitchen, so handed it him directly. I said nothing, though it was clear from the short gasp he made as he picked through his letters that he too had spotted the picture postcard. That gasp allowed me to ask whether anything was wrong.

"Wrong, Miss Lathbury? Word has now come from the other party in this sordid business." He began to read, uttering a few disjointed phrases:

> "'FBL unimpressive on first meeting'...'this year added maturity'...Does she mean him or her, I wonder?...'poetic'... 'dreamy'...'cat's meow'...Hmm.... 'Your favourite adopted granddaughter'..."

"Don't you find it somehow fitting, Mr. Lovecraft," I said, once again standing up for young love, "that your favourite grandson and granddaughter should be...friends?"

"Believe me, Miss Lathbury," he said solemnly. "No good will come of this. I can feel it in my old bones."

Rather to my disappointment, I had to conclude that Mr. Lovecraft was not a romantic. I vowed not to let that fact discourage me, however. After little more than a month in his service I was certain that I wanted our relationship to move beyond the strictly professional. His age, his atheism, his far from matinee-idol looks—none of these things really mattered. But how was I to make progress without coming across as too eager? I decided to confide in Mrs. Angel, with whom I remained on cordial terms.

While Mr. Lovecraft had soon given me my own key to his front door, I continued to enter his part of the house through the Angels' flat, at their urging. Joan, as she asked me to call her after about the second week, always enjoyed a friendly chat before I went upstairs and I think Edward, as a break from the wireless, liked listening in.

Mr. Lovecraft's movements, in the aftermath of his riding accident, was a natural topic for discussion, and they became of greater interest as his mobility increased. His solitary rambles were one thing, but what did he do with himself in the evenings? One had to wonder, did he have a favourite pub? As far as Joan could tell, he completely abstained from alcoholic beverages. She believed he mostly spent his nights writing, often far into the early morning, but she did catch him recently at the Compton Arms.

"This past Saturday Edward was in the mood for a pint, so we went out to the Compton," Joan was saying at the kitchen table a few days after I heard Mr. Lovecraft voice his disapproval of the romance between his "grandchildren." "The Hen and Chickens is closer, but the Compton has a nicer sort of clientele. As we stood at the bar, who should walk in but Mr. Lovecraft. With him were two disheveled-looking men in tweed jackets patched at the elbows—more the type for the Hen and Chickens I should have thought.

"In short order we were introduced, to Mr. Darnell and Mr. Hillyer, proprietors of Faunus Books in the Holloway Road. It seems they were in the habit of stopping by the Compton after closing shop on Saturdays and inviting their regular customers to join them, even if certain regular customers only drank ginger beer. This prompted a chuckle from Mr. Lovecraft. Within minutes another three or four men arrived, and the group retired, full of book talk, to a table in the snug."

"Were there no women, Joan?" I asked.

"None that I saw, dear," she said.

"Don't women patronise book shops as much as men?"

"Yes, but do such women accept invitations to go out to pubs afterwards with the shabbily-dressed owners?"

It was both comforting and unsettling to hear that Mr. Lovecraft seemed to prefer exclusively male company. For a moment I feared that he was one of those men who had no interest in women, as a failed marriage might suggest, but I dismissed this thought as unworthy. Mr. Lovecraft might be a man's man, but that didn't make him a pansy.

"Oh, Joan, I so enjoy working for Mr. Lovecraft," I said, "especially our conversations over tea." Then I whispered in case Edward could overhear in the next room: "I only wish tea would, well, sometime lead to supper. Do you understand me?"

Joan smiled, then whispered back, "From the beginning I've felt you deserved to be more than simply Mr. Lovecraft's typist, Leonora.

And while he may seem indifferent to feminine charms, how can he not appreciate you? No doubt he realises a respectable, educated woman is all he requires to make his life complete."

Yes, I thought, but did he envision *me* filling that role? I was not as optimistic as Joan on this crucial point.

"Speaking of supper," she continued in a normal tone, "I hope you're not busy Guy Fawkes night. Edward and I traditionally have friends over before the firework display in Highbury Fields."

"That would be lovely, thank you."

She must have sensed a hesitant note in my voice, for she hastened to add, "Mr. Lovecraft, you'll be pleased to know, dear, has already accepted."

It already being past the hour, I thanked Joan again and entered Mr. Lovecraft's part of the house through the connecting door. In the front hall I almost stumbled over a man's bicycle parked next to the stairs. Later, over tea, my employer confirmed that it was his, purchased second-hand from a bicycle shop in the Essex Road. He couldn't wait to explore some of the more remote and obscure byways of London that his new means of transport now made accessible.

When I casually mentioned that I was looking forward to the Angels' Guy Fawkes party, he said he could supply me with enough work that afternoon to keep me occupied until the hour guests were due. I couldn't tell whether he was surprised or pleased I would be among the guests.

In the event I worked until five o'clock that day, a Friday, then went downstairs to help Joan with the party preparations. There wasn't a lot to do, as only one other couple were able to make it in the end, Mr. and Mrs. Caldwell, who were retired and lived in Canonbury Square. Soon after six the Caldwells arrived, with the makings of a salad. Mr. Lovecraft emerged through the connecting door a few minutes later, bearing a bottle of lemonade, for which he professed he had developed a liking despite discovering it was not at all like American lemonade. Some less than fresh flowers which I had brought that morning were my barely adequate contribution.

At first we gathered in the drawing-room, where Edward took the drink orders. Like Mr. Lovecraft, I asked for a lemonade. The Caldwells each requested a sherry. Edward then shuffled into the kitchen, where Joan would do the actual pouring. While we waited, Mr. Caldwell asked our American guest his opinion of the recent election results in his country. Mr. Caldwell wasn't shy to express his approval of President Roosevelt's handy victory, though as a man of the left he worried that the New Deal would not go far enough toward socialism. He and Mr. Lovecraft immediately plunged into deep political discussion.

With the arrival of the drinks and a plate of hors d'oeuvres, the conversation took a lighter turn. Mr. Caldwell, who gave local walking tours and had a ready supply of literary and historical anecdotes, proved an amiable raconteur. He and Mr. Lovecraft eventually got on to "Old London" with particular reference to Arthur Machen, whom Mr. Caldwell seemed to know at least by reputation. Evidently thrilled to have found a fellow connoisseur of the master, Mr. Lovecraft proceeded to relate a rather involved tale of an eighteenth-century murder on Highbury Fields which he had read about in one of Mr. Machen's essays.

At this point Mrs. Caldwell and I joined our hostess in the kitchen, where she had retreated earlier. As Joan removed the roast chicken from the oven, some debate ensued whether one of the gentlemen might carve. Mrs. Caldwell settled the matter by taking knife and fork to the bird herself. I called the men to supper after everything—chicken, gravy, lettuce salad, mushy peas and mash—was on the kitchen table.

Throughout the meal the convivial Mr. Caldwell regaled the company with stories of unusual people he had met on his walking tours. Not until the trifle was I really able to talk one-on-one with his wife, who I was pleased to learn was an Arthur Ransom enthusiast and collector of children's books. We had just finished the coffee when we heard the first boom of the fireworks. While the view from the back garden was largely unobstructed, the consensus was we should go out to the Fields to watch. Even Edward was game for this.

It was a pleasant night, clear with only a moderate chill. Mr. Lovecraft wore an overcoat that seemed unduly heavy, in addition to hat and gloves. On the way to the park he said that he had avoided 4th of July celebrations because as a child he was hypersensitive to loud noises, whilst as an older youth he had done so out of respect for his lawful majesty, King George the Third. Tonight was one firework display that he could in good faith enjoy, commemorating as it did a failed plot against the realm. Before I could make some teasing reply, Mr. Caldwell complimented Mr. Lovecraft on his loyalty to the crown which led to comment on the rumours surrounding the present king. Only a rapid series of huge bangs silenced Mr. Caldwell.

By now we were among the throngs in the Fields, and any sustained conversation was impossible. Too, with so many people milling about, it was not easy to stay together as a group. In the flashes from the fireworks I could see Edward on Joan's arm and the Caldwells holding hands. Mr. Lovecraft stood a short distance from the rest of us, gazing raptly at the sky, his hands thrust in his coat pockets. Might I sneak up on him in the dark and jump into his arms at the next overhead burst? This was but a fleeting fancy. Instead I stayed put, my thoughts straying to Mr. Lovecraft's retelling of Mr. Machen's morbid account of murder on this spot two centuries earlier. I was not in a festive mood.

Too soon there was a sustained crescendo of fireworks almost directly above us and the show was over. Half-deafened, I mumbled my thanks to the Angels and bade farewell to the Caldwells. I looked for Mr. Lovecraft, but he was lost somewhere in the crowd. Feeling weary and defeated, I headed toward Highbury Corner to catch a bus home.

The following week I considered giving Mr. Lovecraft my notice. Without hope of any real intimacy developing between us, what was the use of continuing as his typist? I made a mental note to telephone Jane to see if she could place me in a new position. At the Angels' I paused in the connecting doorway just long enough to tell Joan what fun I'd had at the party Guy Fawkes night. I don't think she was fooled.

Upstairs my employer was waiting for me in the drawing-room, dressed in his familiar dark suit like some drab City clerk.

"Good afternoon, Miss Lathbury," he said with more than usual animation.

"Good afternoon, Mr. Lovecraft," I answered coolly.

"I trust you got home all right the other night."

"Yes, the number four bus came almost immediately."

"I regret, Miss Lathbury," he said haltingly, "that I missed you at the end of the fireworks. I had spotted a cat, you see, under a street lamp in need of comforting. The poor animal was clearly frightened."

"Surely there were human beings frightened by the firework display in need of comfort, too." As a cat lover myself, I had to applaud Mr. Lovecraft's generous impulse, but I wasn't mollified.

"Yes, but one could hardly…" He stopped and laughed nervously. I wasn't about to help him out. "As I was saying, it was negligent of me not to offer at least to escort you to the bus stop."

"I managed fine on my own, thank you."

Again Mr. Lovecraft hesitated and I said nothing.

"See here, Miss Lathbury," he said finally. "I am afraid I have no work for you today."

"I had better head home then." I'd been unbuttoning coat, but now started rebuttoning it.

"No, please. Allow me to explain. I was expecting a parcel from Mrs. Machen in this morning's post, but it failed to arrive. The new chapters might come in the afternoon delivery, but it occurs to me, instead of waiting for the post, that we might…go for a walk."

"*Go for a walk?*" I replied, as if he had just made the most outlandish proposition. I was caught wholly by surprise.

"Why yes, I thought we might visit Highgate Cemetery, where I have only recently learned Arthur Machen's first wife is buried."

Well, there it was. Nearly everything he did seemed to be connected in some way with his literary mentor. However, I was not about to refuse this unexpected invitation.

"A cemetery visit would be *lovely*, Mr. Lovecraft," I said with more warmth than I'd hitherto shown. "I like viewing old tombstones."

"Good, such is a favourite pastime of my own, Miss Lathbury."

Downstairs Mr. Lovecraft collected his hat and coat where they hung on pegs by the front door. So quickly had plans for the afternoon changed, I had only got as far as removing my gloves, which I now pulled back on.

Outside the sky was grey, though there seemed little chance of rain. Given the hour we agreed it made sense to take a bus up the

Holloway Road past Archway and disembark at the stop nearest the cemetery entrance. When I remarked on the heaviness of his overcoat, Mr. Lovecraft confessed that he was extremely sensitive to low temperatures and could become physically ill if it became too cold. For much of the ride on the number forty-three bus he discoursed on the salubriousness of the English climate, despite the damp and the sparse sunshine.

At Highgate we first strolled around the west side of the cemetery, where many notables lie buried. With the aid of a little printed guide, we were able to locate Karl Marx's grave and from there that of one of our finest English authors, George Eliot. Mr. Lovecraft professed not to care for Eliot's work or for the Victorians in general, though in *Middlemarch* he did find the scholarly Mr. Casaubon's researches into the fish-deity Dagon highly suggestive. Mr. Machen, he added, also held Eliot in low esteem.

At last we crossed the road to the east side, the older part, where a gate attendant directed us to the plot containing the grave of the first Mrs. Machen. In future officious guardians would restrict access to this section of the cemetery, but at the time we could wander the grassy grounds freely. Mr. Lovecraft said that Mr. Machen in one of his autobiographical volumes refers cryptically to a "great sorrow." Delicate inquiries had led the Welsh mystic to reveal in a letter that he was speaking of his first wife's death, after a long bout with cancer, in 1899.

"Is your first wife, sorry, *former* wife, still alive, Mr. Lovecraft?" I asked.

"I have heard nothing to the contrary," he said. "We lost touch several years ago, shortly after she moved to California, where for all I know she may now be pushing up the daisies—though California boasts no spot as quaint and as redolent of ancient mystery as this!"

We were standing by the grave of Amy Hogg Machen, whose simple stone was one of the more recent. The light, such as it was, was fading, and a mist had arisen, lending a ghostly glow to the marble monuments that crowded the cemetery. We were alone, with the gate attendant the nearest human presence. What I could scarcely articulate about this melancholy scene Mr. Lovecraft shortly put into words, starting with the sinister aspect of a nearby crumbling tomb.

"Who knows, Miss Lathbury," he intoned, "what grisly Tartarus, what black wells of Acherontic fear or feeling, what impious catacombs of nameless menace might lie beneath yon sepulchre?"

I wasn't sure whether to laugh or scream, but the utterly serious *manner* in which he spouted this nonsense was most unsettling.

"Might not a hidden vault," he continued, "lead to those grinning caverns of earth's centre where Nyarlathotep, the mad faceless god, howls blindly in the darkness to the piping of two amorphous idiot flute-players?"

If this was Mr. Lovecraft's idea of fun, I wasn't having any. I had an impulse to flee, but as he droned on about the "boundless daemon-sultan Azathoth," I did what I had to do to stop him— I removed my gloves *and slapped his hideous, leering face as hard as I could!*

Chapter 4

Icannot tell you who was more stunned. For the longest time we stared at each without saying a word. Then Mr. Lovecraft broke into a laugh more alarming than any of his insane utterances. Again, I had to fight an urge to run for my life.

"My dear Miss Lathbury," he said. "I do apologise. I did not mean to frighten you."

"You didn't? Well, Mr. Lovecraft, what *did* you mean by reciting such dreadful rubbish?" When he didn't answer, I turned and started to walk briskly toward the way out. He followed at my heels.

"Is this your idea of a lark," I went on, "luring an innocent young woman to a lonely cemetery in order to scare her out of her wits?"

"Miss Lathbury, I beg your pardon, I was only…I was only trying to impress you."

"You could have impressed me a lot more by complimenting me on my clothes or giving me flowers or inviting me to dinner or performing any of a hundred other courtesies a gentleman normally pays a lady. After all, Mr. Lovecraft, you've been married. You should know what pleases our sex."

"Alas, knowing how to please the fair sex is not one of my strengths, Miss Lathbury," he said in a tone that suggested he almost took pride in the fact. "Just ask that endlessly forbearing woman, my erstwhile wife!"

We shortly reached the road outside the cemetery, where Mr. Lovecraft hailed a passing cab. I didn't object, as it was now getting dark and a cab was a welcome alternative to waiting for a bus in the cold. As we headed down Highgate Hill, Mr. Lovecraft broke the silence by asking if I cared to join him for dinner at a curry restaurant he knew of in Highbury. I pretended to have to think about it, but in the end got off my high horse and said yes.

"Excellent, Miss Lathbury, but would you mind if we first stopped at Faunus Books in the Holloway Road? In order to put my graveside maunderings in context, to convince you they were not wholly the ravings of a lunatic, I want to give you one of my books, of which I have no spare copies at home. It is entitled *The Call of Cthulhu and Other Weird Stories.*"

"The call of *what*?"

"Ah, perhaps you had better read the title story before I try to explain."

We arrived at Faunus Books a few minutes before closing time. Mr. Lovecraft introduced me to Mr. Hillyer and Mr. Darnell, who both exuded a sort of musty, mouldy air in keeping with the contents of their shop. My employer pointed out that while the proprietors primarily offered second-hand volumes, they also carried current titles in such specialised fields as supernatural horror. While I studied the new arrivals shelf, he purchased a copy of his book, at author's discount. When I asked him to inscribe it, he said he would do so later, after he had had time to think of something suitable.

Over dinner at Rasa, a south Indian vegetarian restaurant just off Highbury Corner, Mr. Lovecraft admitted that a damning notice of the book by Edmund Wilson, the leading American literary critic, had been devastating. Mr. Wilson's ruthless appraisal had essentially killed any desire to produce new horror tales. In turn, a letter praising a magazine article of his on the Depression and its possible remedies from no less a personage than President Roosevelt largely accounted for his present career path. Mr. Orwell, he added incidentally, had in his youth aspired to write ghost stories in emulation of M. R. James, though of late his work had become entirely political. The death in June of Dr. James, a weird fictionist of the first rank, was a sad loss for the field.

While Mr. Lovecraft drank some Indian fruit beverage, I indulged in a fizzy Indian beer that helped embolden me to speak of my own literary preferences. He listened politely to my talk of contemporary writers, but only brightened up when I mentioned Sylvia Townsend Warner, who he informed me was related by marriage to Mr. Machen. As a confirmed antiquarian, he rarely paid attention to new novels, unless of a supernatural cast. When I mentioned that

Miss Warner had published a novel about a witch, *Lolly Willowes*, he said this was news to him. I made a mental note to give him a copy of *Lolly Willowes*, which seemed only a fair return after his generosity in presenting me with his ghostly volume.

By the end of the meal, when Mr. Lovecraft called for the bill, I was feeling sufficiently mollified to ask if I might pay my share. He wouldn't hear of it, and I made no further fuss. After the earlier episode in Highgate Cemetery he owed me a nice dinner, which this certainly had been, despite our finding little common literary ground. Like a gentleman, he walked me to my bus stop on the St. Paul's Road and waited with me there.

"I've had a lovely evening, Mr. Lovecraft," I said when my bus came into sight in the distance.

"I have enjoyed myself as well, Miss Lathbury. And again my apologies for my behaviour this afternoon."

"I forgive you," I said in all sincerity.

"I am not a naturally sociable man, Miss Lathbury, but there are times when I appreciate female companionship. I hope you will do me the honour of joining me for another outing soon."

"Yes, I would like that."

Mr. Lovecraft bowed stiffly as I boarded the bus. Clearly it was too much to expect a handshake let alone a kiss on the cheek. Before the doors closed I turned to thank him again for the book, but he was already striding toward home.

Over the weekend Mr. Lovecraft was much on my mind. He may have acted strangely at Highgate, but I counted it a victory that he had initiated a purely social excursion—and had promised another soon. I happily anticipated reading his story collection, in the hope it might give me some added insight into his character.

Well, was I in for a shock! I had expected traditional ghosts or vampires or devils or witches, perhaps of an American variety, but his fiction was like nothing I'd ever encountered before. His typical hero seemed to be a solitary male scholar who, after stumbling on evidence of supernatural mischief with an extraterrestrial origin, despairs of human existence. Religion provides no consolation whatsoever. Such, anyway, was the thrust of the title tale with the unpronounceable name!

Some stories had rather pleasant landscape descriptions, but in no tale was there much action or plot. Romantic love figured not at all, unless one counted the odd marriage at the centre of a sordid domestic tragedy called "The Thing on the Doorstep." One of the more lurid tales, "The Dunwich Horror," seemed to parody the scriptural account of our Lord's death and resurrection. It did human beings scarcely more credit, though good does prevail in the end. I could read no more than a few pages of "Herbert West–Reanimator," an updated and far inferior *Frankenstein*, before skipping on to the next tale. "The Rats in the Walls" was the most disturbing of the stories I finished. By its horrifying end I couldn't help thinking it a pity that the cat and dog quarantine hadn't gone into effect a few years earlier, thus perhaps giving the unfortunate Mr. Delapore second thoughts about moving to England with his feline pet, Nigger-Man.

Overall the stories struck me as likely only to impress boys of twelve or thirteen. I couldn't imagine any grownup person reading such peculiar stuff and taking it seriously. I could only applaud Mr. Lovecraft's decision to abandon it for political writing!

I reconsidered giving him *Lolly Willowes*, which I now suspected would not be to his taste, but I was curious to see what he might make of a work where the devilry is subordinate to the human feeling, not the other way around. I duly presented him with Miss Warner's novel the next time I went to Highbury. While I was well into his story collection by then, I held off expressing any opinion, having not yet made up my mind just how frank I should be.

About a week later, having finished the volume and had time to think about the contents calmly, I brought the book with me to Highbury. Over our tea that afternoon, as I handed it to Mr. Lovecraft for inscription, I murmured something about his lyrical descriptions of the New England landscape. Beaming, he put his pen to the title page.

"To Miss Leonora Lathbury, May you now have a better understanding of the Old Gentleman and Your Obedient Servant, H. P. Lovecraft," he repeated.

"Well, to be honest, Mr. Lovecraft, I'm not sure I do understand. Why are *people* so unimportant in your fiction?" When it came to the test, I couldn't resist challenging him at the most fundamental level. In addition, I felt a bit annoyed that after theoretically pondering the matter, the best he could produce were these formal and formulaic words.

"I am a cosmic indifferentist, Miss Lathbury. Our human race is only a trivial incident in the history of creation. It is of no more importance in the annals of eternity and infinity than is the child's snowman in the annals of terrestrial tribes and nations."

"But what of human suffering?"

"I hasten to add that I am no advocate of standing on the sidelines in an age like this whilst so many are suffering."

Well, this was somewhat reassuring. But I continued to press the attack:

"And what is one to make of your unearthly monsters? I mean *really*, when there's so much real horror in the world. Can any adult take seriously, for instance, *Yog-Sothoth*?"

"I agree that Yog-Sothoth is a basically immature conception, and unfitted for really serious literature. The fact is, I have never approached serious literature and may never achieve it at my present rate." He might have gone on in this self-deprecating vein indefinitely had I not interrupted and asked what he thought of *Lolly Willowes*.

"If I may return your candour, Miss Lathbury," he said, "Miss Warner's charming fairy tale is at heart concerned with mundane social matters and as such does not fall within the mainstream of the weird tradition."

To my mind this was a positive virtue of *Lolly Willowes*, but I realised it would be useless to argue the point with Mr. Lovecraft. Instead, I put down my tea cup and announced that it was time for me to go.

"Can you not stay and accompany me to the cinema, Miss Lathbury? There is a five-fifteen showing of Laurel and Hardy's *Our Relations* at the Screen on the Green on Upper Street."

"I'm afraid I have a women's committee meeting at church this evening, Mr. Lovecraft. I have nothing against spontaneity, but sometimes it helps to plan ahead."

"A point well taken. *Our Relations* will be playing all this week. Perhaps when you come in Thursday?"

"I'll let you know, Mr. Lovecraft."

I let him know on arriving early Thursday afternoon that going to the pictures after work would be a treat. I wasn't going to play that hard to get. *Our Relations* had its amusing moments, but on the whole it was rather too busy and talky. Mr. Lovecraft agreed, saying it was a pity that the need for belt-tightening had prompted Mr. Hal Roach to shift from making two-reelers to feature-length films. We had gone to Rasa for a bite to eat afterwards, and it was there that Mr. Lovecraft made a startling admission:

"Miss Lathbury, I hope you will not hold it against me, but I was, incredibly enough, for several months a supporting actor under contract to the Hal Roach Studio. I appeared briefly in a number of Our Gang and Laurel and Hardy shorts."

"My goodness, Mr. Lovecraft. I had no idea—and certainly don't hold it against you! That must have been glamorous really, working in pictures. How did you ever get started in that world?"

"Ironically, it was the sale of subsidiary rights to a six-part serial written down to the herd level, 'Herbert West–Reanimator,' that took me to Hollywood. Have you by chance seen *Reanimator*, as the so-called adaptation was titled?"

"No, I've never even heard of it."

"Lucky for you, Miss Lathbury."

Mr. Lovecraft proceeded to relate how Mr. Roach had originally intended to hire him as a screenwriter, but one look at his ugly mug had decided the comedy kingpin to put him in front of the camera instead—as a reanimated corpse and, later, as an all-around heavy. As for the suitableness of a stage career for a gentleman, Mr. Lovecraft observed that Arthur Machen had once been a strolling player whilst Edgar Allan Poe's parents had both been theatre people.

"And what of *your* parents, Mr. Lovecraft? Are they still alive?" I asked, emboldened by the Indian beer.

"They are both deceased," he replied after taking a long sip of his mango juice. "When I was a small child, my father was stricken with a complete paralysis resulting from a brain overtaxed with study and business cares. He lived for five years at a hospital, but was never again able to move hand or foot, or to utter a sound."

"How dreadful!"

"My mother lived until 1921. She was a person of unusual charm and force of character, accomplished in literature and the fine arts— a French scholar, musician, and painter in oils. She was, in all probability, the only person who thoroughly understood me."

"Well, Mr. Lovecraft, I hope you will give me credit for at least *trying* to understand you."

"Miss Lathbury, you are most tolerant of an old Yankee gentleman and his eccentric ways. But what, may I ask, of your family?"

For the first time since our initial interview, I had the chance to talk of my people, and with pride mentioned noble connections in certain collateral lines. He might profess socialist views, but by now I'd recognised that Mr. Lovecraft was an aristocrat at heart. At any rate, he appeared to listen closely to my family account, making approving noises at appropriate intervals. He allowed that genealogy was a passion of his, and hoped whilst in England to dig deeper into his family's history, in particular the Devon roots of the Lovecrafts. The previous year he'd spent a day in Broadhempston, where he'd found a Lovecraft or two buried in a centuried churchyard, but had been unable to locate the ancestral seat of Minster Hall. Perhaps he would return for a more thorough search in the new year.

The weather, in the meantime, was curtailing activity. In the days following our cinema outing, Mr. Lovecraft ventured outdoors less and less. It was too often raining or dark too early in the day for bicycling, other than to nearby Highbury Barn for groceries. The gas was now constantly lit in the drawing-room fireplace, the windows shut and the curtains drawn. The stuffiness could be unbearable at times, but I never complained to my employer, who thrived in this hothouse atmosphere. One of the principal advantages of living in a low-rent area like Highbury, he admitted, was being able to afford the luxury of ample gas heat.

Mr. Lovecraft remarked that he had a gas fire to keep him warm at night in his bedroom, which of course I'd never seen, other than a glimpse from the loo on the half-landing leading to the second floor. If he continued to be physically aloof, I was content with what I felt was a greater emotional bond between us since our excursion to Highgate. Slapping his face seemed to have snapped him to his senses!

I confess I really didn't mind this platonic state of affairs, for though I might have welcomed the occasional chaste kiss on the cheek or arm around the shoulder, give a man an inch and he'll take an ell, as the old expression goes. Our relations remained absolutely correct, and here I think we had a perfect if tacit understanding.

I continued to perform my secretarial chores cheerfully. I was especially pleased to type up a recent lengthy political poem of Mr. Lovecraft's own which was later published in *The Adelphi*. Mrs. Machen's memoirs passed the halfway mark, and I was delighted to learn that their marriage had produced two children, a boy, Hilary, and a girl, Janet.

For the American holiday of Thanksgiving the Angels generously entertained their lodger and me to a traditional turkey supper. It was then that Mr. Lovecraft announced that his aunt, Mrs. Gamwell, would be coming to England for Christmas and New Year's. Mrs. Angel had a spare bed that could be set up in his study for use by his "daughter."

I happened to be in Highbury on the day of the abdication, and at Joan's invitation joined her and Edward, together with Mr. Lovecraft, in their drawing-room to hear the king's speech over the wireless. Mr. Lovecraft expressed no opinion on a monarch sacrificing all for love, but was genuinely impressed by the historic moment and the technological marvel that made such a live broadcast to millions possible. We all sat too moved to speak in the aftermath, until Mr. Lovecraft declared: "Of George the Sixth one may well say, as did his abdicating brother, *God Save the King!*"

As Christmas approached, my social calendar filled up, mainly with church related events. I had to decline Mr. Lovecraft's invitation to join him and Mr. and Mrs. Orwell for a restaurant meal before the couple departed for Spain. My alternative proposal that he go with me to an Advent supper led him to suggest that he might fancy attending a Christmas service instead, once his aunt had arrived. He was curious to observe an Anglican service on native English soil. Though disappointed not to have him as my escort to the Advent supper, I was grateful that he was willing to attend a service, however cerebral his motives. It was some comfort that he indicated his preference for the C. of E. in a broad, low form as against silly Anglo-Catholic high-churchery.

In the end Mr. Lovecraft and his aunt came to St. Columba's for a service of lessons and carols Christmas Eve. I couldn't help wishing that the candlelight, the sweet singing of the boys' choir, the splendid pageantry and ritual would touch Mr. Lovecraft's emotions and shake his materialist beliefs. After the service he said that the religious programme rivalled the annual Kingsport Yule festival in awesomeness, but I suspect this was a private joke. Mrs. Gamwell was a bright, lively little woman, who told me she hoped I might help her beloved nephew to see the error of his radical political views!

As I had for most of my adult life, I spent Christmas with Jane and her family. On Boxing Day I went to Highbury, where I exchanged gifts with Mr. Lovecraft. My present to him was a very practical one, a wool jumper, while he gave me a copy of the English edition of his novel, *The Case of Charles Dexter Ward*, with a suitable seasonal inscription. I had already given him a second present—three tickets to the Christmas pantomime at the Hackney Empire, as at one point he'd expressed an interest in this traditional entertainment. That afternoon the three of us took the bus to Hackney for the show, which was played far more broadly than I remembered from pantos in my childhood. The audience of mostly working-class children quite enjoyed themselves, though, judging by the noise level. Afterwards Mr. Lovecraft and Mrs. Gamwell said they were charmed, but I think they returned to Highbury feeling less than enraptured by this example of popular English culture.

I saw Mr. Lovecraft at home one more time before the New Year. A gaily decorated tree stood in one corner of the drawing-room, and Christmas cards were everywhere displayed—on the mantel, table tops, and those bookshelves which still contained open space. Mrs. Gamwell was upstairs napping while we sat in our respective seats, Mr. Lovecraft in the wing chair and I on the sofa, and drank our tea and nibbled Christmas biscuits baked by Joan. We exchanged some banalities about resolutions for 1937, but my employer seemed to have lost the holiday spirit that had been in evidence a few days earlier.

"I don't wish to pry, but is there anything troubling you, Mr. Lovecraft?"

"You are kind to ask, Miss Lathbury."

"I hope the service at St. Columba's wasn't too tiresome for you."

"No, no, not at all."

"And the panto at the Hackney Empire, I must say—"

"Please, Miss Lathbury, I am preoccupied by another matter entirely."

"Yes?"

Mr. Lovecraft sighed, then the truth came out. The day after Boxing Day two late Christmas missives arrived: one from his former secretary, the other from his best friend. Mr. Lovecraft had made no mention of their relationship since the initial romantic revelation, but now there was an update. It seems that Sonny Belknap had recently shared with Clarissa correspondence that he, Mr. Lovecraft, had sent his young friend going back many years. Some of these letters contained what Clarissa construed to be racist, specifically anti-Semitic, remarks and she was highly upset. That he owed his success to a Jewish publisher particularly rankled. Belknap was upset too, in particular because she had passed on some of these private remarks to another old friend, Sam Loveman, who happened to be Jewish.

"I have been indiscreet, Miss Lathbury. Not so long ago, alas, I was not as enlightened as I am today. I could not help reflecting the prejudices of my class."

"You're a good man, Mr. Lovecraft," I said, wondering who among us could claim to be wholly free of race and religious prejudice.

"On the other hand, how could Belknap have been so thoughtless! Of that bushy-haired nitwit one may well say, like the exasperated Oliver Hardy, 'Well, here's another fine mess you've gotten me into!'"

Chapter 5

In the New Year there would be further repercussions from this unfortunate incident. Mr. Lovecraft received a terse letter from his Jewish friend, Sam Loveman, saying in effect that they were no longer friends. Mr. Lovecraft didn't show me this letter, but he described it in enough painful detail to make me feel extremely sorry for everyone concerned. At the same time I took it as a sign of our new intimacy that he would discuss such a sensitive personal matter with me.

One friend whose occasional note or brief letter he gladly shared from this period was Mr. Orwell, who was now a soldier with a Republican militia group in Spain. More than once Mr. Lovecraft expressed his regard for the man's courage and commitment in journeying to an actual battlefield to fight for his democratic Socialist ideals.

Overall I had good reason to feel pleased with the way things were progressing with Mr. Lovecraft as the winter wore on. We soon established a routine of going to the pictures every week, though sometimes for variety we attended a play instead. Once at my suggestion we attended a classical concert at the Albert Hall, but this was not a success. Mr. Lovecraft afterwards confessed that the trauma of playing the violin as a child had left him with a permanent aversion to serious music.

I respected his need to spend much of his free time with his male friends. Mr. Caldwell became a regular lunch companion. Saturday evening at the Compton with the Faunus Bookshop "gang" was sacrosanct. As a rule we never saw each other on a Sunday, though one unseasonably mild day after church I did join Mr. Lovecraft on Mr. Caldwell's historical walking tour of Islington Village. On another occasion the Caldwells invited us to dinner at their flat in Canonbury Square, where I had the pleasure of admiring Mrs. Caldwell's Arthur Ransome collection.

Books remained a favourite topic of conversation. Mr. Lovecraft was particularly keen on a new novel by an American author named J. P. Marquand. Entitled *The Late George Apley*, the book provided a penetrating and mildly satiric portrait of Boston, Massachusetts, society. I found it almost as amusing as Mr. Lovecraft did. Less appealing was George Santayana's *The Last Puritan*, which I also read at his urging. Although it dealt with similar themes, such as the decline of the traditional Yankee ruling class, it was far more philosophical and long-winded than *The Late George Apley*.

One afternoon shortly after arriving for work I was startled to spot Mr. Lovecraft sitting at his kitchen table cleaning a pistol. He admitted that this was a recent purchase and he would later be going to a rifle club near Finsbury Park to practice shooting. When I asked him if this was yet another instance of his taking up a new gentlemanly pursuit, he replied that as a youth he had loved firearms and could scarcely count the number of guns he had once owned. This struck me as a somewhat dangerous hobby, and I could only wish him better luck with it than he had had with riding.

As might be expected of a literary man of his calibre, Mr. Lovecraft was fascinated by the English language—especially its spoken forms. One article that he put a great deal of research into over the winter was a survey of English dialects, supplemented with lively anecdotal observations from his own experience. He treated the class aspect with a freshness and frankness that only an enthusiastic, non-native amateur could have brought to the subject.

I ploughed on with the typing of Mrs. Machen's edited memoirs, which were now drawing near to the present and presumably to a close. A comment of mine on their charm after I'd finished working for the day and we were having our tea elicited a startling admission from Mr. Lovecraft.

"Charming is the word, Miss Lathbury," he said brightly. "They form an incomparable chronicle of Mrs. Machen's youth and family. And her account of her meeting with her future husband is of course uniquely important."

"But what about the years since their marriage? I've noticed she hasn't a lot to say about Mr. Machen."

"Ah, there is the rub," he said with some heat. "By this stage she should have told the reader something of real consequence about that literary Titan her husband, but so far all she has supplied is domestic trivia."

"Can you not suggest she add more about *him*?"

"I have tried to hint as much, but my advice on this score goes unheeded. In one letter to me Machen states that the missus should be left to write whatever she wishes to write. He is perfectly content in her pages to play a mere walk-on role."

Mr. Lovecraft sounded truly disappointed, though I had to wonder if the wife of a great author should feel obliged to share private details about him in print. Wasn't it enough that she was a supportive and loving partner?

"Well, I suppose your fee must be some consolation," I said.

"It is not the money, Miss Lathbury. The truth is, they cannot afford to pay me a penny!"

"How terrible!"

"How terrible indeed that a writer of Arthur Machen's talents should have to scrape for the bare necessities at his age. A few years ago he was awarded a Civil List pension, but the loss of a reader's job for a publisher shortly thereafter more than offset this gain. I tell you, Miss Lathbury, the life of an artist is hard!"

"Then the editing you've done on the memoirs has been an act of charity," I said. I refrained from saying "Christian" charity.

"Yes, though I have not gone without *some* material reward. Machen has given me inscribed copies of his two latest books. Let me show you." Mr. Lovecraft went over to the main set of bookshelves, which by now contained a sizable Machen collection. A moment later he handed me two slender volumes.

"*The Cosy Room* and *The Children of the Pool*," I read on the jacket covers. "What comforting titles." Inside were inscriptions that seemed more heartfelt than any of Mr. Lovecraft's in his books to me. Both appeared to be story collections.

"Which one do you recommend I read first?" I asked, feeling sorry for the poor author, not a word of whom I had read. Perhaps it was high time that I did so.

"Neither collection represents their author at his best. You should start with *The Hill of Dreams*, his memorable epic of the sensitive aesthetic mind. It is his finest work of fiction."

Mr. Lovecraft put *The Cosy Room* and *The Children of the Pool* back on the shelf, and returned with *The Hill of Dreams*.

"I hope it isn't too frightening," I said, examining the murky and vaguely sinister frontispiece by S. H. Sime.

"Other than a dream vision of Roman Britain it contains nothing supernatural, I can assure you. It is in fact the perfect introduction to Machen's native Wales—where I hope you will soon accompany me."

He said this last bit in a low, hurried voice, and for a moment I wasn't sure how to respond, delighted though I was by the implied invitation.

"Are you asking me to Wales *alone*, Mr. Lovecraft?" I said, playing the innocent ingénue. "I hear Wales is a wild and dangerous place. Do you think it would be *proper?*"

"Please, Miss Lathbury," he said, blushing. "Allow me to explain. I have yet to mention one other compensation for editing Mrs. Machen's memoirs. We are invited, both of us, to attend a luncheon in Machen's honour in Newport on March 3rd. He is finally to receive some official recognition for his achievements on the occasion of his seventy-fourth birthday. The committee responsible originally believed it was going to be Machen's seventy-fifth, and only later discovered they were a year off."

Well, of course I accepted, arranging to take a couple of days off from my distressed gentlewomen. I read *The Hill of Dreams* beforehand, a beautiful if in many ways baffling book. The writer-hero is an utterly impossible character, who sacrifices all chance of human happiness out of some perverted sense of dedication to his art. When I raised these objections, Mr. Lovecraft conceded that the protagonist was a neurotic given to emotional hysteria, but he was marvellously appealing for all that!

On the train to Newport the day before the luncheon, I brought along Mr. Machen's autobiography, *Far-Off Things*, which Mr. Lovecraft had insisted I read after hearing my objections to *The Hill of Dreams*. I was relieved to find it more accessible than the novel, a more straightforward, less ironical account of the life of a struggling writer.

We spent the night in an inn near the railway station, in separate rooms, I scarcely need add. As always, Mr. Lovecraft insisted on paying for everything. After a late breakfast the next morning we took a bus to Caerleon, to visit the recently excavated Roman amphitheatre there. Mr. Lovecraft had made a special point of getting to Caerleon-on-Usk, to give the town its full name, on his first trip to Britain. It was, after all, Arthur Machen's birthplace.

We had been barely begun our tour of the site, mostly earth-covered stone walls, when Mr. Lovecraft exclaimed, "By the Great God Pan! Here is the man of the hour himself!"

I turned away from the mosaic fragment I'd been inspecting and saw a group of people, three men and a woman, approaching us across the grass. Mr. Machen was unmistakable—a short, pear-shaped gentleman, whose fringe of unruly white hair and Inverness cape perfectly fit my image of the bohemian author. The diminutive older woman at his side was surely Mrs. Machen. Mr. Lovecraft made the introductions. Their two younger companions, Mr. Stonor and Mr. Summerford, were as cordial as the celebrated couple they were escorting. Mr. Machen expressed his pleasure at the excavation in language as extravagantly lovely as his writings, while his melliflu-ous voice was as arresting as his appearance. Mrs. Machen was the soul of kindness, telling me how much she appreciated my labours on her memoirs.

An hour or so later Mr. Lovecraft and I joined the crowd of guests filling the dining room of the Westgate Hotel in Newport. Presiding at the head table was the Lord-Lieutenant, Sir Henry Mather-Jack-son. Local dignitaries included the Bishop of Monmouth and the mayors of Newport, Monmouth, and Abergavenny.

We had the pleasure of sharing a table with Stella Gibbons, au-thor of that wise and amusing novel, *Cold Comfort Farm*. She ad-mitted to Mr. Lovecraft that she had a fondness for ghost stories, and was considering writing one herself. He suggested she might do a sequel to Mr. Machen's celebrated tale of the Great War, "The Bowmen," in which an angelic host of mediaeval archers, led by St. George, comes to the rescue of British forces during the retreat from Mons—but from the point-of-view of the angels.

A university professor and a newspaper editor each spoke learn-edly and sympathetically of the guest of honour and his work. But it was Mr. Machen himself who left the strongest impression. In his speech, after first acknowledging the inspiration of the natural beauty of Gwent, he dwelt on the effort and disappointment that had been the price of trying to capture this beauty in prose. No one had encouraged him to persevere in the writer's trade. His total earnings from eighteen volumes produced over twenty-two years was £635. When Mr. Machen finished his litany, no one applauded harder than Mr. Lovecraft.

At the close of the proceedings Mrs. Machen received a bouquet of flowers and a painting, while Sir Henry presented the venerable author with a cheque for two hundred guineas. All in all, the honoured guest's sobering remarks notwithstanding, it was a most festive occasion.

We were to see the Machens again toward the end of the month. With the editing finally complete on Mrs. Machen's memoirs, we accepted their invitation to visit them at home in Amersham. Mr. Lovecraft had been there twice before, in the summer of '35 and the previous September. It was during this latter visit that he had offered to edit Mrs. Machen's memoirs on such generous terms.

On the 3:25 train from Marylebone Mr. Lovecraft was preoccupied with the work of another literary friend, one who was wholly of the present world, unlike Mr. Machen, who was quite beyond it. This was Mr. Orwell, whose latest book, *The Road to Wigan Pier*, about poverty in the industrial North, he had just finished. It was a devastating account, with a certain personal resonance. Had his literary fortunes not taken a sudden turn for the better in 1934, Mr. Lovecraft declared, he would by now be as bereft as the unemployed miners of benighted Wigan.

Mr. and Mrs. Machen occupied a flat on the first floor of a red-brick house, Lynwood, in the Amersham High Street. Compared to Mr. Lovecraft's maisonette, or even my own modest quarters, the place was small and cramped. Unfortunately, the brisk, rainy weather precluded our going into the garden, where they'd entertained Mr. Lovecraft in the past.

Instead we gathered in the sitting-room, where Mr. Machen served us what he called Dog and Duck punch, which he pronounced "poonch" in the manner of Dr. Johnson. With elaborate ceremony he poured this libation from an earthenware pitcher into ornate goblets such as mediaeval priests might have used when performing the Mass. This mild, herbal beverage in fact reminded me of the type of concoction brewed by the vicar for the church bazaar or bridge party. It was only after my second glass, when my head started to reel, that I realised the punch was spiked with alcohol. Out of politeness I said nothing, but was firm in refusing a third glass. I couldn't help feeling somewhat alarmed when Mr. Lovecraft complimented our host on the punch's warming qualities and accepted his second or third refill. By this point his long face was a healthy pink.

In the low lamp light Mr. Machen's ruddy complexion seemed to glow like a furnace fire. He was going on in that distinctive voice of his about a radio talk which he'd given the other day at the BBC for the Welsh Home Service.

"They shut me up all alone in a severe little room," he said, "with its lights turning from white to red, and its faint suggestion of an electrocution in New England."

If this was an attempt to needle his New England guest, Mr. Lovecraft didn't take the bait. He merely nodded and encouraged our host to continue his narrative. The talk had no title, according to Mr. Machen, but touched on several literary controversies linked only by his opinion that the majority view was mistaken.

"People often praise books for their realism and lifelike portrayal of character," he asserted, "whereas the greatest characters in fiction are singularly unlifelike. Who has ever met, or would expect to meet, Falstaff, Don Quixote, or Mr. Pickwick?"

"Not meeting Mr. Pickwick would suit me, sir," replied Mr. Lovecraft, "for I cannot bear Dickens. He is the worst sort of sentimentalist."

"And you, Lovecraft," retorted Mr. Machen, "are the worst sort of materialist!"

I looked anxiously at Mrs. Machen, but her twinkly expression betrayed no concern. Perhaps she was used to her husband's pugnacious pronouncements.

"On the contrary, sir," said Mr. Lovecraft, after a swallow from his goblet, "I am the best sort of materialist. I am an *indifferentist*. That is, I know that the interplay of forces which govern climate, behaviour, biological growth and decay, and so on, is too purely universal, cosmic, and eternal a phenomenon to have any relationship to the immediate wishing-phenomena of one minute organic species on our transient and insignificant planet."

"Cant, Lovecraft," countered Mr. Machen. "Materialist cant. Or 'indifferentist' cant if you will. It all amounts to the same thing—rubbish. See here, I tackled a materialist once who took a very similar line…"

Mr. Machen proceeded to argue the benefits of religion to the development of English agriculture, painting, and architecture, a course of reasoning that made perfect sense to me.

"The good effects of Christianity are neither to be denied, nor lightly esteemed," said Mr. Lovecraft after hearing our host out, "though candidly I will admit that I think them overrated. Meanwhile, sir, you seem wilfully to miss my point…"

If Mr. Machen was as tolerant of his materialism as Mr. Lovecraft had once claimed, this tolerance clearly didn't rule out vigorous debate of the subject.

The verbal thrust and parry continued at the King's Arms, a short distance down the High Street, where we went for an early supper. At our host's suggestion, we all ordered bangers and mash. When Mr. Lovecraft declined a pint of traditional English ale, Mr. Machen declared, "I keep forgetting, Lovecraft. You are a Puritan as well as a materialist."

A smile and a wink in my direction confirmed my impression that Mr. Machen was playing a role—the foxy Welsh wizard?—in a mischievous effort to twit Mr. Lovecraft. His sparring partner, however, remained unruffled.

"Like the Puritan, I am an enemy of drink," said Mr. Lovecraft primly. "I've never been able to figure out why people seem to find the artificial paradise of alcoholic excitation so necessary to their happiness."

"You astound me, Lovecraft," said Mr. Machen, lifting his own pint of ale. "Next thing you'll be telling me is that you've never been able to figure out why our art galleries and museums don't remove so-called works of art displaying the naked human form."

"No one but a ridiculous ignoramus or a warped Victorian, sir, sees anything erotic in the healthy human body, either as revealed in Nature, or as depicted in its normal proportions by painting and sculpture."

"Against eroticism, are you?"

"Eroticism belongs to a lower order of instincts, and is an animal rather than nobly human quality."

"May I remind you, Lovecraft, that we are among ladies. Such ribaldry—"

"Our verdict on a bit of risqué wit must always be provisional and tentative," said Mr. Lovecraft in a nervous, high voice. "Clearly, there is bad taste in the overdoing of any subject *not necessitated by the laws of truth-telling*, which may contravene the sensibilities of…"—and here he looked sheepishly at me and Mrs. Machen—"…of a refined female audience."

After further fruitless to-ing and fro-ing over religion and, more delicately, eroticism, the two men got on to politics, specifically the war in Spain. Mr. Lovecraft spoke passionately for the Republican cause. Mr. Machen listened politely, then declared:

"I am, and always have been, entirely for General Franco!"

At this Mr. Lovecraft came out with an expletive not usually heard in mixed company. I dare say for the first time since our arrival in Amersham Mr. Machen had succeeded in provoking him. Then he said something that gave me a terrible jolt:

"I shall be sure to give the general your regards when I get to Spain, sir, *at the end of a bayonet!*"

"Are you planning a trip to Spain, Mr. Lovecraft?" asked Mrs. Machen, as if Spain were a normal tourist destination these days.

"Yes, I am," he answered, his tone suddenly subdued. "I've been meaning to join a friend there who's been fighting on the Aragon front. I've been waiting for warmer weather…"

"Mr. Lovecraft, are you *serious?*" I asked, wondering if the Dog and Duck punch had thoroughly addled his brain. "Do you really mean to…*to endanger your life?*"

"Miss Lathbury, don't worry," he said, but he sounded far from reassuring. "I've been meaning to tell you… This is not the proper time and place… I regret—"

"Say no more, Lovecraft," interjected Mr. Machen. "Let us leave the present troubled age and speak instead of a century remote enough from us not to spark controversy. As Dr. Johnson tells us…"

The rest of the meal passed in comparative serenity, though I was too agitated to finish my plate. When the bill came, Mr. Machen insisted on paying it. "After all, I am a rich man," he said. "Not because I have recently received a gift of two hundred guineas, but because Purefoy and I have such friends and helpers as you, Lovecraft, and you, Miss Lathbury."

"I once knew a poor man," he continued on the pavement outside the King's Arms just when I thought we'd exchanged our farewells.

"He was a country squire with an income of ten thousand a year..." The gist of this story was that the "poor man" wanted both a coach and four and a steam yacht, but could not afford both. He bought a coach and four, yet ever afterward longed for a steam yacht. "I was sorry for him," concluded Mr. Machen.

Chapter 6

I'm sorry for Machen," Mr. Lovecraft was saying wearily on the train back to London. "He's too old, too set in his views, to see the error of his political conservatism. He reminds me of an Irish plumber I once tried to disabuse of his rabid anti-British outlook. This was in the period leading up to America's entry into the Great War. He was equally stubborn, and my efforts were for naught."

"Why, then, do you bother?" I had to ask.

"Argument—either oral or epistolary—is something I can't resist."

Mr. Lovecraft was looking a little greenish around the gills, and I had to wonder whether the potent Dog and Duck punch was finally taking its toll. Had Mr. Machen served this beverage on his previous two visits? And if so, had the results been as dire? Instead I merely asked how he was feeling, and he admitted that the bangers and mash possibly hadn't agreed with him. That he had touched "demon drink" was, I decided, not a suggestion he would want to hear, especially in his present state. Besides, I had a more pressing question on my mind.

"Speaking of war, Mr. Lovecraft, I'd appreciate your telling me why you wish to fight in Spain."

"It's a complicated story, Miss Lathbury, one that I promise to tell you another time. At the moment I confess…"

Mr. Lovecraft abruptly got up and dashed out of the compartment. He was gone a long while. When he returned, he collapsed on the seat and promptly fell asleep. I woke him when we reached Marylebone station. He made no protest when I saw him into a cab.

On my next visit to Highbury, during our usual afternoon tea, Mr. Lovecraft was more subdued than usual. True, he looked as if he were still recovering from an illness, but that was only half the story. I knew that he knew he had to give me a full explanation for why he was keen to participate in the Spanish war. Finally, he raised the subject:

"First, Miss Lathbury, you should know that my decision is no idle or impulsive one. I have been contemplating this action since soon after my arrival in England last year. Remember the day we first met? I did not get on a horse simply to emulate a gentleman. Knowing how to ride was a skill Orwell thought might be useful to a soldier. Riding had been part of his training when he was a police officer in Burma.

"Later I resumed my boyhood hobby of bicycling to improve my physical fitness. As for pistol practice, well, the value of that is obvious.

"The real obstacle to my departure has been the weather. Whilst I might plead a hypersensitivity to cold, who am I to ask for special treatment? If my orders are to fight in frozen, vermin-filled trenches, who is Private Lovecraft to disobey?"

"But why can't you continue to *write* in support of the cause you believe in?" I said. "Can't you do more good with your pen than a gun? Your talents would be wasted on the battlefield, and if the worst were to happen, why…" I was on the verge of tears, but did my best to keep my emotions under control. Acting the hysterical female I was sure would only lower me in Mr. Lovecraft's eyes.

"You have to understand, Miss Lathbury. It is more than principle that motivates me. It is also shame."

"Shame? What on earth have you to be ashamed of?"

"In my young manhood, Miss Lathbury, I was a virtual invalid, subject to all manner of nervous complaints. Still, I used to fancy that were I stronger, I might have gone to West Point, adopted a martial career, and found in war a supreme delight which scribbling can but faintly adumbrate.

"Then in May 1917, after America declared war on Germany, I saw my chance for glory and resolved to enlist. I accordingly presented myself at the recruiting station of the Rhode Island National Guard and applied for entry into whichever unit should first proceed to France. Since the physical examination only related to major organic troubles, of which I had none, I soon found myself, as I thought, a duly enrolled private in the R.I.N.G.

"However, I had embarked on this venture without informing my mother. The sensation caused at home on my return from the recruiting station was far from slight. In fact, my mother was almost prostrated with the news, since she knew that only by rare chance could a weakling like myself survive the rigorous routine of camp life. She soon brought my military career to a close. It required but a few words from our family physician regarding my nervous condition to annul the enlistment."

"Couldn't you have served as a clerk?"

"I later sought to be placed in a class that would permit me to help in a clerical way as much as I could. I was even prepared to become a typist! But the head physician of the local draft board—who happened to be a family friend and even a remote relative—knew too much of my constitutional ailments, and had me classified as totally and permanently unfit."

"So you spinelessly allowed your mother to use her influence to get you out of the American army," I said.

"Precisely. Now you can understand why I must go to Spain. As it is, I am on the old side at forty-six and may be pretty useless, but if I am to salvage any vestige of self-respect I have to do it."

"When do you leave?"

"I have yet to determine that. Like Orwell, I have joined the International Labour Party, which should help ease my entry into one of the Republican brigades. I may not depart until late April."

"I'm relieved to hear it."

"Believe me, Miss Lathbury. Spain will be an interesting experience, and will either kill me or cure me of any lingering neuroses."

The longer, milder days of spring would ordinarily have lifted my spirits, but in the weeks following this revelation I was in an almost perpetual state of heightened nervousness. I did my best to follow my daily routines and concentrate on the work at hand.

I read the page proofs of Mr. Lovecraft's latest novel, set in an imaginary world, entitled *The Dream-Quest of Unknown Kadath*. Knopf, his American publisher, was bringing it out in the summer. Compared to the stories in *The Call of Cthulhu*, it was a light, at times even humorous work. It had its darker moments, though. At one point the hero, Randolph Carter, leads cats and fabulous creatures called night-gaunts into battle against horrible monsters, the moon-beasts. I couldn't help wondering if this was a political allegory. But, no, Mr. Lovecraft said he had written the novel a decade earlier, shortly after returning to Providence from two years exile in New York City. A pure fantasy, *The Dream-Quest* was if anything a celebration of his coming home to New England.

He added that he had his doubts whether such a personal work would appeal to a wide audience. On the other hand, given that his previous books with Knopf had all been successful, there was every reason to hope that his fans would be just as welcoming of this idiosyncratic, once repudiated work. Since there were all sorts of problems with spelling inconsistencies and what was and what wasn't a proper name, the proof-reading was far from a straightforward task.

During this period Mr. Lovecraft received a letter from a journalist he knew in Providence named Winfield Townley Scott, who had just heard report that he intended to go to Spain. Mr. Lovecraft had begun to circulate the news to various friends, and clearly the word had spread. Mr. Scott asked for permission to do a lengthy profile of perhaps Providence's most notable—and heroic—living author. Would interviewing people who knew him for background be okay?

Preoccupied with travel arrangements, Mr. Lovecraft didn't give this flattering request much thought. But since he respected Mr. Scott as a man of integrity and a fine writer, he could hardly refuse. In any event, he would likely still be in Spain when the piece was published, assuming it was done quickly.

One important person with whom he had yet to share his plans was his aunt, Mrs. Gamwell. As with his mother twenty years before, he was hesitant to upset her with the prospect of his dying in battle. Nonetheless, he promised me he would write her with full particulars before he left England. According to Mr. Lovecraft, those of his American friends who had responded to his great announcement were to a man supportive. Some of the Faunus Bookshop crowd were taken aback, but they all rallied round and planned to give him a rousing send-off at the Compton. The only negative voice was that of a casual correspondent and American novelist living in Paris, a Mr. Henry Miller, who wrote to say that to go to Spain at this time would be the act of an idiot.

I couldn't help thinking that maybe Mr. Miller was right. I kept such fears to myself, however. Indeed, I never mentioned Spain, unless Mr. Lovecraft brought it up first. I didn't dare ask, for example, how long he expected to stay there. Joan was no better informed than I was, though one day she told me he had paid her three-months rent in advance. And what was I to do, if anything, in his absence?

If Mr. Lovecraft was anxious, he did a good job of pretending things were normal. On one occasion I looked up from my typing and caught him standing in the drawing-room doorway—staring at me. His face had that same oddly disturbing expression it had had when he tried to scare me in Highgate Cemetery. He immediately flushed and turned away, muttering something about some chore that needed doing in the kitchen.

At last, towards the end of April, as we were having our afternoon tea, I could tell that the time had come. Mr. Lovecraft, who was settled in the wing chair with his coffee mug, seemed unusually quiet. When he did speak, he refused to meet my eye. Then, after a wistful disquisition on the beauty of the English spring, he said:

"Miss Lathbury, I must speak plainly. Tomorrow I take a boat to France. By the end of next week I expect to cross the Spanish frontier."

"Oh, Mr. Lovecraft! Please do be careful!"

"I have packed plenty of warm clothes, including the wool jumper you gave me for Christmas. I am well supplied with cash."

"I'm pleased to hear it," I said in a whisper, staring into my teacup. I could hardly bear to look him in the face.

"There is a practical matter or two we ought to discuss at this point. First, I hope you will continue to come to Highbury at least once a week to go through my mail and answer any letters that require answering. Is that agreeable to you?"

"Yes," I murmured. "Do you know how long you will be away?"

"I cannot tell. I may be gone for some time."

"You will write?"

"Of course." There was a painful pause. Then Mr. Lovecraft produced from his suit pocket a standard A4 envelope. He had to rise slightly from his chair to hand it to me. Written on the outside were the words "Instructions in Case of Decease."

"I give this to you, my dear Miss Lathbury, for safekeeping. It is best to prepare for the worst."

At this I burst into tears. The next thing I knew Mr. Lovecraft was sitting next to me on the couch, and he had actually taken my hand in his. It felt very cold.

"Miss Lathbury, there is one last thing. If I do happen to return in one piece, will you do me the honour of becoming my bride?"

Chapter 7

*W*ell! I suppose at some level I must have been hoping to hear words like these for ages, and I suppose there was really no doubt how I was going to respond.

"Yes, oh, yes," I said through my tears, "to become Mrs. H. P. Lovecraft…" Here I broke down into sobs and couldn't continue. What if there were no Mr. H. P. Lovecraft alive to marry?

"My dear Miss Lathbury," he said, squeezing my hand. "That an attractive young lady of your character and background should consent to accept an old gent with a mug like mine pleases me infinitely."

At this point, realising my "mug" must look a mess, I excused myself to go clean up in the lavatory. When I came back, I resumed my seat next to him on the couch. When he made no attempt to take my hand again, I put my hand on his and asked:

"Do you love me?"

"I cannot tell you how much I appreciate you, Miss Lathbury." With this he hooked my little finger with his little finger and said, "Umph."

"Yes, I know you *appreciate* me—for my secretarial work, most obviously. But do you *love* me as a man does a woman?"

"Miss Lathbury, I—"

"And, oh, don't you think it's time we started addressing each other by our Christian names?"

"Why, certainly, I—"

"Mine's Leonora, in case you've forgotten. But what shall I call you? H. P., as you're known to your vast and adoring public? Or Howard, as you are to your fond and devoted aunt?"

"Howard will do."

"Do you love me, Howard?"

"My dear Miss...sorry, Leonora...yes, I...I...I love you—though when I use the word *love* I should explain that—"

"I'd rather not hear your qualifications, if you please, dear," I said firmly.

"Very well, but—"

"I'm curious about so many things. First off, do you feel any bitterness that your first marriage failed?"

"Not at all. You might say that I agree with Dr. Johnson when he observed of the man who married twice that it was the triumph of hope over experience."

"Wasn't Dr. Johnson being cynical?"

"Perhaps, but remember that Dr. Johnson was happily married to his Mrs. Porter to the end of her life."

"Why did you and your wife divorce?"

"In a nutshell I mistook superficial for basic congeniality. Small similarities did not, as expected, grow greater—nor did small differences, as expected, grow less. Instead the reverse process occurred in both cases. Aspirations and environmental preferences diverged increasingly until at length—albeit without real blame or even bitterness on either side—the Superior Court of Providence County was permitted to exercise its corrective and divisive function, and I was ceremoniously reënthroned in a dour celibate dignity."

His reticence about the nature of these differences and similarities concerned me less than his mention of "celibate dignity." Despite his seeming monkishness and his dim view of eroticism as expressed to Mr. Machen, was the man whose proposal I'd just accepted, like every other man, really only interested in one thing? And if so, how could I refuse if he asked me to give myself to him the night before he was due to leave for possible death in battle?

"Howard, dear, there's another, related topic I think we ought to be clear on," I said, shifting slightly away from him on the couch. "I understand it will be my duty as your wife to share a bed, but to be perfectly frank I have never much cared for...the physical side of things." I didn't say that past romances had tended to sour once my suitors lost patience with my "coolness."

"Believe me, Leonora," he replied, "this sex business is highly overrated."

"I'm glad to hear you say so."

"I never thought pre-marital experience worth the attendant ig-nominiousness, and doubt very much I was the loser thereby. I see no reason not to observe the proprieties until we have entered a state of domestic harmony."

"Are you sure?" I still couldn't quite believe that any man would be so self-denying.

"I hasten to add, however, that I will not shirk my conjugal du-ties, as I earnestly hope to have children. I have discovered in my re-searches that the name Lovecraft appears to be as extinct in England as it is in America. If I die without issue, I am the last of my line."

"Like some tragic gothic hero."

"Orwell has confided in me that he and his wife are keen on producing offspring—and look at Machen, a first-time father at the grand old age of forty-nine!"

"Yes, children would be lovely," I said, but then I remembered that he was about to leave for Spain and might not be coming back. "You know, Howard," I said, as the tears started to flow again, "I'd be willing to…to disregard the proprieties, if you like, your last night in England."

"That is noble of you, Leonora," he said, "but no, you need not sacrifice your virtue for my sake. In any event, I must keep an eye on the clock. I promised the lads I would meet them at the Compton for a farewell ginger beer."

Since it seemed to be assumed that I, his new fiancée, was not included in this party (Howard wished our engagement to remain a secret until his return), we didn't have a lot of time to discuss such practical matters as where we might live or whether I might still do his typing. But, as we parted with more tears on my part at the bus stop nearest the Compton, Howard did say that he looked forward to continuing our discussion of matters matrimonial through episto-lary exchange. Later that night, after he finished packing, he would have to write the long-postponed letter to his dear aunt disclosing his Spanish plans.

I received his first letter about a week after his departure. It was postmarked Paris, where he met his correspondent, Mr. Henry Miller, whose apolitical attitude he found incomprehensible. On the other hand, besides being a fellow admirer of Mr. Machen's work, Mr. Miller gave him a box of chocolates for the "Red" train from the Gare d'Austerlitz, loaded with foreign volunteers for the Republican cause. On the trip south he fully intended to share the chocolates in comradely fashion.

His second letter, evidently written on the train, ran on for pages and was full of his views on love and marriage. I quote a couple of representative passages:

> *I don't believe in the existence of sentimental 'love' as a definite, powerful, or persistent human emotion. I have always regarded marriage as composed of friendly regard, mental congeniality, social foresight, and practical advantage; to which at first the element of biological eroticism is added. I dare say my future bride might go so far as to suggest it need never be added!*
>
> *There are, of course, persons difficult to adjust to any sort of marriage; but so far as the vast majority are concerned, I believe that a well-chosen and highly discriminating entry into that state (mostly possible, I suppose, only after one or more unsatisfactory trials and divorces) affords a greater promise of reasonable felicity, and a larger quota of high-grade emotional values, than any other arrangement which can be envisaged. Certainly, it does not provide an ideal happiness—but then, nothing else does, either! Still, it approaches much more closely to tolerableness than any other condition (always assuming that the right sort of partner has, through a combination of luck, intelligence, and persistence, been secured). And in you, Leonora, I know I have secured the right sort of partner!*

All this was a bit impersonal and theoretical, and I wished that he wouldn't qualify his love as he did, but at least I was foremost in his thoughts.

His next letter was sketchy and very alarming. He arrived in Barcelona in the midst of what amounted to a pitched battle between the Communists and a rival political faction, the P.O.U.M. (whatever that stood for), of which the International Labour Party was a part. For days he had to lie low, dodging the bullets of supposed friends and allies, until security forces restored order to the streets. Fortunately, he had avoided exposure to any direct bloodshed. Now he was about to head to the front. The only good news was the tolerably warm weather.

I wrote back immediately to the *poste restante* address in Barcelona he supplied, imploring him to take care and expressing my love in far less dispassionate terms than he had used. I said I prayed constantly for his safe return in the not too distant future. At church, too, I saw to it that the vicar mentioned his name among those in sickness or adversity.

While I awaited further word from my fiancé, I attended to Howard's correspondence as best I could. Mrs. Gamwell was reasonably accepting of her nephew's going off to Spain, though apparently he had misled or otherwise confused her as to his allegiances, for she wished him well serving General Franco and the Nationalist cause! I decided it wasn't my place to correct this misunderstanding. Mr. Scott reported that he was making good progress with his biographical article, and had through Mr. Long got in touch with Howard's former wife, who was now Mrs. Davis and proving fully cooperative. That the woman had recently remarried in distant California I found a comfort.

Mr. Machen wrote to say that efforts to find a publisher for Mrs. Machen's memoirs had so far yielded no results.

It was near the end of June, after anxious weeks of hearing nothing, that I finally received a letter postmarked Paris from my husband-to-be, saying he was well and on his way back to England! The letter provided details of his doings since the unpleasantness in Barcelona. As part of a half-English, half-Spanish unit, led by Mr. Orwell, he had proceeded to the front near Huesca. In the trenches he hadn't minded the bad food, much of it out of tins and no worse than what he used to consume in his lean years. Given his advanced age, his fellow enlisted men called him *el viejo* (the "Old One") or, better yet, *abuelo* ("Grandpa"), while the officers tended not to assign him anything too onerous. He spent his fair share of time in the line, though once he was threatened with court-martial when he was almost caught dozing on sentry duty.

It was in fact while he was on sentry duty that a terrible thing happened at dawn one morning less than a fortnight after his arrival at the front. He was standing guard behind a wall of sandbags when Mr. Orwell showed up to take over his post. Seconds later he heard a rifle crack and saw Mr. Orwell fall to the ground. Evidently a sniper had shot him when he looked over the sandbags—his head silhouetted by the rising sun! This being the first casualty that Howard had witnessed at close hand, he had immediately fainted.

When he regained consciousness, he joined some other men in attending to Mr. Orwell, who was alert but unable to speak. They carried him on a stretcher about a mile to the nearest hospital, where he was treated for a throat wound which could easily have been mortal. The bullet had barely missed the carotid artery! It was after this incident that Howard was discharged and reassigned to a civilian post behind the lines—as a typist in the same office where Mrs. Orwell was working as secretary to the International Labour Party representative in Barcelona.

Of this unglamorous phase of his Spanish experience Howard said little. Given the deteriorating political situation (and quite candidly the dreariness of his office chores, for which as a two-finger typist he felt utterly unqualified), he had decided to join the Orwells in their flight from the country a month or so later. By this time Mr. Orwell had recovered sufficiently from his wound, and they were able to escape across the Pyrenées just ahead of certain arrest by the Communists as Trotskyite deviationists.

Some thirty-six hours after receiving this extraordinary missive, the phone rang as I was preparing for bed. It was Howard, who said he was overjoyed to be back in the sane atmosphere of storied London. Since he was exhausted, he could only speak briefly. Could I come around the following afternoon? I said I would be counting the minutes to our reunion. As soon as he rang off, I tore up the envelope marked "Instructions in Case of Decease" and threw the pieces in the rubbish.

Howard was waiting at the top of stairs when I arrived in Highbury. His face had more colour than usual, as if he had just returned from a Mediterranean holiday, but otherwise he looked the same as when I saw him last. He didn't resist when I embraced him.

"Hail the conquering hero!" I cried.

"Hardly," he protested. "The truth is, Leonora, I did not acquit myself well in Spain."

"Nonsense, dear. You survived. That's enough for me."

"You are too kind."

"No, I'm not. I'm just a supportive fiancée. You must tell me all about your adventures."

"I have already conveyed their essence in my letters to you, Leonora. In due course I will write up a complete account. For now I would prefer to discuss a pleasanter topic, namely our forthcoming nuptials."

His first wedding having been a furtive affair, with no one informed until after the deed was done, Howard was determined that this time he would give the world more than ample notice. He wanted to share his good fortune with others, particularly his aunt, who would need to make arrangements to cross the Atlantic during the height of the summer season. A date had to be set as soon as possible.

When I said I wanted us to be married in my church, Howard didn't object. He even agreed to meet the vicar and go through all the necessary ecclesiastical rigmarole. It now occurred to me that his being divorced might present obstacles, and here we conspired in a little harmless deception—not to tell the vicar that he had been previously married. As far as Howard was concerned, he wished he could expunge the record of his first marriage as if it had never existed, as happened to a certain mythical king in a story by Lord Dunsany.

During this first serious discussion of our future together, I made it clear that I wished to raise our children in the church. Howard magnanimously agreed to this, though he hoped that if any child of ours should reject religion in later years I could abide that choice. If I was prepared to marry a "cosmic indifferentist," I suppose I would just have to take the risk of having a child who might follow in its father's unbelieving footsteps. As long as that child maintained high moral standards, however, I couldn't be too dismayed. I flattered myself that mine was a charitable faith that allowed for weaknesses in others.

The next day we met at the lower end of Upper Street and shopped for a ring among the antique stores in Camden Passage. The one we decided on was suitably understated and tasteful. Our engagement was now official!

When over our next lunch I broke the news to Jane, my friend grinned and asked if she might use my example as a testimonial to her firm's placement record. She cheerfully agreed to be my matron of honour, and later helped me select a simple if smart wedding dress at a Mayfair shop she knew that wasn't too expensive. At another Mayfair emporium I ordered stationery with the initials LLL. *Leonora Lathbury Lovecraft*—now that was a name with style!

Since time was short, Howard cabled Mr. Long, asking him to serve as best man. He also cabled Mrs. Gamwell, inviting her to come to England for the wedding. Both responded with delight and promised to attend. In discussing the guest list there was some question of whether to include Miss Stone, but the matter was settled when Mr. Long revealed in the letter confirming his best man role that the two of them had broken up for good after a big fight. Howard was so pleased with this development that he wrote back insisting on paying all his friend's travel expenses.

In the busy weeks that followed we met with Mr. Wood, the vicar at St. Columba's, and reserved a wedding date for the second Saturday in August. At a subsequent pre-marital counselling session Howard declared that he had been raised a Baptist (without mention of his later apostasy) and that he was agreeable to a Church of England ceremony (without mention of his first marriage by Anglican rites). Mr. Wood granted his approval and the banns were posted.

We decided that we would honeymoon in Devon, where Howard anticipated doing further research into his paternal ancestry in the vicinity of Broadhempston. Afterwards we would go to America, to take up residence with his aunt in Providence until larger quarters could be found for us all. Howard was sure Mrs. Gamwell would welcome this arrangement. I wasn't so sure I liked the idea, though I had the impression the ménage would be only temporary. In principle I was perfectly willing to accept unknown Providence as my future home, as long as we made regular visits back to England.

Amidst all the preparations Howard managed to find time to write, while I did my part to type his chief literary effort of the moment, a book-length personal and political narrative called *The Shadow Over Catalonia*. From it I gained a good deal of insight into the dreadful situation in Spain, while I had to chide the author more than once for the "slapstick" role in which he cast himself.

The only cloud to spoil our happiness at this juncture was the news of the poor reception in America of Howard's new book, *The Dream-Quest of Unknown Kadath*. My sensitive fiancé stopped reading the reviews after the first one or two (one critic gleefully pointed out a host of typos and spelling inconsistencies), though he was able to joke that if he received enough such "bombs" he might collect them all in a single volume, as Mr. Machen once did his negative reviews. In mitigation, the Gollancz edition of his previous American book, *At the Mountains of Madness*, was published shortly thereafter to respectful notices.

With little prompting Howard put in an appearance at the St. Columba's summer jumble sale, where his enthusiastic purchase of some cheap ties and an ancient suit made a most favourable impression. One weekday morning he surprised me by appearing at the church annex while I was attending to my distressed gentlewomen. He was an instant hit with the ladies, whose mothering instincts he seemed to arouse. Happily, they indicated that they didn't mind his soon stealing me away from them. Later Howard said that he had felt a real affinity with the old women, since they had so reminded him of his aunt and her Providence social circle.

Mrs. Gamwell or Aunt Annie, as I was now to call her, and Frank or Belknap—just what I was to call him was unclear—arrived in early August, having crossed the Atlantic on the same ocean liner. Frank, as I'll refer to him for convenience, was a shy, nervous little man, who at first I couldn't believe was Howard's best friend. Despite his silky moustache and ubiquitous pipe, he seemed like a child playing at being an adult. I didn't see a lot of him, as Howard kept him busy touring bookshops and old London neighbourhoods. I finally warmed up to Frank the night before the wedding, when several friends, including the Angels and the Caldwells, joined me and Howard for the "rehearsal dinner" in the snug of the Compton. Raising his champagne glass, Frank gave a splendid speech, florid and full of classical allusions, in which he paid tribute to my character, intelligence, and beauty. In contrast, when Howard made his bridal toast, with glass of ginger beer in hand, he highlighted my virtues by way of a series of wry, self-deprecating comments that drew universal chuckles from the company, not least myself. Later, as I got into bed for what I imagined would be my final night as a spinster, I was still basking in the afterglow. Was I not the happiest woman alive?

Chapter 8

Jane came the next morning to my flat to help me dress. This she accomplished in short order, as only adjusting my veil required any real effort. The day had dawned drizzly and overcast, but it was going to take a lot more than bad weather to dampen the spirits of an ebullient bride. At a quarter to twelve Jane's husband, Simon, met us in his car outside my building, and we drove the few short blocks to St. Columba's. The ceremony was due to start at noon.

In front of the church we encountered a number of arriving guests, including Mr. and Mrs. Machen, shepherded by Mr. Darnell and Mr. Hillyer. There was a break in the clouds, and for a moment strong sunlight illuminated St. Columba's beautiful neo-Gothic facade. Was not this an auspicious omen? Nervous as I was, I felt a trifle calmer when the warden informed me that he had just seen the groom and best man go in the side entrance leading to the chancel.

We who made up the procession waited in the vestibule, where we could hear the strains of Bach from the organ whenever the main door opened. The last few guests straggled in, among them a sensitive-looking man with large ears whom I didn't recognise. He didn't return my smile, but hurried on inside. Might he be one of the less socially adept members of the Faunus Bookshop circle? Some of Howard's friends invited to the wedding I had met only fleetingly.

At the last toll of the bell marking the noon hour, we entered the church. The organist commenced the wedding march, and Jane proceeded slowly down the aisle toward the altar. After a suitable interval, Simon and I followed in similar stately fashion. Glancing at the pews, I was struck that the guests on the bride's side were mostly female, in their flowered hats, while those on the groom's side were predominantly male. Ahead loomed the vicar, holding the prayer book. My intended, dressed in a new dark suit (I'd been adamant that he not wear the one acquired at the jumble sale), and his best man stood like wooden soldiers at the communion rail.

Simon delivered me to Howard's side as the music stopped. Mr. Wood began the service, concluding the preamble with these normally rhetorical words:

"Into this holy estate these two persons come now to be joined. If any man can show just cause why they may not be lawfully joined together, let him now speak, or else hereafter for ever hold his peace."

The vicar paused, but before he could go on a man's voice boomed from behind: "Stop!"

Howard and I turned. The sensitive-looking man with oversized ears whom I'd observed earlier was striding up the aisle. No longer wearing his hat, he was quite bald. I realised then that this individual was a total stranger to me. He was, however, apparently familiar to my fiancé.

"My God," croaked Howard, as if he had just seen a ghost or a reanimated corpse.

"This marriage is a put-up job," said the intruder in a strong American accent, addressing the vicar. "You can't lawfully wed these two."

"You mean to say, sir, you know of an impediment?" asked Mr. Wood.

"I sure do," he answered, removing a folded sheet of paper from his suit pocket. "I have here a subpoena from the Superior Court of Providence County on the behalf of Mrs. Sonia Davis, the former Mrs. Howard P. Lovecraft, that proves he already has a wife."

"But Sonia remarried!" cried Howard.

"Yeah, but you never filed the final divorce papers. In the eyes of the law you and Sonia are still man and wife—and now you've turned her, one of the kindest and most beautiful women I ever met, into a bigamist. Believe me, you smug hypocrite, this time you're going to pay for your deceit."

"Sam, I—"

"Who are you, sir?" interrupted the vicar.

"I am Samuel Loveman, bookseller, and I have come all the way from America to see justice done."

"Do you know this gentleman, Mr. Lovecraft?"

"Yes, I do," said Howard softly. "He was once my friend."

For a moment Mr. Wood seemed at a loss, then he shut his prayer book and took the paper from Mr. Loveman.

"Howard, is this charge true?" I asked. Up to this point I had been too stunned to speak. But I was now collected and in no danger of swooning like the jilted bride of some tawdry gothic romance.

"My dear, I cannot tell you how much it grieves me… I fully intended… I never meant…"

"Mr. Lovecraft," said Mr. Wood sternly, "were you once married before?"

"Yes, I cannot deny it," said Howard in a barely audible voice.

"To a Mrs. Sonia Davis?"

"She was Mrs. Sonia Greene when I married her. But, yes, I understand she is presently Mrs. Sonia Davis."

"And yet you made no mention of this prior marriage when we discussed your upbringing and religious views?"

Howard made no reply. The vicar sighed, then said:

"I am no expert in American legal documents, Mr. Lovecraft, but in the light of this evidence and your admission, I must take the prudent course."

Hitherto those in the pews observing this unexpected drama had been as still as church mice, but now there arose a general murmuring and muttering.

Mr. Wood stepped forward and announced in a sorrowful voice, "I regret to inform you that an insuperable impediment prevents me from completing the service. You may all go home." Then he leaned toward Howard and said quietly, "And you, sir, must answer to this poor, misled woman—and I daresay to your Lord and Maker."

At this the colour drained entirely from Howard's face, and he fainted dead away. Fortunately, he toppled onto Frank, who cushioned his fall. The murmurs and mutterings exploded in an uproar.

"Sorry to spoil your wedding, lady," Mr. Loveman said, putting on his hat, "but one day you'll thank me. The guy's an insane racist. So long."

As I knelt to succour Howard, the best man crawled out from underneath his friend.

"Oh, what a terrible mess," moaned Frank. "And it's all my fault, too. If I hadn't shown Clarissa those letters, then she wouldn't have told Sam. And then Sam wouldn't have told Sonia—not that she was altogether surprised, mind you."

When Howard didn't respond to my ministrations, Mr. Wood called for a doctor among the guests. When none responded, he said he would ring for an ambulance. In the meantime Frank continued his plaintive lament:

"All this was bad enough, but the worst was when that journalist fellow up in Providence, Scott Winfield I think his name is, started interviewing everybody about Howard. For some reason, maybe from something hinted at by Mrs. Gamwell—I assure you it wasn't from me—he got the idea it would be worth checking the court records. And there in the county courthouse he discovered Howard was never officially divorced. I'm sure Mr. Winfield didn't plan to use this information in his article, but a lot of people in Howard's circle soon got wind of it, including Sam. It all happened so fast, and I didn't want to upset Howard by mentioning the fact, you see. Oh, it's all such an awful mess."

The vicar returned with a cup of communion wine, which he put to Howard's lips. Howard finally revived, gasping and sputtering. He seemed dazed, however, and when he tried to talk he was incoherent. The ambulance attendants who arrived on the scene a few minutes later decided it would be best to take him to hospital.

Soon after recovering from what amounted to a mild nervous breakdown, Howard returned to America, accompanied by Frank. One may well wonder how I was bearing up in the aftermath of this shock. Of course, I was initially *very* dismayed, even angry, to have had my marital plans all dashed in an instant, but I refused to abandon hope.

At his hospital bedside, when he was well enough to receive visitors, Howard convinced me, or perhaps I convinced myself, that his failing to file his final divorce papers was an oversight, a careless error. He had meant to do all that the law required. At the time the business had been so painful he simply hadn't paid sufficient attention to the details. Long afterwards, in his joy at the prospect of marriage with me, he had entirely put the matter from his mind. He never imagined that a little mistake would come back to haunt him in such a devastating manner.

Howard assured me that, upon getting home to New England, he would quickly put his legal house in order, then return with the proper documentation to prove he was a free man. We would resume where we left off—though we both realised we would have to settle for a civil ceremony. No Anglican clergyman was going to marry us in the light of the debacle at St. Columba's.

Alas, in the event it was not so simple, as Howard explained in his voluminous letters to me. The price for Sonia granting him a divorce, he learned bitterly, would be a share of his income. She claimed to have supported him financially during their years together, her lawyers arguing that it was only fair for him to make her restitution. He was, after all, an established author. Then there was the psychological suffering he had caused her. The problem was, Howard's last book, his idiosyncratic fantasy novel, had been a complete flop. Moreover, his other Knopf titles were no longer selling, as a fickle public seemed to be deserting him. His royalty cheques were ever diminishing. He could barely afford his lawyer. At the same time Howard would be damned if he was going to surrender to his former wife's unreasonable demands.

The months dragged on with no settlement. Howard tried fruitlessly to place the manuscript of *The Shadow Over Catalonia*. In the end he was forced to conclude that the Spanish war was no longer fashionable with book publishers, now that Herr Hitler was making such trouble elsewhere in Europe. Howard kept vowing he would return to England to visit, but he was never able to save enough dollars to pay for the trip. And then his aunt was in poor health again, and this added to their financial woes. Efforts to regain employment with the Hal Roach picture studio were to no avail.

After about a year of this unsatisfactory situation, I suggested coming to America, but he discouraged me from making the voyage. When I asked him why not, Howard wrote frankly that he could not bear to face me unless and until he could support me properly. Never again would he place himself in the humiliating position of having to depend on his wife for his very survival. It was clear to me that the emotional cost of his divorce case was distorting his judgement. Gloom and despair were his watchwords.

As for myself, it was a trial to adjust to an indefinite engagement. At first I told my friends to hold on to their wedding gifts—the time would soon come when I could accept them in good conscience as a married woman. Eventually, I had to tell Jane, as I did others, that she should try to return her gift if still possible.

At last a letter arrived from Howard saying that the battle over his divorce was over. He was sparing of the details, and I had to infer that the result was far from his liking. Still, he was once again a bachelor and we could dare dream of a reunion. In addition, his financial picture was looking brighter, thanks to the efforts of his friend Mr. August Derleth. It seems many writers were producing stories that borrowed heavily from Howard's so-called "Cthulhu Mythos," and Mr. Derleth had worked out a licensing arrangement whereby these writers paid Howard a fee for the use of his fictional concepts.

Alas, this good news arrived shortly before Germany invaded Poland and Britain declared war. I had the opportunity to get a berth on one of the ships carrying civilians which sailed regularly to America in those months of the phoney war, but a higher loyalty kept me at home. I joined the W.R.E.N.s, where I soon got caught up in a social whirl involving any number of attractive, single naval officers. By this point, after so many upheavals and disappointments, I was resigned to my fate—that I would in fact never marry Howard P. Lovecraft.

A formal breaking-off of the engagement was unnecessary. As the battle of France gave way to the battle of Britain, Howard's letters became fewer, their tone less personal. I will say, however, that his patriotic fervour, his impassioned support for Britain in her finest hour, never for a moment wavered.

Bobby

Chapter 1

When my train late that gray, overcast morning pulled into Providence's Union Station, after an overnight ride from my home in the Midwest and a brief change-over in Manhattan, I considered myself an extremely lucky fellow. Unlike other new graduate students arriving at Brown University for the first time, I knew precisely where I would be living and how to get there. A Hoosier born and bred, I had never before set foot in "His Majesty's Province of Rhode-Island and Providence-Plantations," but my landlord-to-be had given me *very* thorough instructions, along with an apology for being unable to meet my train in person (he just didn't dare leave the workmen alone for an instant).

As a taxicab whirled me up a steep hill past stately colonial homes and ivy-trimmed university buildings, I got an idea of what Charles Dexter Ward must have felt on returning to the old town from his European travels. But instead of taking me to a great brick house with bayed facade and classic Adam porch, the cab deposited me in front of a three-story Victorian, half-hidden by ladders and scaffolding that couldn't disguise the distinctly Charles Addamsish air of the place. What else was I expecting? After all, this was 454 Angell Street, the birthplace and recently reoccupied home of my literary hero, our century's Edgar Allan Poe, who had generously agreed to my proposal, despite knowing me only through correspondence, to rent me a room in his Gothic manse.

The cabbie kindly carried my hefty suitcase as far as the front door, which was set back on a veranda that ran the length of one side of the house. Before I could press the buzzer, the door swung open—and out of the gloom stepped the fabled author, dressed in a black, old-fashioned suit, looking for all the world like a senior, silver-haired relative of the silent, hulking butler in the Charles

Addams cartoons. In fact, from photos he had sent me at my request, I was well prepared for my first sight of the solemn, grotesquely long face of Mr. H. P. Lovecraft, creator of the Cthulhu Mythos cycle of stories, of which I had been a passionate devotee from age twelve or thirteen.

But the intimidating features lit up as soon as he shook my hand—a quick jerk, not unlike that of a politician in a receiving line—and I immediately felt somewhat more at ease.

"Mr. Robert Pratt, I presume?" he said in a deep stage voice with the hint of an aristocratic Yankee accent.

"Grandpa, uh, sorry, Mr. Lovecraft! I can't tell you what a pleasure it is to meet you in person!" It was one thing to call him "Grandpa," albeit at his insistence, in letters—quite another to address him so familiarly in the flesh.

"Welcome to the House of Lovecraft, Bobby," he replied in a lighter, presumably more normal tone. "Please come in."

I entered a dark, wood-paneled hall, whose predominant color scheme was black and yellow. Hardly what I was expecting, given what I knew of my host's Georgian tastes.

"You may wonder at the ornate decor, but to my naïve and undeveloped aesthetic sense the ebony and gold combination represents the apex of dignified beauty. Such was the front hall in my grandfather Whipple Phillips's day, and so after untold eons has it been restored to its former glory."

Mr. Lovecraft grabbed my suitcase before I could stop him. For a man of seventy he seemed remarkably fit. As he led the way up the exquisitely carved mahogany staircase, he pointed with his free hand toward the front parlor.

"There is again today, as formerly, an almost Oriental richness in that room, as in the palace of a caliph. As a boy I used to read the *Arabian Nights* there with an especial zest."

Glancing to my left, I could see into an overfurnished room whose predominant color scheme appeared to be pink and yellow.

A marble statue of some discreetly draped nymph rested in a niche at a turn in the stairs, while an oversize painting depicting some sylvan scene from classical antiquity dominated the head of the stairs. Sconces with flame-shaped electric bulbs provided just enough light to prevent me from tripping over the Persian carpet on the second-floor landing. (Scaffolding obscured any natural light from the windows.)

Much of the artwork, he allowed, had been in storage since 1904, the year of his grandfather's death, which marked the start of his family's precipitous decline. Happily, as I knew from his letters, the sale of movie rights to several of his stories had brought him a financial windfall. He had tasted such success once before, back in the thirties, but it was only now, thanks to this present boon, that he could realize his life's greatest ambition—the acquisition of the old homestead. Over the decades the place had been profaned and altered, at last transformed into a warren of doctors' offices. He had just been able to outbid a crass developer who wished to clear off the lot, like Wilbur Whateley threatened to clear off the earth, and build some hideous abomination of an apartment block in its stead. Paradise had been regained!

"Wow!" I exclaimed. "You mean to say you've had the house changed back to exactly the way it was when you were a kid?"

"Not exactly, but as near as my pocket book will permit. See here, for example." By now we had reached the third floor, where a narrow twisting corridor took us to an isolated garret room. "I have opened up only one of the old servants bedrooms—which is to be yours, as I wrote you. I hope you will find it to your satisfaction."

He set my suitcase down on a narrow iron bedstead. Of other furniture there was a dresser and mirror, a small table, and a large bookcase. A bit Spartan perhaps, but there was a splendid treetop view from the single gable window.

"Oh, this is *perfect*," I said, wondering if I might be permitted to hang some posters or prints to brighten up the walls. Fresh flowers would also be a big improvement—or should that be an arrangement of deadly nightshade? As before, I couldn't help feeling I'd stepped into a Charles Addams cartoon. Or maybe an H. P. Lovecraft story. What *thing* might be shut up in the attic?

"About half the rooms, chiefly on the second and third floors, remain closed off and unused. Whilst I may be a householder for the first time in my preternaturally extended existence, I am not un-mindful of the high cost of oil heat."

After showing me the bathroom across the hall, Mr. Lovecraft said he would go fix lunch in the kitchen. I should join him there when ready via the backstairs. I was pleased to find the bathroom fitted with all the conveniences, even if there was no shower, just a tub with ball-and-claw feet, and the toilet was the almost forgotten type with chain and overhead tank though plumbers tell us…tell us what? That there are none left in Providence? Not likely. That only an eccentric stuck in the past would favor such an antique commode? I mean, not every situation lends itself to witty Lovecraftian paraphrase!

After washing up and unpacking, I went down to the kitchen, which had a decidedly turn-of-the-century feel—the most modern appliance was an undersized Frigidaire. Or was that a "Cool-aire"? A loaf of French bread lay on the kitchen table, but Mr. Lovecraft was nowhere in sight. Then I heard voices through the open window over the sink. My host was outside, evidently engaged in some earnest conversation.

A door at the rear of the kitchen led out to the yard, where I spotted the Sage of Providence talking with a swarthy individual in paint-spattered overalls. Because there seemed to be some sort of dispute, I kept my distance.

"Mr. Defazio, I still do not understand," Mr. Lovecraft was saying. "How did one of your men get his hands stuck in a window frame he was replacing and another man destroy it in the process of trying to help him out?"

The man said something under his breath, threw up his hands, and walked away. I decided it was safe to approach.

"The last workmen are just finishing their labors," said Mr. Lovecraft with a trace of a smile. "The restoration has been a stupendous task, but because—" Here he paused and gave a short, dry laugh.

"But because it had been the seat of my ancestors I let no expense deter me," I replied, completing the sentence from the opening of "The Rats in the Walls."

"Alas, I am no wealthy retired manufacturer, Bobby, like the ill-fated de la Poer. As I indicated earlier, I can only afford for now to approximate the past. In truth, the house was only the seat of my grandparents, although I suppose by some standards that represents a long heritage. Certainly longer than any of which the excitable Mr. Defazio can boast."

As long as we were outside, Mr. Lovecraft proposed giving me a quick tour of the "estate." The grounds, muddy from recent rain and littered with debris from the workmen, reminded me of the farm in "The Colour Out of Space" in its "blasted heath" phase. Somebody had a formidable gardening and landscaping job ahead of him. For the moment, as part of our deal, I could look forward to raking leaves as the fall progressed and otherwise keeping the yard in trim.

Much had changed since the 1890s. A house now occupied the vacant lot next door where the coachman had built him a combination grand terminal and roundhouse and where he had played railway man with cars made out of packing-cases. Likewise ruthless time had annihilated the barn-like stable on the grounds of 454, though there had been a period after the departure of the coachman, along with the horses and carriages, when he had had the great stable as a gorgeous, glorious, titanic, and unbelievable playhouse.

I could listen to the man rhapsodize about his childhood endlessly—in person he was as mesmerizing as in his letters—but when I asked about dining accommodations on his imaginary railway line, adding that I had eaten nothing on the train from New York, he took the hint and agreed it was time for lunch.

Back in the kitchen, Mr. Lovecraft instructed me to sit at the table while he prepared the food. I offered to help, but didn't push it. In fact I relished being waited on by my god of fiction. Soon enough I would be enrolled in classes and taking most of my meals at the Ratty, the Brown University refectory.

"Do you care for coffee, Bobby?" inquired my host.

"Sure, coffee will be fine, Mr. Lovecraft."

"Would instant be all right?"

"Yes, sir."

"Bobby," said Mr. Lovecraft, turning on the gas under the kettle, "Let us dispense with the formalities. Now that I have entered on my eighth decade it seems only fitting that you, like the vast majority of my friends, should call me 'Grandpa.'"

"Okay…Grandpa," I said, confident that I would soon get used to this familiar form of address.

"I have fancied myself an old gentleman for so long it seems miraculous finally to have reached my dotage."

"You don't seem *that* old to me. How many people your age would willingly take on the responsibilities of looking after a big old house?"

"Thank you, Bobby. I knew there was a reason I agreed to let you be my tenant. How do you take your coffee?"

"With milk please. And sugar."

From a cupboard above the kitchen counter the celebrated author produced a jar full of sugar packets and put it on the table. These turned out to bear the names and logos of a number of New England area restaurants.

"In my youth I was so foolish as to saturate my coffee with sugar, but no more. Too much sugar is unhealthy."

Lunch was indeed simple and healthy—bread and cheese and a lettuce and tomato salad. Grandpa confessed that he used to eat poorly, taking only two meals a day, relying heavily, too heavily, on canned and packaged goods. Then in his mid-forties he lived for a spell in California, where his diet consisted largely of fresh fruits and vegetables. Ever since he had taken care to eat well. Why he had moved to the opposite coast, he discreetly left unmentioned, but I, as a fan of the "Laurel and Hardy" and "Little Rascals" films shown on TV in recent years, needed no explanation.

"What do you miss most about California?" I asked.

"The idyllic weather and the Mexican food, in that order," he answered.

"How about the people you worked with at the Hal Roach Studio?"

"I enjoyed a relationship with my colleagues that was entirely professional."

"I bet you could tell some good stories about your fellow actors."

"No, I have largely forgotten the studio routine. Believe me, Bobby, my career as a minor Hollywood actor was far from glamorous. Perhaps the single most powerful emotional experience of that period was my first glimpse of sunset, all flaming and mystical, into the Pacific Ocean."

"Didn't you meet any really famous movie stars, not just comedians?"

"Not that I remember," he replied matter-of-factly. "As I may have mentioned in my letters, I have always been tremendously sensitive to the *general visual scene*—external, objective, mysterious and full of potential cosmic suggestion—while relatively indifferent to people."

"Did California inspire your writing at all?" I realized I was getting nowhere pursuing the Hollywood line.

"I wrote only one story during my California exile, 'The Shadow Out of Time.' The subtropical vegetation of the region did in part color the prehistoric vistas my disembodied hero sees in his dreams."

"I probably asked you in a letter, Grandpa, but why have you written so few stories?" His epistolary response to this question had been evasive, so I was seizing the opportunity to ask again. "As near as I can figure out, 'The Shadow Out of Time' was about the last thing you published. And it was one of your best!"

I owned a complete set of Lovecraft hardcover editions—the five Knopf volumes, including his scholarly study, *Supernatural Horror in Literature*, all long out of print. In addition I had the World reprint of the best of his supernatural fiction plus assorted paperbacks, notably the Armed Forces editions that came out at the end of World War II. The copyright page listings indicated that he had published no new fiction since the late thirties. I'm of course not counting the various authorized "Mythos" volumes by others that began to appear in the forties and that still on occasion sullied the literary landscape.

"Soon after I began to publish story collections a particularly damning critique from his eminence, Mr. Edmund Wilson, killed my career as a weird fictionist. In the later Depression years I shifted from amateur to professional journalism, focusing on politics and economics."

"Weren't you living in England then? And didn't you fight in the Spanish Civil War?" I had only recently learned these facts, from an old magazine article.

"True, I did have the pleasure of residing in England. And true I did play a less than distinguished part in the Spanish Civil War," he said, reddening. "But all that was long ago. Of late I have returned to one of my earliest passions—science."

"Yes, isn't your latest book *The Cancer of Superstition*?" While I possessed this Lovecraft volume, I had barely cracked the spine.

"Combating the charlatans and crackpots who would foist fads and fallacies in the name of science on a gullible public has become something of a crusade of mine."

"Good for you, Grandpa," I said as sincerely as I could. Frankly, this was an area of interest that held no appeal for me. When I'd casually put in a good word for astrology in one of my letters, I'd received a severely rationalist rebuke, in which he mentioned that a dispute over the purported influence of the stars had led to a lasting break between him and an old friend, a fellow writer and professional astrologer, who had had the temerity to do his chart. Chastened, I never brought up the subject again.

"Superstitious nonsense is no idle threat, Bobby." I finished my lunch while the great man held forth on this topic so obviously close to his heart. I pricked up my ears when he concluded, "That said, I will say your original question prompts a confession."

"Oh, yes?" I wasn't sure what my original question was.

"Very few of my friends and correspondents are in on the secret."

I nodded, eager to be initiated into this select band.

"You remember that as part of our bargain you agreed to do some typing for me?"

"Yes." I'd actually sort of forgotten that part of the bargain, though I'd been willing to promise anything to secure lodgings with my idol.

"I admit it took a while, but I did finally recover from the emotional devastation wreaked by Mr. Wilson's review. In recent years I have been working on a dynastic chronicle or saga dealing with the hereditary mysteries and destinies of an ancient New England family, a family tainted and accursed down the diminishing generations by cosmic outsideness."

"Boy, sounds like you're back to your old form!"

"Despite the distractions of the work on 454 Angell, I have nearly completed the epic. I estimate it will run to some two hundred thousand words. I hope you will be able to spare a few hours from your studies each week to type this monstrosity."

"Goodness me! What an honor!"

"Of course, like any author, I alternate between thinking of it as my magnum opus and thinking of it as a verbose and undistinguished mess, only too worthy of the scorn of the likes of Mr. Wilson."

"Let your readers, not some high-falutin' know-it-all critic, be the judge of that, Grandpa!"

"In all fairness to Mr. Wilson, I hasten to add that the man is extremely erudite and his literary judgments thoroughly sound outside the field of the fantastic. His review of my *Cancer of Superstition* was perceptive and sympathetic. When I wrote him a note of thanks, he responded graciously. We have since exchanged several cordial letters—"

I was curious to hear further comment on Edmund Wilson, but at this juncture the doorbell rang, and my landlord excused himself. He returned a minute later and explained it had been the mailman, bearing a couple of packages that required his signature. He brought a load of what appeared to be mostly personal letters back to the kitchen table. From his suit pocket he produced a pair of reading glasses. I had had some notion that I was only one of many correspondents, but if this was a daily average then it was a wonder he had time to do more with his waking hours than answer his mail.

I cleared the dishes and washed up—how readily I slipped into the servant role!—while Grandpa, wearing his glasses, which gave him a distinctly professorial look, slit open his letters with a penknife and provided a running commentary on their contents. A check from his fellow author August Derleth was especially welcome. As I well knew, Mr. Derleth had started a publishing house in the early forties to publish "Cthulhu Mythos" fiction by other writers. As part of a licensing deal, I now learned, Grandpa received a percentage of the earnings from his imitators. He was grateful to "Comte d'Erlette" for his generosity and foresight in thinking up and enforcing this arrangement—all the more so as the "Wisconsin Thoreau" was by far the leading producer of the derivative stuff.

He was also pleased to hear from an English correspondent, a brilliant young philosopher named Colin Wilson (no relation to Edmund). Despite Wilson's claim to have detected a sado-masochistic strain in the old gentleman's more gruesome work, Grandpa welcomed the epistolary debate fed by his correspondent's outlandish theories and assertions.

"Finally, let us see what 'Sonny' Belknap has to say for himself," he announced. "It has been an age since I heard from the young rascal."

"Are you referring to Frank Belknap Long, author of various tales of the 'Cthulhu Mythos'?"

"Indeed, though I have waived the usual fee in his case. The poor kid needs the money far more than I do."

A passing mention of Long in one of Grandpa's letters had led me to read a couple of the guy's science fiction novels, but I hadn't been impressed. Typical cheap paperback fare.

"My God!" croaked my companion. The penknife dropped unheeded on the kitchen floor. A few strangled phrases from his friend's letter followed:

> *"My romantic recklessness has surprised and astonished me…I met Lyda at the National Arts Club…a romantic and impulsive and a very extraordinary girl in all respects…she has exquisite taste and is brilliant in everything she undertakes… Lyda believes it is much wiser to live every moment to the full and let the future take care of itself…we are both very much in love…"*

"Are you okay, Grandpa?" I asked in alarm. At that moment he looked like a de la Poer scion who'd just read the ancestral letter detailing the revolting hereditary rituals practiced below Exham Priory.

"By God, Bobby, *Sonny has eloped*!"

Chapter 2

Why a pal's tying the knot should so upset Grandpa was far from clear to me. Was he hurt to be informed after the fact? Was he jealous? I'd heard that wives could undermine male friendships.

"Listen to this," Grandpa continued after recovering from his initial shock. "The impetuous imp says he proposed to this Lyda Arco person after knowing her only a week! The Maryland marriage was his idea, because there was no waiting or red tape!"

"Do you think Mr. Long is too young?" I asked.

"Too young? Belknap is fifty-eight years old!"

"And Miss Arco?"

"He declines to give her age, although her being 'a psychiatric nurse, a gifted singer, a poet, a painter, and an art promoter' indicates a certain maturity."

"If she's that talented, she must make good money."

"Alas, it would seem not. Belknap says here that the woman lost her job with a Park Avenue internist three days after they were married. Let me quote you: 'Getting the right job will take time, as she has executive qualifications and executive jobs are very scarce right now in New York.'"

Grandpa removed his glasses and sighed. In a voice more sad than angry he said, "Poor Sonny, for all his excitement and optimism, I fear he and his bride may face a rocky road ahead."

I was aware that Grandpa had once been married. When we first corresponded I asked him a lot of probing personal questions. Without being too specific, he'd admitted that financial trouble had dogged his marriage from the start. Within a year he and his wife had separated. Divorce proceedings, incomplete on a technicality, had ultimately led to a costly court battle that had left him nearly ruined. I knew enough not to point out the obvious parallel between his own experience and what he projected might be that of his close friend.

For the moment there was nothing more to say on the subject of Frank Long and his dubious marriage. Grandpa suggested we finish the house tour. Once more I passed through the ebony and gold front hall and followed my host up the mahogany staircase, though at the head of the stairs he took a different turn from last time. At the end of a long corridor lined with bookcases he opened a door to an empty corner room that he said had once been his mother's. None of her furnishings had survived, but he intended eventually to make it his guest room. With a fireplace and two exposures it had the potential, I agreed, to be a pleasant place for overnight visitors.

Rather perfunctorily Grandpa showed me the former bedrooms of his aunt and his grandparents. All I could see were piles of boxes. These boxes, he said, contained his collections of newspaper cuttings, amateur press publications, travel brochures, and miscellaneous printed items. He planned eventually to organize these materials and put them in proper storage compartments. He saved the study, which had once been his grandfather's office, for last.

Here, finally, was a room, despite the drawn shades, that looked lived in. Bookshelves and filing cabinets lined the walls, while among the pieces of furniture were a dresser, a Windsor chair, a typing stand, and a large central table heaped with papers and magazines. An Oriental carpet covered most of the floor. Nearly every inch of wall space was filled with pictures, including a number of drawings by such artist friends as Virgil Finlay and Clark Ashton Smith. One print of a Welsh village he'd acquired while living in England. A couple of insipid landscapes in oil Grandpa proudly identified as the work of his mother.

"Golly, this looks cozy. But where do you…sleep?" Between a lamp and a bookcase was a door that looked as if it might lead to a small bedroom.

"Well you might ask," said Grandpa. "Let me show you." Opening the door, he revealed a closet holding an upright Murphy bed. "I roll it out whenever Morpheus beckons."

"How come with so much space you don't have a separate bedroom?"

"Old habits die hard, Bobby. I have become so used to working and sleeping in the same room over the years I cannot as yet contemplate any other arrangement."

I guessed that Grandpa hadn't shared his bed with anyone in a very long time. Perhaps not since his brief marriage.

On top of the bookcase next to the closet I noticed a framed letter. On closer inspection this turned out to be a fan letter from President Franklin Delano Roosevelt dated 1935. Very impressive! Also in a seeming place of honor atop this bookcase were two yellowed issues of the *Saturday Evening Post*. Grandpa explained that these contained his tale of alien miscegenation in a decadent Massachusetts seaport, "The Shadow Over Innsmouth." It was the first and last time that one of his hell-beaters slipped past the editorial guardians of this popular bastion of literary Babbitry.

This same bookcase held on its lower shelves a complete run of *Weird Tales* and miscellaneous issues of various other pulps. He used to throw away his story manuscripts after they achieved magazine publication, but at a certain point he learned to save them. A Providence friend and journalist, Winfield Townley Scott, now resident in New Mexico, had once tried to persuade him to donate his papers to Brown University's John Hay Library, but he sincerely doubted a prestigious institution like the Hay would be interested in his scribblings.

Another bookcase I saw was largely devoted to his own works. Besides the familiar Knopf and the austerely designed British editions from the thirties, there were a fair number of paperback reprints and, new to me, several recent French translations. He admitted that he was particularly pleased that one French critic had hailed him as "ce nouvel Edgar Poe." The French had also translated a number of Cthulhu Mythos anthologies that had gained equally admiring reviews.

Grandpa confirmed that the American hardcover editions of his fiction were out of print. His friend August Derleth, however, had been pestering him of late about collecting all his tales into a single omnibus volume. Such a book Grandpa estimated would be about the size of a Modern Library Giant. He was far from sure this large format made sense. In any event, he and Derleth had agreed that his novel in progress should be published first.

"Do you have a title for your new novel?" I asked.

"Provisionally I am calling it *The House of the Worm*. Here, let me show you part one. It is a ghastly thing."

From the central desk Grandpa picked up a batch of manuscript pages and handed them to me. I could see right away that it would be a ghastly thing to type. The penciled text was written in a minute script filled with crossings-out and complicated interlineations. As in his letters, he seemed unfamiliar with margins.

"I can't wait to get started, Grandpa, but right now I could really use a breath of fresh air. Would you mind if I took a walk around the neighborhood?"

"I would offer you my services as a guide, Bobby, but I feel I should remain at home in case I need to consult again with the at times less than competent workmen. May I lend you a map of College Hill?"

"The music department sent me a campus map. Thank you. If I don't get back till late, though, could you recommend a place to eat?" Having been treated to lunch, I dared not further impose by also expecting dinner.

Grandpa suggested any of several low-cost eateries on Thayer Street, gave me a house key to keep, and said not to worry about disturbing him on my return. He was invariably up well past midnight.

I would later wish that Grandpa had accompanied me, or that I had lingered at the house longer that afternoon, despite the threat of having to start typing his manuscript, for as it turned out our subsequent interactions would be all too rare. On my initial tour of the College Hill neighborhood I stopped at a book shop near the Brown campus and purchased a notebook in which I intended, à la Boswell, to record the great man's conversation. In the next three months I would barely fill three pages.

I was soon immersed in my graduate studies, a seminar on the great nineteenth-century Italian opera composers being my principal delight, and was out the door every morning on my way to classes long before he got up. While Grandpa had expressed polite interest in my passion for classical music in his letters, in person he showed little inclination to discuss the subject, pleading a tin ear. He preferred the long-forgotten popular songs of the turn of the century.

He was, to my disappointment, underwhelmed when I played him LPs of *My Fair Lady* and *Camelot*—on a used record player I had to invest in because he possessed only an old gramophone that once belonged to his late aunt.

Grandpa had an equally ancient and bulky radio, to which he hardly ever listened. The one notable exception was election night, when he stayed up to cheer Senator Kennedy's narrow victory over Vice-President Nixon. Where he had at one time been an anti-capitalist democratic socialist, he was now, he told me, a plain old Democrat. Needless to say, there was no television in the house.

Grandpa's idea of fun was to go for a long walk or a lecture at Brown or R.I.S.D. or one of the local museums. One evening I caught him leaving the house carrying, of all things, a mathematics textbook. This prompted the sheepish confession that he was going to night school in order to pass his high school equivalency test. He had been working toward this end for years, and if he passed his math exam in January, math having nearly killed him in his student days, he would at last earn his high school diploma. He asked that I keep this information under my hat. This was evidently a greater secret than his work on *The House of the Worm*.

The last movie Grandpa had seen was *Psycho*. He was a great admirer of Hitchcock, but his chief interest in this disturbing film was its having been based on a novel by a friend of his, Robert Bloch, who was doing far better in Hollywood than he ever did.

At home Grandpa occupied himself primarily with reading and writing. The sole telephone, located in the kitchen, seldom rang, and not once to my knowledge did he get together with a friend of either sex socially. He did on occasion exchange a neighborly word with Mr. Wright, who with his family lived in the house next door that now occupied the former vacant lot.

Grandpa used to travel a great deal, but with work still remaining on the new house he had no plans to go anywhere for the foreseeable future. When I asked him if he hoped someday to return to England, he said that London had suffered so severely during the blitz he couldn't bear the idea of going back and seeing the damage—or the contemporary so-called architecture that desecrated the sites of so many lost Georgian treasures.

Grandpa did, however, proceed with his plans to create a guest room. To this end he enlisted my help in furnishing his mother's former room. He had considered getting a single or at most a pair of twin beds, but I insisted that he get a double—just in case any couples came to visit. In the end he conceded the wisdom of my choice, though he left it to me to select queen-sized sheets. For him bed linens seemed about as unmentionable as ladies' underwear.

Because it was sunny, the future guest room initially served as my study. When I wasn't raking leaves or doing light chores around the house (most of my studying I did at the university library), I was busy typing the manuscript of *The House of the Worm*. With practice I mastered Grandpa's inscrutable scrawl, and at times could produce as much as a thousand words at a sitting, though the effort always left me feeling on the verge of nervous collapse.

What can I say about Grandpa's masterpiece? From the opening it appeared to be a far more ambitious variation on the themes of *The Case of Charles Dexter Ward*. Where summary had sufficed to describe Ward's lengthy European travels, here the time-defying hero's adventures in such places as London and Paris and even the Basque region of Spain received the full technicolor, panoramic treatment. One could believe the author had visited the places he wrote about. Providence and its history again assumed a central role, but Southern California was also a living presence. Bolton, a passing name in Grandpa's fiction, was now a major focus of supernatural shenanigans. Grandpa confessed that when he first mentioned the town in such tales as "The Picture in the House" and "Herbert West—Reanimator," he was unaware that there really was a Bolton, Massachusetts!

In addition, *The House of the Worm* had a psychological complexity only hinted at in such late tales as "The Thing on the Doorstep" and "The Shadow Out of Time." Charles Dexter Ward was a stock figure, a single-minded fanatic, but in this late epic the hero actually grew, his personal concerns forming a poignant balance to the cosmic intrusions that threaten civilization. Female family relationships figured in a way they never had before in the Lovecraft canon. And the style was fully mature, a perfect blend of formal and vernacular language. There were even some passable attempts at dialogue, though transcripts of letters, diaries, and other hand-written documents mainly punctuated the narrative.

When I praised the novel to Grandpa, he made his usual self-deprecatory remarks, but I knew he was pleased. Despite his lack of confidence, he had to realize that this was his best work to date, a triumphant return to the weird realm after years of pursuing lesser literary paths.

By comparison, I became acutely aware, the Cthulhu Mythos fiction from the pens of others was all too painfully pedestrian or worse. How could he bear to allow his concepts to be so bastardized? When I pointed out the faults of his imitators, Grandpa refused to say an ill word against any of them. Pressed further, he conceded merely that time would ultimately vindicate quality.

On certain questions of literary merit, Grandpa didn't hold back on expressing his views. When I asked him if he was familiar with the work of the poet Allen Ginsberg, he said he most certainly was. In the past year he had taken particular offense at a so-called poem of Mr. Ginsberg's entitled "A Supermarket in California," a sort of paean to that erratic and degraded bard, Walt Whitman. Incensed ("'eyeing the grocery boys' indeed!"), he had sent the bearded beatnik a poem of his own on Whitman that spoke for the sounder faction of American taste, but had yet to receive a reply.

On Oscar Wilde he was even more scathing. Since I'd been a Wilde admirer for nearly as long as I'd been a Lovecraft fan, I couldn't help feeling a bit dismayed. At any rate, I got the message that if Grandpa was indifferent to sex in general he was positively hostile to sexual deviance.

Of modern writers he spoke reverently of George Orwell, author of the magnificently grim *Nineteen Eighty-four*, and Arthur Machen, author of that exquisite autobiography of the mind, *The Hill of Dreams*. He had been privileged to count both men as friends whilst living in London. One of Orwell's least appreciated works, in his view, was the man's personal account of fighting in the Spanish Civil War, *Homage to Catalonia*. In the late thirties Grandpa had tried his hand at a similar narrative, based on his far less heroic experiences in Spain, but had never found a publisher for *The Shadow Over Catalonia*.

He lamented the passing of his fellow New Englander, J. P. Marquand, over the summer. It was a pity that Marquand never equaled *The Late George Apley*, but to have produced one masterpiece in a lifetime was more than most writers could boast.

Among living authors he was partial to Barbara Pym and Anthony Powell. Miss Pym's wry novels of genteel spinsters and church jumble sales struck a particular chord, perhaps because they reminded him of certain appealing aspects of English life. As for Mr. Powell, who had favorably reviewed the British edition of *The Case of Charles Dexter Ward*, his multi-volume chronicle, *The Music of Time*, gave an incomparable, and highly amusing, portrait of the better class of Englishman in the interwar period. Grandpa's one concern was that he wouldn't live long enough to see the completion of the saga. In the most recent volume, *Casanova's Chinese Restaurant*, he was sure he detected a trace of the late George Orwell in the figure of Lord Erridge, the eccentric leftwing revolutionary who goes to Spain to fight in the civil war.

Before leaving Providence to join my family in New York for Thanksgiving (my parents had decided this was a convenient meeting spot for us all), I was bold enough to ask Grandpa if he had any regrets in his life (other than possibly not finishing *A Dance to the Music of Time*). Looking back over the years, was there anything he wished he had done differently? Grandpa thought for a while, then declared that his greatest regret was having failed to produce a child. His closest relatives were second cousins on his mother's side whom he rarely saw. The Lovecraft name would die with him. His modest literary output was his only legacy.

When I returned to Providence after the Thanksgiving break, Grandpa called me into his study. From his grave demeanor I braced for bad news. Was he unhappy with how slowly I was coming on typing the manuscript of *The House of the Worm*? Was he going to raise my rent if I didn't get cracking?

After inquiring about my Thanksgiving and my impressions of New York, he said, "Bobby, have you and your family made plans for Christmas?"

"I expect I'll be going home to Goshen."

"Do you know when?"

"We didn't discuss dates. I just assumed I'd leave Providence as soon as vacation starts."

"I have a favor to ask. Might you consider not leaving right away for Indiana? I have house guests due a few days before Christmas who plan to stay through the holidays. I would be infinitely grateful if you could be present to lend a hand when they first arrive."

"I don't see why not. Who are they?"

"Mr. and Mrs. Frank Belknap Long, Junior."

Chapter 3

The week before Christmas I helped Grandpa erect a tall spruce in the ebony and gold front hall, next to the mahogany staircase. He had not put up a Christmas tree in twenty years, not since before his aunt died, but he still had a goodly supply of lights and ornaments. These were no family heirlooms, he added, merely cheap replacements purchased from Woolworth's in the thirties.

As we went about the tree trimming, he reminisced about Christmases past. Before the war he usually spent the week following Christmas in New York, visiting friends from his days of exile in the "pest zone." (What had made life there endurable were the regular meetings of his informal literary gang, the "Kalem Club.") Invariably he stayed with Belknap and his parents, who were always the most gracious and generous of hosts. Christmas celebrations chez Long were among his fondest memories. Tragically, when Frank B. Long, Senior, a dental surgeon, died in 1940, he left no savings to support his wife and writer son. The Long family fortunes plunged just as precipitously as the Lovecraft ones had in 1904.

After Mrs. Long's death in 1950 following a long illness that entailed high hospital bills, the last of the Longs was virtually penniless. The pulp markets had nearly disappeared by then, and despite zealous efforts to churn out paperback novels Frank could barely afford the rent on a studio apartment in an unfashionable part of Brooklyn. The move into Manhattan with his bride was at least a step up. The painful truth was that Frank had only himself to blame for his present financial plight. In his youth he should have pursued other, more reliably paying work in case he couldn't support himself solely by his pen. Grandpa's career had taken a similar course, but he had been far luckier and eventually found his salvation in professional journalism.

"So come the Yule," I said, as I leaned over the banister and hung the last, cat-faced bulb on a slender branch, "the Longs will journey to ancient Providence to keep festival with you."

"Only the poor and the lonely remember," quipped Grandpa, "not that I suppose poor Frank feels very lonely these days hitched to the old ball and chain."

"How long do the Longs plan to stay?"

Grandpa had stepped back and was surveying the big tree with a skeptical eye. There were some spots in the greenery that begged for another dozen or so ornaments to fill the gaps.

"We have yet to discuss the matter," he said, "although they are welcome to impose on the Old Gentleman almost indefinitely. Now that it is within my means to do so, how can I refuse them the hospitality Doc and Mrs. Long once so freely extended me? As an early Christmas present, I have sent them roundtrip first-class train tickets, with open returns."

As darkness began to set in on the shortest day of the year, I was the one who answered the phone and accepted the collect call from New York. The thin, whiny man's voice at the other end said that they had missed their train but would surely catch the next one. They were still at home, packing. At the time Grandpa was taking one of his increasingly rare walks, given the ever more seasonable weather. (Being extremely sensitive to low temperatures, he couldn't stay out in the cold for long.) When I told him this news on his return, he expressed the hope that the reserved tickets would be valid on a later train.

On his walk, Grandpa informed me, he had purchased a bottle of sherry at a liquor store. While he might be a teetotaler, he was no Puritan and wanted to be able to offer his guests a drop if they desired one. In our correspondence I'd gathered that he frowned on drinking, so as his tenant I'd been careful not to imbibe alcoholic beverages in his presence.

That night I did some more typing of *The House of the Worm*. Since the guest room was shortly to be occupied, I had on Grandpa's instructions converted one of the vacant rooms on the third floor to an office, to which I removed both typewriter and manuscript. Around midnight, I went downstairs to check on the Old Gentleman, who was studying an advanced algebra textbook before the fire in the Arabian Nights parlor. I'd just announced I was too weary to stay up any longer when we heard a car pull up out front and cut its motor. Then a car door slammed and there was a loud commotion as of several people talking at once. The noise grew louder, and we knew the guests had finally arrived. Grandpa reached the front door just as the bell sounded.

The porch light had been left on, so we had a clear view of the trio that stood revealed on the doorstep. In a prima donna voice a short corpulent woman dressed in a crimson coat and matching fur hat was haranguing a man, evidently a cab driver, to be careful with her guitar, which he was propping up against a steamer trunk. At her side, an elfin, goateed fellow, similarly bundled up if in a drab, ill-fitting overcoat, was muttering as he carefully counted out a handful of change.

"Hullo, Howard," said Frank Long, giving a nervous nod in the direction of his friend. "I'd like you to meet the girl who has made me the happiest man in the world. Dear, this is Howard."

"How do you do, madam," said Grandpa, bowing. "I hope you enjoyed a pleasant train ride."

"Train ride?" exclaimed Lyda. "What train ride? We came by bus!"

"Yes, that's right," chimed in Frank. "Lyda quite sensibly realized it would be a lot cheaper to take the bus. We had to go to Penn Station first, though, to cash in the tickets you sent us. A big nuisance *that* was, let me tell you."

"Please come in," said Grandpa, betraying no annoyance at this capricious change of plan.

It was at this moment that I noticed that Lyda walked with a crutch, as if she were crippled.

"Do you need any help?" I blurted. I'd been lurking in the shadows, but now seemed the moment to present myself.

"Allow me to introduce Robert Pratt," said Grandpa. "He is my—"

"Butler!" shrieked Lyda. "You rich people have all the amenities. And what a handsome boy he is, too!"

"Can I help you with your bags?" I said. If I'd felt any offense at being mistaken for the butler, I was instantly mollified by her

compliment. Anyhow, she wasn't so far off the mark. What was I after all but a well-educated house boy?

"Yes, you certainly may," responded Lyda. "Our chauffeur should have the rest of our luggage shortly."

The steamer trunk and the guitar were only the beginning. I joined the cab driver in lugging several suitcases, hat boxes, and shopping bags filled with papers and what-not into the front hall. Evidently the Longs were prepared to spend the winter in Providence if need be. As the cabbie left, I noticed Grandpa slip him an extra dollar.

"Well, here we are at last at the home of that celebrated author, Horace P. Lovecraft," said Lyda, removing her fur hat to reveal carrot-red hair done up in an untidy bun. "At first I didn't believe Frankele when he said you, a lowly horror writer, could afford to live in a palace. I'm very impressed. It's clear you have excellent taste—for a Victorian."

"I should explain," said Grandpa evenly, "that this house used to belong to my grandfather Phillips. I have made every attempt to restore it to period, which is of course late Victorian. My own tastes, I should say—"

"Bah! Don't apologize," said Lyda, as she shrugged off her coat, underneath which she was wearing a dazzling peacock shawl and beaded black gypsy dress. "This dark heavy look suits your personality. Before you hit the big time were you an undertaker?"

Grandpa gave a short, dry laugh. What else could he do?

"After you're gone this place will make the perfect funeral home."

"Dear, give Howard our gift," said Frank, who had the sense to change the subject.

From one of the shopping bags Lyda produced a bottle of Russian vodka. It didn't look like one of the premium brands, and was about two-thirds full. "It got cold on the bus, so we each had a nip," she said. "I hope you don't mind."

Grandpa gave another short laugh and said nothing. How strange to see him at a loss for words! When, seemingly paralyzed, he made no move to accept this unexpected Christmas present, I took it and placed it under the tree.

"I tried to explain to Lyda that you weren't much of a drinker," said Frank, "but she wouldn't listen. I promise we'll get you something you really like later on."

By now Frank had removed his hat and coat. With his wavy gray hair and worn tweed sportcoat and shiny flannel trousers, he cut a dapper if slightly seedy figure—a latter-day Edgar Allan Poe perhaps, had Poe survived into his late fifties. At Grandpa's biding, I took the guests' coats and hung them in the front hall closet.

Tired from their journey, the Longs said they were ready to turn in immediately. Getting them and their belongings upstairs and into the guest room was, however, a major exercise. A team of obliging ghouls to handle all the luggage would have been handy. Lyda could proceed up the stairs only slowly, clutching the banister. She was quite free with her comments on the Christmas tree, pitying her host for not having more and better ornaments. Before retiring to his study for the night, Grandpa for the first time, I thought, truly looked his age. I couldn't get up to the third floor and in bed fast enough myself.

Nobody arose early the next morning. I was eating breakfast in the kitchen around eleven when first Grandpa and then Frank appeared, the former fully dressed in his usual formal casual attire of white shirt and dark trousers, the latter in a ratty brown bathrobe and slippers. Frank poured some coffee to bring up to Lyda, along with some toast and cold cereal.

"She said she expected the butler to provide room service," grumbled Frank good-naturedly before mounting the backstairs with a tray, "but she'll just have to settle for her humble husband. Don't bother to make anything for me—I'll just share some of her food."

After Frank left, Grandpa gave me an imploring look, muttered something about needing to go do his algebra homework, then stalked out of the kitchen. I felt guilty. The next day I was scheduled to leave Providence for the Midwest. How was he going to cope with the Longs on his own? But I could only do so much. I had already done enough grocery shopping to last a week—and I was in fact looking forward to fixing dinner that evening, a genuine Yule feast.

In the afternoon, while I was baking cookies in the kitchen, Frank wandered in and asked if I wouldn't mind taking Lyda some tea. She had said she was curious to talk to me. In the meantime he had some very important things to discuss with Howard, so the longer I engaged Lyda in conversation the better.

How could I refuse? Anyway, I was curious, too. She seemed so much more lively than her timid, self-effacing husband. So I prepared a proper pot of tea, set it on Grandpa's nicest tray with cups and saucers and a plate of chocolate chip cookies straight out of the oven, and proceeded upstairs.

In response to my knock on the guest-room door I heard a shrill cry of "Come in!"

Lyda was sitting up in the queen-sized bed, in a pink dressing gown, her fiery hair hanging loose to her shoulders. On her nose was a pair of flared, ruby-red reading glasses. The bed itself was covered with an array of magazines and newspapers. Clothes were strewn over the dresser, the armchair, the floor, everywhere.

"Thank you for my tea, Jeeves," she said, shifting some of the papers to make space for the tray.

I had to navigate around some half-unpacked suitcases, and just managed to avoid stumbling over her crutch.

"It's cold in here. That boss of yours is too cheap to turn up the heat!"

"Would you like me to light the fire?" Earlier I had laid a fire in the guest-room fireplace. It had turned decidedly colder that day, and Grandpa may have forgotten to adjust the thermostat.

"No, on second thought, why don't you just bring me my shawl. It's hanging over the radiator."

I brought her the shawl, which was patterned with pink roses.

"How gorgeous," I said, as I helped her drape it around her shoulders.

"It's Russian—like me!" she proclaimed. "Here, sit down on the bed and have some tea. You must tell me all about yourself."

"What is there to say?" I said, perching demurely on the edge of the bedcover.

"Don't be coy. Tell me about your people. Where do they come from?"

I began to tell her about my parents and my upbringing in Indiana, but when I incidentally mentioned my love of music Lyda interrupted. She also was a music lover. The next thing I knew I was listening to a lengthy monologue about herself, starting with her birth in Russia to actor parents, both of whom had been prominent in the Yiddish theater in czarist days. Her father's name was Arco. Childhood polio in one leg had ruled out a career for Lydasha on the stage. Her family had escaped to China after the Russian Revolution, and eventually made their way to Canada and later the United States. From among the newspapers and magazines she pulled out a number of old clippings, many in Yiddish, about one member or another of her illustrious family.

I was able to have more of a back-and-forth conversation with her ladyship when the subject got on to contemporary music. She claimed to know everyone of importance in New York connected with the theatrical and classical music worlds. I was enthralled. When I complimented her on the quality of her voice, she proudly admitted that she had received some training as an opera singer and had once performed as part of a program at Carnegie Recital Hall.

After about an hour of this I said I had to go back to the kitchen to resume dinner preparations. But Lyda wouldn't let me go until she had expressed her views on horror fiction and horror writers, a species that was totally unknown to her before she married Frank. Based on the horror people she'd met so far, they were utterly uncouth and uncultured, the worst riffraff, especially the fans. I couldn't let this judgment pass without asserting that I was a horror fan. And how could she dismiss Grandpa as "uncultured"? She simply answered that I was a nice boy, the exception which proved the rule.

That evening the gentlemen met in the Arabian Nights parlor for the "cocktail hour," no doubt the first time such a ritual had been observed in the Lovecraft household. I put out the bottle of sherry, with crystal glasses, on the coffee table. Frank, decked out in an old-fashioned smoking jacket, filled a glass, from which he thirstily drank in between trying to light his pipe with a large silver cigarette lighter. Grandpa, in sober black, sipped a ginger ale that I provided from the kitchen. I poured myself a ginger ale as well, since the chef needed to stay alert. The two older men scarcely spoke, seemingly having exhausted their conversational store after their long afternoon tête-à-tête.

The sound of her crutch on the stair announced the arrival of Lyda, a good half-hour after the rest of us had assembled. She made a stunning entrance, in her crimson off-the-shoulder gown, scarlet lipstick and nails, and matching cigarette holder. She had arranged her orange hair in an elaborate coiffe. Frank hastened to light her cigarette and escort her to a seat on the room's most elaborate piece of furniture, a horsehair sofa. Frank sat beside her, and soon was puffing contentedly on his pipe. Lyda, casting a disdainful eye on the sherry bottle, asked for a martini. Since the vodka bottle was already open, there was no reason to stand on ceremony and I retrieved it from under the tree. A minute or two later I served her a vodka martini *sans* vermouth.

When Lyda asked Grandpa about his musical tastes, his terse answers didn't satisfy her. She had heard of none of the old tunes he mentioned, and was unfamiliar with the names Leroy Shield and Marvin Hatley, as was I for that matter. Grandpa seemed in no mood to elaborate. There was a long silence, during which I considered suggesting we crank up the Victrola that once belonged to Grandpa's aunt or bring my modern record player downstairs, but Lyda saved the day by ordering me to go get her guitar. She would give a solo performance.

I listened to about five minutes of the recital—snatches of operatic passages, accompanied by not unmelodic if unrelated strumming of the guitar strings—before excusing myself and retreating to the kitchen. I left Frank refilling his sherry glass, and Grandpa doing a passable imitation of a night-gaunt at rest.

Soon after Lyda came stumping into the kitchen. In her opinion "Horace" was a musical idiot. She needed to talk to someone with culture. I rose again to Grandpa's defense, but then she spotted the telephone on the wall by the refrigerator and in the next instant she was dialing somebody she knew in New York. She in fact got through to several friends, some on the west coast apparently, before I took the roast beef out of the oven.

Since what had once been the Phillips family dining room was shut off and out of commission (given over to Wilbur Whateley's twin brother perhaps?), we ate around the kitchen table. Lyda was kind enough to light the candles. Along with the roast beef, cooked a perfect medium rare, if I do say so myself, there were scalloped potatoes and succotash (if you don't know what succotash is, ask a New Englander).

"Frankele talks about you all the time, Horace," Lyda began once we were all seated. "And what's so special about H. P. Lovecraft,

Esquire? I ask. What has he written that I've heard of? Do his books make the best-seller lists? Do literate people recognize his name?"

Ever the stoic, Grandpa did not deign to reply.

"And who is he to charge other writers for using his ideas," the woman continued, "when he's too lazy to write a word himself. Is that fair, I ask you?"

"Are you ready for a glass of sherry, Lyda?" I said. Somebody had to try to switch the subject.

"No, but I'm ready for another martini, young man. And could you bring me my shawl? This old kitchen is drafty. Thank you."

Once her glass was replenished and her shoulders covered, Lyda resumed the offensive.

"Frank tells me you were once a movie actor. In your biggest role you played a living corpse. Sounds to me like perfect typecasting."

I suppose I could have done more to distract Lyda, but I have to say that after a while I took a guilty pleasure in her outrageous pronouncements. For his part Grandpa steadfastly refused to be provoked. If Frank was embarrassed by his wife's behavior, he showed no sign of it as he wolfed down everything on his plate. Besides myself, he was the only one to have seconds, helping himself to more beef, which I'd been keeping warm in the oven.

As I cleared the dishes and prepared dessert—bowls of coffee ice cream and Christmas cookies—Lyda got on to the subject of marriage.

"Frank tells me you once eloped with a Russian Jew, Horace," she said. "I find that hard to believe."

Grandpa made no comment.

"I understand you didn't tell a soul. Whatsamatter, were you ashamed of your bride? Were you afraid those stuck-up Yankee relatives of yours would disapprove?"

Again Grandpa deigned not to reply. Then in a less accusatory voice, she said:

"They say imitation is the sincerest form of flattery, so Frank had to go ahead and marry a Russian Jew, too!"

Lyda claimed to have had several husbands, or perhaps only lovers. By this point she was on her fourth "martini" and not everything she said made sense. At any rate, the men in her life had all been distinguished and virile, each a highly accomplished musician or artist, but in the end she had settled on Frankele, who was like a child.

"So naïve, so unassuming! How could I not fall in love with him?" she trilled.

"What do you mean naïve? What do you mean unassuming?" said Frank testily.

"So unworldy. So innocent. Like a little boy—and later I learn he's fifty-nine years old!"

"I beg your pardon, madam, but if I am not mistaken your husband is fifty-eight years old," said Grandpa, finally showing some fight. "Perhaps you meant to say that Frank is in his fifty-ninth year."

"Frank was born on April 27, 1901," she thundered, emphasizing the oh-one. "You do the arithmetic."

"Belknap," said Grandpa faintly, "You told me you were born in 1902."

"No, Howard," said Frank in a peevish voice, as he emptied the last of the sherry into his glass, "I never told you that."

"Then how…"

"Remember when we first met, in April of '22, in New York? I told you then I was twenty. What you didn't realize was that I was almost twenty-one. A year later, when you sent me that coming-of-age poem for my birthday, I didn't have the heart to tell you I'd turned twenty-two."

"And I have been deceived ever since," said Grandpa. "For thirty-eight years I have had my favorite grandson's age wrong."

"All this time I've been worrying you'd find out, but now that we've both got one foot in grave, what does it matter?" Then turning to me, Frank said, "These cookies are delicious, by the way. They taste almost like homemade."

On this note the party ended. Grandpa bade everyone a hasty good-night and shuffled off into the shadows. The Yule spirit, such as it was, seemed to have utterly deserted him. The Longs soon followed, though first I had to retrieve Lyda's guitar from the parlor. I left the dirty dishes soaking in the sink, blew out the candles, and retreated to my third-floor eyrie, where I did some packing in anticipation of my early departure the next day. Around midnight I collapsed into bed and fell instantly asleep.

Chapter 4

I don't know if I smelled the smoke or heard the crackling of wood first, but all of a sudden I was wide awake. Outside the gable window there was a rosy glow bright enough to enable me to read my watch. It was a few minutes past three o'clock. I sprang out of bed, threw open the sash, and immediately an acrid burning smell assaulted my nostrils. As my eyes started to water, I could see below and to the right flames shooting out of a second-floor window. A muffled female cry of "You idiot!" confirmed that it was a window to the guest room.

As fast as I could I pulled on my bathrobe and stepped into my slippers before racing down the back stairs to the second floor. The hallway was dark, but then the guest-room door opened and out staggered Frank and Lyda, coughing and sputtering, dressed in their night clothes. I took one look inside the room, and saw that the bed and half the furniture were ablaze. Smoke poured out into the hallway.

Two things were clear—first, someone had to call the fire department, and second, we all had to get out of the house. I bolted down the backstairs to the kitchen, trusting the Longs would follow close behind. To my horror, when I turned on the kitchen light, I discovered that the telephone had disappeared from the kitchen counter. Later I would learn that Lyda had noticed a phone jack in the guest room and sometime in the early morning had ordered Frank to retrieve the telephone from the kitchen, because she preferred to ring people from the comfort of her bed.

When the Longs didn't appear, I ran back up to the second floor, where in the light of the flames now leaping from the doorway of the guest room I spotted them hobbling toward the front stairs, Lyda supported by her crutch on one side and by Frank on the other. Later Lyda would tell me that she went the longer route to safety because she was sure the main staircase would be far easier for her to get down than the steep and treacherous back stairs.

Then it hit me that we hadn't seen Grandpa. I dashed through the smoke and flame and burst into his study yelling, "Fire!" Since I'd never been inside his room at this hour of the night, I barged right into the Murphy bed, barking my shin. My scream of pain had the salutary effect of waking up the Old Gentleman from what must have been a profound slumber. "Good Lord!" exclaimed a sleepy-sounding Grandpa. "What the devil is going on?"

One of us finally switched on a light, and there before me in his bare feet and old-fashioned flannel nightshirt stood my literary idol. In the next instant Grandpa grasped that the house was on fire and we had to exit as fast as possible. We caught up with the Longs floundering near the top of the stairs. Here in the beneficent glow of the Christmas tree lights, which had been left on, we consulted briefly. Against her protests the three of us men lifted Lyda and carried her, shrieking all the way, to the bottom of the stairs. We paused only long enough in the front hall to grab our winter coats and hats from the closet.

Once outside we hurried as fast as we could across the lawn to Mr. Wright's house next door. Luckily, we didn't have to bang long on his door before we were let in. It seems the noise of the fire and the smell of smoke had aroused Mr. Wright, who reported that his wife had just called the fire department.

Grandpa had barely passed his neighbor's threshold when he gasped, "My God! My manuscript. *The House of the Worm*!"

Before anyone could stop him, he was loping back across the lawn, his overcoat flapping in the light from his burning house. I ran after him. By now sheets of flame had engulfed the top two stories at the rear of 454 Angell. For a second or two the Christmas tree lights were visible as Grandpa opened then shut the front door behind him.

Was I going to risk my neck by following him into the house? I'll admit I've since felt some guilt because I didn't. I halted just short of the porch. After all, it wasn't *my* magnum opus that was in danger of fiery destruction. Hero worship has its limits. I waited for Grandpa until I heard the sirens of the fire engines, then shivering with cold trotted back to the neighbors' house.

From the Wrights' living room window we had a view of much of the action. Unlike me, the firemen in their protective helmets and coats had no fear of going inside, though I didn't see why they had to break so many windows with their axes. Other firemen aimed hoses at the flames. In the meantime we were joined by a fire marshal, who asked whether anyone was still in the burning house. There was, though Mrs. Wright informed him she'd already called an ambulance.

The fire marshal then asked us how the fire started. Frank and Lyda were soon deep in argument and mutual recrimination. While the details would change in future retellings, the basic facts were these: at Lyda's insistence Frank had started the fire in the fireplace just before they were ready for bed. Because the logs had been slow to catch, Frank had tried squirting them with lighter fluid from the can he used to refill his cigarette lighter. This had an immediately invigorating effect on the smoldering logs. By the time Frank had returned with a glass of water from the bathroom, the papers and articles of clothing in the fireplace's immediate vicinity were burning. Frank did his best to battle the flames while Lyda shouted guidance from the bed, but his efforts were in vain. In no time it seemed the fire was licking at the chintz curtains. The smoke soon made it hard to see and breathe. By the time they realized they should call the fire department, the phone was dead.

Later the investigating authorities would conclude that other factors contributed to the swift spread of the fire. Sparks from the chimney had flown on to roof, which had caught fire due largely to the cheap reshingling job. The third floor might have escaped with only minimal damage had much of the roof not gone up in flames.

The ambulance, siren wailing, arrived just as a team of firemen emerged on the front porch carrying a large bundle in a blanket. The Christmas lights were still glowing. In another minute the ambulance siren started up again, then slowly receded in the distance.

Grandpa's rescuers, as I would later learn, found him lying near his study. He may have gotten as far as the third floor, then turned back, unable to get past the searing heat. Next to him was a broken guitar, over which it appears he tripped in the dark, smoke-filled hallway.

At the Jane Brown Memorial Hospital, Grandpa was treated for smoke inhalation and third-degree burns. He was in intensive care, still unconscious, when I went to the hospital a few hours later, after getting some restless sleep on the Wrights' living-room couch. (The Wrights naturally gave the Longs their guest room.) Since the doctors said Grandpa's condition, though critical, was stable, I decided to proceed with my plan of returning home to the Midwest. Although I'd lost everything in the fire, including my train tickets, my parents wired me enough money to pay for my train fare. Mr. Wright kindly loaned me some of his clothes.

The Longs would stay on as guests of the Wrights through Christmas. Talk about Christian charity! Frank and Lyda faithfully visited Grandpa every day in the hospital, though he remained in a coma. It was soon after their visit to him Christmas day that they received the terrible news from the doctor—Grandpa had taken a sudden turn for the worse and died. Lyda phoned me from Providence that evening to tell me of his sudden passing. I was undone. Lyda could supply only the bare facts, but years later Frank would grumble that during that final visit his better half should never have wished the patient a speedy recovery so he could write a new novel to replace the one lost in the fire.

The following semester I moved into graduate housing on the Brown campus. I didn't return in time for the funeral, attended by the Longs, the Wrights, and a few distant cousins. Grandpa of course never saw my Christmas present to him, a box of ornaments, which had been resting under the tree. My tears flowed again when I started to receive, forwarded from 454 Angell Street, his Christmas present to me—a subscription to the *New Yorker*.

While Grandpa had been virtually unknown in his lifetime in his native Providence, the local press gave his death and its aftermath a fair amount of coverage. His heroic, doomed effort to rescue the manuscript of *The House of the Worm* was picked up by the Associated Press and widely reported. It was some consolation that this was the only major Lovecraft work to perish. Apart from smoke damage, Grandpa's study, where he kept the bulk of his papers, had survived unscathed. These, among them many story manuscripts, would find a safe home at the John Hay Library several months after his death. More than one snob wrote to the Providence *Journal* wondering at the decline of the library's standards in agreeing to add to its collection the papers of a mere horror writer. I was happy to see the *Journal* print a number of letters in rebuttal, including one from me.

Within a year August Derleth published his omnibus Lovecraft volume, *The Outsider and Others.* Further movie sales followed, much to the benefit of Grandpa's principal heir—Frank Belknap Long— who would be eternally grateful for the royalty checks that arrived punctually every six months from the saintly Mr. Derleth. Years later Frank admitted to me that the income from the Lovecraft estate was sufficient to meet all their financial needs. He was so relieved to be able to retire and not have to write another word of fiction. At the same time he had the satisfaction of Mr. Derleth publishing a couple of collections of his old stories and a volume of his poetry, and of being a frequent honored guest at the conventions that began to pro- liferate during the fantasy boom of the late sixties and seventies.

While the house at 454 Angell had not been adequately insured, the sale of the property still gained Frank a tidy sum. The new owner tore down the remains and put up an apartment building in its place, a modern structure not altogether lacking in taste.

It's only fair to point out that Frank and Lyda did experience a few bumps in their years together. After I completed my graduate studies at Brown I settled in New York, where I got to know the Longs probably as well as anyone. Lyda, it may now be told, suf- fered from manic-depression. At times she would run up huge phone bills or check into expensive hotels where she'd order room service and rack up even larger phone charges. Fortunately, she fell under the care of a psychiatrist, who happened to be an old girlfriend of Frank's. Incredibly enough, as a teenager living in Providence, she had even known Grandpa. Under this strong-willed woman's guid- ance, Lyda took her medication and didn't suffer the extreme ups and downs that could make life such a trial in the Long household. I made a point of playing their Boswell, recording many of my more amusing (and amazing) encounters with Frank and Lyda. One day soon I will put my memories of them in proper form for publication, now that they too at last are gone.

One anecdote, however, seems appropriate here. When he was in his cups Frank would often reminisce about the master of weird tales, for whose death he couldn't help feeling some responsibility. If only he hadn't lit that fire and the fire hadn't gotten out of hand. Mostly, though, he regretted that there had been some ill feeling between them at the end. That afternoon before the fatal fire, when the two of them had been closeted in Howard's study, his old friend had hinted that he was thinking of cutting him, Frank, out of his will because he highly disapproved of Lyda. It was the first time Frank learned of this intended legacy. The memory was extremely painful. Because husbands and wives can have no secrets between them, however, he had conveyed the gist of their discussion to Lyda, but not until the morning before Howard died. Lyda, for her part, felt no guilt. In her view, as she would often remind me, they had received only their due from "Horace's" timely demise.